Secluded coun[illegible] unexpected deaths, fiendishly clever plots, and the reassuring presence of a master detective.

MURDER MOST COZY

"The Danger Point" by Margery Allingham
Mr. Campion stops a cunning jewel thief between courses at a fashionable West End dinner party.

"Mistress of Shadows" by Hugh B. Cave
Take a gabled house in Salem, Massachusetts, add an eccentric old lady, and mix in a young woman who has gone missing after she tries to trace a lost ancestor, and Hugh B. Cave has cooked up a treat.

"A Young Man Called Smith" by Patricia Moyes
A valuable stamp collection, a rich wife's diamonds, and a young beauty's virtue are all at risk when two young men named Smith turn up at a country estate, and one of them is surely an imposter.

"Holocaust at Mayhem Parva" by Julian Symons
An eerie feeling of familiarity will steal over readers of this erudite tale of crime wherein a Professor Plum meets a dastardly end . . . and so does a Colonel Mustard . . . and a Mrs. White . . . and, of course, only Miss Harple knows whodunit!

MURDER MOST COZY

Mysteries in the Classical Tradition from *Ellery Queen's Mystery Magazine* and *Alfred Hitchcock's Mystery Magazine*

Edited by Cynthia Manson

A SIGNET BOOK

SIGNET
Published by the Penguin Group
Penguin Books USA Inc., 375 Hudson Street,
New York, New York 10014, U.S.A.
Penguin Books Ltd, 27 Wrights Lane,
London W8 5TZ, England
Penguin Books Australia Ltd, Ringwood,
Victoria, Australia
Penguin Books Canada Ltd, 10 Alcorn Avenue,
Toronto, Ontario, Canada M4V 3B2
Penguin Books (N.Z.) Ltd, 182–190 Wairau Road,
Auckland 10, New Zealand

Penguin Books Ltd, Registered Offices:
Harmondsworth, Middlesex, England

First published by Signet, an imprint of New American Library,
a division of Penguin Books USA Inc.

First Printing, January, 1993
10 9 8 7 6 5 4 3 2 1

(*The following page constitutes an extension of this copyright page*)

 REGISTERED TRADEMARK—MARCA REGISTRADA

Printed in the United States of America

PUBLISHER'S NOTE
These stories are works of fiction. Names, characters, places, and incidents either are the product of the author's imagination or are used fictitiously, and any resemblance to actual persons, living or dead, events, or locales is entirely coincidental.

CONTENTS

Foreword 9

Mistress of Shadows
by Hugh B. Cave 11

A Young Man Called Smith
by Patricia Moyes 53

The Dressing Table Murder
by C. M. Chan 88

A Matter of Taste
by Dorothy L. Sayers 132

Arrie and Jasper
by Amanda Cross 148

A Case of Headlong Dying
by Michael Innes 168

Cruise to Death
by Alexandra Allan 189

The Danger Point
by Margery Allingham 214

Holocaust at Mayhem Parva
by Julian Symons 239

FOREWORD

Before you begin reading the stories in this book, I suggest you make yourself a cup of tea, find a soft lap blanket and an old-fashioned rocking chair, and settle yourself by a blazing fire. If, by chance, you happen to have a furry companion, you may also wish to have your cat nearby for some extra comfort as you begin reading these chilling mystery stories from *Alfred Hitchcock's Mystery Magazine* and *Ellery Queen's Mystery Magazine.*

The title seems a paradox—how can murder be *cozy*? The term "cozy" is used quite often these days to categorize a type of mystery story. There are numerous definitions of cozies. Particular thematic elements emerge, however, and form a pattern. Cozies never contain graphic descriptions of violence (not much, anyway; some fistfights are permitted). The real violence is almost always offstage. A cozy is a whodunit, a puzzle in need of a solution. A cozy's central character can be an amateur sleuth or a private detective or a cop, but the latter two operate away from any suggestion of the "mean streets" and with few visits to the precinct. A good bit of time spent in Scotland Yard is okay, though.

Now, don't get confused—just see for yourself. I think you will find that this anthology contains a wide variety of cozies, from Margery Allingham, Patricia Moyes, Michael Innes, Amanda Cross, Julian Symons, Dorothy L. Sayers, and their ilk.

And all, we think, are most entertaining—and murderously cozy!

—Cynthia Manson

MISTRESS OF SHADOWS

by Hugh B. Cave

The house filled him with foreboding. Old, huge, half a mile from its nearest neighbor, it seemed hostile and menacing, as though surrounded by an invisible wall that defied him to come closer.

Nonsense, he angrily told himself. He was just tired from the long drive from Connecticut. From so stupidly getting lost on the outskirts of old Salem and having such trouble finding the place. There was no barrier, invisible or otherwise. The driveway curling up from the two-lane blacktop was even inviting. At least, it appealed to the architect in him.

All right. Witches were hanged hereabouts, three hundred years ago. Our people came from this part of New England. I inherited this feeling, probably.

Stopping his car short of the once-handsome Victorian piazza that ran along the front, he sat for a moment studying the house and what he could see of a weathered old barn behind it.

He didn't know much about his sister's visit, actually. Aware of his indifference to her passion for genealogy, she had been reluctant to discuss her activities with him.

Some woman living in this house had replied to a query of hers in a publication specializing in family pedigrees. There'd been an exchange of letters, a phone call, then Prudence had said quite casually, "I'll be going to Salem on Tuesday."

"*The* Salem? Massachusetts?"

"I'll be back Wednesday."

"You're onto something new?"

"I won't bore you."

"I won't bore you" was a kind of code phrase this talented sister of his frequently used to shut him out of her world. She didn't encourage many people to enter that world. But she *was* his sister and today was Friday, and she had not phoned to explain her failure to return as planned. It was out of character for her not to phone.

He glanced at his watch—only half an hour more of daylight this cool October evening—then got out of his car and climbed the worn, wooden piazza steps. About two hundred years old, he estimated, letting his practiced gaze travel over the house as he pulled the porcelain bell knob. Shamefully neglected.

The wide front door swung open, and he found himself face to face with a small, slender man of about forty who seemed as neglected as the house itself.

"Yes?"

"Good evening. My name is Mark Reeves and I'm looking for my sister. She told me she was coming here."

There was a drabness about the man that infected even his voice. "Here? Today?"

"Tuesday. She came here to see a Mrs. Sarah Woodlin."

"My mother-in-law." The man summoned enough energy to frown. "Owns this place. Victor Mayne's my name. Nobody called here Tuesday that I know of."

Mark felt a return of his unease. "You haven't seen a young blonde woman, very attractive, driving a new blue station wagon?"

Victor Mayne silently wagged his head.

"Could I—do you suppose I could have a word with Mrs. Woodlin? They corresponded, you see. There was at least one phone call to arrange a meeting. Perhaps she will know—"

"Talk to 'er if you like. She's out back, most likely. Come on in. I'll call 'er."

Mark followed him into a large living room filled with old furniture. Not invited to sit, he stood there feeling out of place while his host walked listlessly into a room beyond and called out, "Sarah! Hey, Sarah! Somebody here wants to see you."

Presently a woman's voice answered querulously, "Who is it?"

"Feller named Reeves. Says you know his sister." Mayne returned to the room where Mark waited. "She'll come. Sit down, why don't you?"

Mark sat down. After a moment of apparent indecision, Mayne followed suit, all but losing his tenuous identity in the grayness of the chair he sank into. "Your sister said she was comin' here Tuesday?"

"Yes. She believes we have ancestors who lived in Salem. She put a query in a magazine, and your mother-in-law answered it."

"That's exactly what happened," said a thin voice from the doorway, and Mark turned to find himself staring at two women. The one who had spoken was a diminutive creature probably in her eighties, wearing a floor-length garment of purple velvet that had once been an evening gown. A narrow band of the same material encircled her wisp of a neck and was tied in a bow at her throat.

The other woman was taller, younger, but much less colorful.

"You're Mr. Reeves, and looking for Prudence Reeves?" The old lady briskly advanced, offering a hand so like the hand of a doll that Mark was almost afraid to touch it, lest it break off at its tiny wrist. "Yes? Well, she didn't keep her appointment with me. After I went to all the trouble of answering her letter in the magazine, and she telephoned me and all, she didn't come. I'm very much annoyed with her." She scowled ferociously. "This is my daughter Daphne, my youngest. The other one, Leila, isn't here just now. Mr. Reeves, I'd like to know why your sister didn't come after saying she would."

"I wish I knew."

He guessed the daughter, Daphne, was Victor Mayne's wife. If two persons could look alike from being married to each other, then she certainly was.

"Prudence left home early Tuesday morning to come here," Mark said, and glanced at his watch. "It shouldn't have taken her any longer to drive up than it took me today; she's a no-nonsense driver. She was to have returned Wednesday. But I haven't seen or heard from her."

"The two of you live together?" Sarah Woodlin asked.

"We share the family homestead. There's only the two of us left."

"Well, she never came here." The old gown shimmered like a purple waterfall as Sarah Woodlin defiantly drew herself straighter.

"Just what did she want from you, Mrs. Woodlin?"

"To talk about your family. My people helped settle this part of Massachusetts, and she thought her ancestors were here in those days, too. And they were. When you see her, you can tell her so. I spent days tracing the name Reeves back through—"

"Now, Ma," Daphne said.

"Well, I did!"

"Mr. Reeves don't want to hear about your ancestors, Sarah," Victor Mayne said. "He just wants to know where his sister is."

"Well, all I can tell you, again, is that she never came here." The old lady tossed her head. "She must have changed her mind. Or had an accident on the way."

Mark found himself not liking the way the three of them were eyeing him now. "Well . . . thanks."

"When you find her," Sarah said, "tell her she can still come see me if she's a mind to."

"I will."

"And you. I'd be pleased to talk to you. In the old days the Reeveses and my family were real close. Yes, real close."

Nodding, Mark turned to find that Victor Mayne was waiting to show him out. At the front door, with a shrug, the colorless man said, "Sorry, mister."

It was dark outside as Mark walked across the piazza to the steps. There had been lights on in the house, but evidently Mayne had no intention of putting on the verandah light to help him to his car. The front door closed behind him with an emphatic thud of dismissal, and he groped his way down to the driveway.

But as he reached the bottom, a voice from a mass of dark forsythia bushes to his left suddenly whispered, "Wait!"

He halted. The other sister? It was a woman, anyway.

"Turn left at the foot of the drive," the voice instructed in a rush of whispered words. "Stop down the road where they won't see you. I'll be along in a few minutes."

"All right." He got into his car. Turning as directed pointed him back toward Salem, which was the way he would have gone in any case.

The road was all curves. After rounding the first, he pulled over to the side.

In about five minutes she came, simply opening the car door and sliding onto the seat beside him. Not the other sister, he saw at once. Not nearly old enough. Her hair was dark and short. Were the dark blouse and even darker slacks deliberate, so as to lessen the chance of her being seen by the people at the house?

"I'm Kim Barton," she said. "I have a room back there."

He frankly stared at her, though in the dim light from the dash it was scarcely a searching look. "A room?"

"I rent one. It's directly above the one you were

talking in, and I heard most of what you said. I'm a schoolteacher. Look, Mr.—Reeves, is it?"

"Mark Reeves."

"They're not telling the truth. There *was* a car at the house Tuesday evening."

He caught his breath. "A blue station wagon?"

"A station wagon. I'm not sure of the color. I was in my room when it arrived, and I went to the window and looked down because we don't have many callers in the evening. I didn't see who got out of it. By the time I reached the window, the person was on the verandah. I didn't hear any talk, either; they must have talked in the other living room—the house has two. But the car was there at least three hours. I was in bed, after eleven, when I heard it leave."

"Why do you suppose they're lying?"

"I have no idea."

"What kind of people are they, Miss Barton?"

"Well, I don't know. This is my second year of teaching in this town, and I've had a room there since I started, but I have to say I just don't know."

"The old lady must be dotty. That purple gown—"

"She's eighty-three years old. But the house belongs to her, and when she cracks the whip, the others jump."

"What about Mayne? What does he do?"

"He was a bus driver. A heart attack at the wheel one day caused him to have a terrible accident, and he hasn't driven since. Not even a car."

"Is the other daughter married?"

"Her husband walked out on her, and the old lady never lets her forget it." Kim Barton opened her door. "I have to get back."

"Do they check on you?"

"I don't suppose it's that, but I never know when one of them will knock on my door. I teach history, and the old lady would go on about Salem history for hours if I'd let her. The daughters—well, I think they sneak up to my room to get away from her."

"It sounds gruesome."

She laughed as she slid from the seat, and again Mark noticed how attractive she was. Or, rather, how relaxed and natural she was. "I hope you find your sister," she said.

"Thanks for trying to help me."

"What will you do?"

"I'll have to think about it."

She looked at him, nodded, and was gone.

He was a man who arrived at decisions quickly, and by the time he had reached the village he knew what he would do. It was a small place, just a traffic light and a cluster of stores at a widening of the blacktop. He found a drugstore with a phone booth.

When a long-distance call to his Connecticut home elicited no answer, he called his secretary's home. "Ethel? Mark. Look, I'm in Massachusetts—that town Prue went to. She isn't here. Have you heard from her?"

Ethel Anderson was a woman whose voice invariably disclosed her feelings. He could all but see the frown-lines in her always expressive face as she said, "Heard from her? No, Mark. Is something wrong?"

"I'm not sure. I'm staying, of course, until I find out. Will you be at home this evening?"

"Yes."

"I'll call you later, then, when I've found a place to stop. Meanwhile, give my house a ring every so often, will you? She just might turn up."

Leaving the booth, he stepped to the counter and asked the gray-haired man behind it if there was a motel nearby.

"There's one. Place called Stoughton's. Which way you headed?"

"Salem."

"Just keep goin' four blocks, then."

"And do you have a police station?"

"Right across the road from the motel."

Stoughton's was a red brick rectangle with numbered white doors. The parking strip was empty. Opening a door marked OFFICE, Mark stepped under a tinkling bell to an unattended desk and waited there until an inner door opened and a woman appeared.

"Hello," she said indifferently. "Can I help you?"

"I'd like a room for the night."

Producing a key and a register, she watched him sign his name, then looked at him with more interest. "Mark Reeves? We had a Prudence Reeves here just the other day." Her fingers flipped a page. "Tuesday. But she never used her room."

He frowned at the signature. It was his sister's, without question. As he fixed his gaze on the face of the woman before him, he was chilled again by the foreboding he had felt at the old Woodlin house. "You say she didn't use her room?"

"She never came back that night."

"What time Tuesday did she check in?"

"Well, my husband had just sat down to supper, so it was about six. I checked her in and she looked at the room and said all right, she'd be back later. Paid for it, too. But she never showed up." The woman cocked her head like an outsized bird sensing a juicy worm of scandal. "She your wife?"

"My sister. Did she leave anything in her room?"

"Nope. Nothin'."

"Did she ask any directions?"

"Well, now, she asked me how to get to Mill Brook Road."

"I see." What Mark saw was the old house whose occupants wanted him to believe Prue had never called on them.

He thanked the woman for her information and went to the room she had assigned him. When he had carried in his overnight case, he locked the door behind him and went across the road to an old white house that bore a sign reading POLICE over its colonial doorway. He was beginning to be a little hungry, too.

His only food all day had been a burger and coffee at a drive-in, about eleven o'clock.

A card thumbtacked to the door instructed callers to "knock and walk in." Doing so, he found himself at the foot of a carpeted staircase. To his right an open door revealed what had been a colonial living room but was now something else.

A diminutive, white-haired woman in her late forties or early fifties, wearing a khaki blouse and skirt, sat there, working at a huge walnut desk. The room was full of a John Philip Sousa march booming in stereo from the twin speakers of a tape player.

Mark was halfway to the desk before the woman looked up from something she was writing. She frowned at him. Frowning was probably easy for that stern face. "Yes?"

"Good evening. This *is* the police station?"

"I'm chief here. Name's Kate Kendall. What can I do for you?" Swinging briskly on her swivel chair, she shut off the tape.

Without the booming music, the room seemed vast and empty, and the loudness of Mark's voice startled him as he began his story.

"Well, I can understand Sarah Woodlin acting queer," Kate Kendall said when he finished. "She *is* queer. I don't see why the daughter and her husband would lie to you, but if Kim Barton said she saw a station wagon there, she saw it. I know her. She's a fine young woman." Kendall got to her feet. "It won't do any harm for us to go back and talk to those people, I guess. Is your car handy?"

"Across the road."

"I'll lock up while you go for it."

She was really not a bad sort, Mark decided as they drove to Mill Brook Road. Beneath the brusqueness, the village's only police officer appeared to be a normal, curious, even friendly woman. Once she stopped being wary of him, she was even talkative.

"So your sister's one of those who get all worked

up about their ancestors, is she?" Kate said. "Well, it's easy to see why she'd want to call on Sarah Woodlin. Sarah's another one."

"So Miss Barton told me."

"Now, as I said before, there's a nice girl. Came here from out of town to teach in the district high school, and we're all just crazy about her. By the way, I don't think we ought to tell those people Kim talked to you."

"I was going to suggest the same thing."

"We'll just say Alice Stoughton, at the motel, gave your sister directions and—well, you leave it to me."

Approaching the house, Mark again felt it was somehow sinister. The floor-length windows were aglow with light now, as were two smaller windows upstairs, probably in Kim Barton's room. When Kate Kendall gave the doorbell a yank, the piazza fixture winked on.

Again it was the nondescript Victor Mayne who opened the door.

"Hello, Mr. Mayne," Kate said. "Tell Sarah I'd like a word with her, if you will."

The gray man's gaze shifted to Mark for a second, but then he shrugged. "Okay. Come on in."

Again Mark found himself in the drably furnished living room.

Sarah, still gowned in purple and wearing the purple bow at her throat, was there with Mayne's wife, Daphne, and another woman who appeared to be the other daughter. Several years older than Daphne, she had the same plain face and mousy hair.

The three were watching television, but Sarah got up to turn the set off and said in mock surprise, "Well, bless my soul. Good evening, Kate. And you again, Mr. Reeves? Sit down, both of you."

Seated, Kate said crisply, "We seem to be having a problem, Sarah."

"We? Or the gentleman here who can't find his sister?"

"We, Sarah. You. Because his sister came here."

"But I've already told him she didn't."

"I know what you've told him. But Miss Reeves was directed here by Alice Stoughton at the motel."

"Well, I can't help that. She just never turned up."

"Her car was seen here."

"By whom?" Sarah demanded, bristling.

"Never mind that. Just take my word for it, the car was seen here. A blue station wagon."

"Not blue," Sarah snapped. "Green."

"What?"

"The car that was here Tuesday evening was green, Kate. And it wasn't anything Mr. Reeves's sister would be driving; it was Danny Elder's old wagon. Whoever you talked to has pretty poor eyesight, if you ask me."

Kate Kendall seemed taken aback, but quickly recovered. "All right, Sarah. Is Kim Barton here?"

"Why?"

"I'll ask you to call her."

"If you like." Sarah shrugged. "Go on, Leila."

The cheerless living room was silent as the daughter whose husband had deserted her walked like a zombie into the hall.

As she climbed the staircase, Mark felt a touch of panic. Surely Kate Kendall was not going to reverse herself and let these people know their boarder had accused them of lying!

When Leila reappeared, followed by Kim Barton, Mark held his breath. Seeing the girl's face lose color as she became aware of his presence, he suddenly disliked Kate Kendall intensely.

But Kate spoke quietly before anyone else could voice a word. "Kim, I want to ask a question or two, if you don't mind. But first let me introduce Mr. Mark Reeves, from Connecticut. Mr. Reeves, this is Miss Kimberly Barton, who boards here."

As Mark accepted Kim's hand, her gaze touched his to flash a message of relief.

"Were you here Tuesday evening, Kim?" Kate asked.

"Yes, I was."

"We want to know if you saw a car here."

"Why, yes, I did."

"What kind of car? What color?"

"It was a station wagon—fairly new, I think. I'm not sure of the color. Blue, perhaps, or black."

"It was Danny Elder's old *green* station wagon," Sarah Woodlin snapped, "and you've certainly seen it before!"

"Danny Elder's car? Really, Sarah—"

"Go *ask* him!" Furious now, Sarah swung on Kate. "This is nonsense, when all you have to do is go to Danny's house and ask him! He was over here Tuesday evening to fix a leaky pipe under the kitchen sink. It took him nearly two hours, and his wagon was out front the whole time."

Again Kate Kendall seemed disconcerted. "Well . . . all right. If you say so, Sarah."

"I say so!"

Kate shifted her gaze to Kim Barton. "I suppose you *could* have been mistaken, Kim." Shaking her head, she turned to Mark. "We've no reason to take up any more time here, it seems."

Victor Mayne showed them out, in a silence that endured until Mark's car was descending the driveway. "Turn right," Kate said then.

"We're going to call on this Danny Elder?"

"Might as well, though I don't suppose Sarah was lying. Not about that part of it, anyway. Take your first left."

Their destination, less than a mile from the Woodlin place, was a shabby house in a cluttered clearing. Without Kate's guidance he would have missed it even if given directions, for it was hidden from the road by trees. In the yard stood the old green station wagon Sarah had talked about.

Danny lived here, Kate said, with his aged grandmother and a "no-good" father. "Sound your horn," she added. "Never know if Clay Elder's got his brute of a dog tied up."

A dog did bark somewhere, then stopped and began growling. It was an ugly sound. A voice tersely ordered the animal to "shut up" and presently a youth of about seventeen appeared. His long blond hair bounced on his shoulders as he advanced. Bare and muscular above the belt, he wore only dirty bluejeans and dirtier sneakers. "Oh, hi, Miz Kendall. You lookin' for Pa?"

"No, for you. I've had a complaint about you, Danny." Kate scowled at him. "Where were you Tuesday evening?"

His pale eyes seemed to darken. "Tuesday? Nowhere. 'Cept Miz Woodlin's, that is. I was there for a time."

"Doing what?"

"Fixin' her sink."

"You were over there fixing a sink in the *evening*?"

"Well, I was workin' on my car all that afternoon."

For a moment Kate continued to stare. Then she said with a sigh, "All right, Danny," and the conversation was over.

"Dead end?" Mark said as he drove back out to the road. "Why did he ask if you wanted his father?"

"No special reason, I guess. Clay Elder has a temper and gets into trouble a lot. Tell me about your sister, Mr. Reeves. She younger than you, or older?"

"Two years older. Thirty-one."

"An artist, I believe you said. Attractive?"

"Very."

"So what will you do about finding her now?"

"I don't know, Miss Kendall."

"Just call me Kate. I don't exactly know what to do, either, but it would seem her car disappeared between the motel and the Woodlin house. Unless, of course, she went somewhere else. I'll get on the phone and find out if her car was in an accident. You'll be at Stoughton's tonight?"

Mark nodded.

"I'll call you when I find out something."

There was a phone in Mark's motel room. He called his secretary.

"No, Mark," Ethel Anderson said. "I've called your house every half hour since we talked before, and no one answers." He could just see her shaking her head in distress—she cared about people's problems. She was fond of Prue, too.

Having told Ethel where he was staying, he drove down the road to a diner. Then on his return he threw himself on the bed and lay there gazing at the ceiling, reviewing in his mind what had happened.

There was something evil about the Woodlin house. Why couldn't he put his finger on it?

Kate Kendall did not call. In the morning, after going to the diner for a breakfast he didn't want but felt he ought to eat, Mark returned to the motel to continue waiting. Just as he was becoming restless enough to invade the police station again, someone knocked on his door.

It was the proprietor's wife, to deliver an envelope that had "Mr. Reeves" written on it in a neat, feminine script.

Mark tore it open and unfolded the sheet of paper it contained. The writing was the same. "Dear Mr. Reeves, I believe I have located your sister's car, but my own is giving me trouble and I must send this to you by messenger. If you will drive out Worden Road to the old stone quarry, you will find me there. Yours, Kim Barton."

He felt a thrill of excitement at knowing Kim Barton was still trying to help him. At the same time, a warning bell rang in his subconscious. "Who delivered this, Mrs. Stoughton?"

"A boy on a bike. He rode right off again."

"Did you know him?"

"Uh-uh. I've no idea who he was."

"Well . . . can you tell me how to get to Worden Road, please?"

"Let's see, now. Best way for you, I guess, would be to drive out Mill Brook Road to Creston, and turn right. Worden crosses Creston after about a mile."

"I'm to go to an old quarry on Worden."

She nodded. "Used to swim there when we were kids. Turn left on Worden and look for a side road. Just a pair of ruts leading left into the woods. Drive in a little way and there you are."

Mark hurried to his car. Should he tell the police chief where he was going? He ought to. The door marked "knock and walk in" was locked, though. Kate Kendall was probably out pursuing some idea of her own.

As he passed the old Woodlin house, something about it filled him with revulsion. Somewhere within those gloomy rooms, he was convinced, lay the secret of Prue's disappearance. Whatever had happened to her had at least begun to happen there.

He could have sworn the house furtively watched him as he drove by, and even knew where he was going. The feeling still haunted him when he reached his destination.

A pair of ruts on the left? He found them and drove in at a crawl, searching for proof that Kim's car had preceded him. But the ground was covered by rotted leaves. There were no tire prints.

Then as the woods closed in solidly behind him, seeming to cut off his retreat, he came to a stretch of bare ground that did contain the marks of tires, and he stopped.

New tires had made these prints. Expensive new radials. Prue had bought a set of such tires less than a month ago.

So Kim Barton *had* found Prue's car. At least, the car had been here. But something puzzled him as he peered through the windshield at the patch of bare ground. If Kim had driven in here, *her* car should have left tire prints, too. In fact, these earlier prints ought to be all but obliterated.

He went forward on foot to examine the marks more closely. There was no sign that any machine other than Prue's had been here. Returning to his car, he shut off the engine. The stillness of the place was relieved only by a sound of leaves faintly rustling in a barely perceptible breeze. Apprehensive now, he walked slowly on down the road to reconnoiter.

The quarry was farther in than the Stoughton woman had led him to believe. Or, at least, than he had anticipated. His car was out of sight behind him when he caught his first glimpse of dark water glimmering among the trees ahead. He stopped again.

The place appeared to be an open pit, roughly circular, about sixty yards across. Nothing more—just an excavation nearly full of water. The old road on which he stood must have been used for hauling out the stone.

Suddenly he took in a sharp breath. In a clump of alders and brush near the quarry's edge, something other than water shone faintly in the forest's dim light. Something blue.

He was staring at Prue's station wagon.

With mixed emotions he strode forward. Someone had driven the car in here to hide it, apparently. But who? Not Prue, surely. She would have had no reason to come here at all.

Suddenly something flashed past his cheek. Not an insect but something metallic, shiny, that split the air with a whistling sound and then ripped through a leafy branch behind him. He dropped to the ground.

As he rolled out of the road, a second missile flashed above him, then a third. Both would surely have struck him had he stayed on his feet. Striving to make no sound, he crawled into the underbrush ten, fifteen feet before stopping again. Then he lay flat, listening.

There was no sound except a faint whisper of wind and the heavy thudding of his own heart.

Had someone shot at him? He thought so but could not be sure. If the missiles had been bullets, the weapon firing them must have been equipped with a silencing device. But was it possible to eliminate all sound with a silencer? He did not know.

But someone had certainly tried to hit him—kill him, probably—with a weapon of some sort. Someone, it seemed, had been using Prue's car as bait.

Knowing the risk he took, he began crawling again. The distance back to his car was not great, if he could avoid a blunder. But the slightest sound, even a twig snapping under him, would betray his whereabouts in this eerie stillness. Sweat ran salty over his tight-pressed lips as he crawled.

Was that a footstep off to his right, where the road was? He held his breath, listening. The sound was not repeated, but he was moving away from the road, he saw by raising his head slightly. That was bad. He must get to his car by the shortest route. The farther he had to crawl, the more prolonged the peril.

When at last he saw the car, he was twenty yards from it and had to pause again to let his heart stop racing. Had he left the key in the ignition? Yes. Good. That would eliminate fumbling. Of course, he would not be able to turn the machine around. There wasn't room enough. He would have to drive it out in reverse.

He took in a steadying breath and advanced again. Under his left knee a bit of dry wood cracked. Somewhere, not too close, a man's voice barked, "There! Over there!"

Mark leaped to his feet and ran.

As he ran he heard the whine of missiles again, and louder sounds as the bullets or whatever they were ripped through leaves and branches close to his face. Just as he reached the car, something nicked his outflung arm, sending a shock wave to his fingertips. But he was able to claw the door open with that same hand. He could still dive in behind the wheel and turn the key.

The engine roared to life. Twisting on the seat, peering through the rear window, he sent the machine lurching backward. A pursuing missile struck the radiator grille. Another crashed into the windshield.

But despite its wild swerving, the car ate up the ruts. One final swerve at the main road and, twisting himself around again to face forward, he drove off. How close he had come to being killed or caught was written in the windshield, where the glass resembled a spiderweb.

He drove a mile and got out to inspect the car and himself. The windshield and radiator grille puzzled him. Bullets would have done more damage, he felt. As for his arm, the missile must have just grazed it. There was a painful swelling between wrist and elbow, but he could find no break in the skin.

Lucky, he thought. That was meant to be an ambush.

He heard march music again as he opened Kate Kendall's door. After turning off the tape player, the police chief folded her arms and glowered at him.

"You look like death warmed over. What's going on?"

After telling her, he handed her the note from Kim.

Kate unlocked a drawer of her desk and took out a holstered revolver. "Come!" As she marched to the door he could almost hear the band playing.

In the yard she examined his car. "You're right: this wasn't done by bullets. I'd say somebody was throwing stones."

"I don't think they were stones. They were shiny."

"H'm." She turned to her own car, a black sedan

with the word POLICE in white on its sides. "I'll drive this time."

After a while she said, "How do you suppose your sister's car got there, Mr. Reeves?"

"I have no idea."

"Seems an unlikely place for a stranger to go."

"I agree."

"Strange." Turning onto the quarry road, Kate leaned over the wheel, peering ahead. "Now just where did you leave your car and go forward on foot?"

He showed her. Stopping short of the spot, she opened her door and got out. Mark followed as she went slowly along the road with her gaze on the ground.

Where his car had stood, she stooped to pick up something. "Is this what was fired at you?"

It was a steel ball about the size of a common marble: a ball bearing of some kind, Mark guessed. "It could be, I suppose."

She dropped the object into a pocket of her khaki shirt.

"They didn't have guns, then, did they?" Mark said. "No gun could have fired that."

"No gun that I know anything about. Why do you say 'they'?"

"As I told you, I heard a man call out, 'Over there!' He must have been calling *to* someone."

"You did say that. And you didn't recognize the voice?"

He shook his head.

"Well"—she was marching again—"let's have a look at the car."

But when they came in sight of the quarry, the only glitter in the forest's faint light was that of the water. No station wagon was there in the alder clump.

"It was here?" Kate said.

He pointed to tire marks at his feet. They were indistinct because the earth at that spot consisted mostly of leaf mold, but it was evident a vehicle had stood there. Kate looked toward the pit.

The car had been parked only a few yards from the edge. There were no other tire marks—perhaps the ground could not retain any—but within a foot of the quarry a small sapling had been broken off. Kate marched to the pit's rim.

Gazing down into that dark, shining water, Mark felt himself shudder. It looked deep and inhospitable. He wondered how even a woman as seemingly insensitive as Alice Stoughton, at the motel, could ever have come here to swim. After a moment Kate said, "I'll have to get help, of course. I can't go diving down there myself."

"You think the car is in there?"

"We have to find out."

He shuddered again, wondering what kind of devilish business his sister had got mixed up in. It was a relief when Kate said gruffly, "Well, let's go," and he was able to turn away from that unwholesome-looking place.

On the way back she turned up the Woodlins' driveway, but instead of getting out of the car, simply blew the horn until the front door opened. Leila, the older daughter, was the one who opened it.

"Tell Kim Barton I'd like a word with her, please."

"Can't you come in?"

"Haven't time."

When Kim appeared, Kate handed her the note. "Did you write this, girl?"

Kim frowned at it in obvious bewilderment. "No, I didn't. What in the world—"

"Can't stop to explain now. You want to ask questions, you'll have to come with us."

Kim jumped into the car, and Kate sent it squealing down the driveway. The front door of the house was open behind them, Mark saw while recovering his balance. On the piazza, staring, stood old Sarah Woodlin, her two daughters, and the gray man, Victor Mayne.

Why did they make him think of vultures?

Kate Kendall must have been a demon when demanding action from others! Mark and Kim were not present when she phoned for assistance in exploring the quarry; she had dropped them off at the motel, promising to call when she had anything to report. But Mark was still answering Kim's questions about his work as an architect and his life in Connecticut when the phone rang.

"No car there," Kate said. "Nothing. But why don't the two of you come over here?"

At the station she said, "Frankly, Mr. Reeves, I thought we'd find your sister's car at the bottom of that quarry, with her in it. Does that shock you?"

"I was braced to accept it, I'm afraid."

"So let's get down to brass tacks. Your sister came here to talk to Sarah Woodlin. Something happened—we've no idea what. We do know those people couldn't have handled her disappearance by themselves, though. They'd have needed help."

"Danny Elder?"

"That's what I think. I don't believe he went there that evening to fix any pipe; he was sent for to get rid of your sister's car. Victor Mayne hasn't driven since his accident." Kate stood up. "I'm going to the Elders' right now to bring that boy here for a talk."

"I'd like to be here," Mark said.

"Of course. Both of you. But for the moment why don't you go for a little walk or something while I write down what I want to ask that boy?"

Kim and Mark went out together.

The road there was bordered by woods. As they walked side by side along its shoulder, their hands sometimes touching, Mark returned to the conversation begun at the motel. "How did you happen to come here to teach?" he asked.

"There was a job here, and I thought it might be fun to teach history in a place where so much of it happened."

"Has it been fun?"

"I'm sure it would have been, had I been able to find a less spooky place to live."

"I don't like the idea of your being at the Woodlins' after what's happened."

"I'll be all right."

The house on Mill Brook Road was not something Mark wanted to talk about at the moment. "Where are you from, originally?"

"The western part of the state. A town no bigger than this."

"A small-town girl."

"That's bad?"

"Of course not. It's just that I've never known a small-town girl before, and you keep doing things that surprise me. The chance you took to tell me the Woodlins were lying about my sister's car, for instance. What made you do that?"

She turned to face him. "Do you remember some time ago, in New York, a girl was brutally beaten on a crowded street in broad daylight? And of all the people who watched it happen, not one tried to help her?"

He nodded.

"Something like that happened to a schoolmate of mine. I resolved then and there never to be the kind of person who would turn her back when she could help someone in trouble."

"So that was your motivation."

"Well, it was my original motivation."

"And now?"

"Now I like you."

Now I like you. The forthrightness of it haunted him even after they returned to the police station. He thought about it all the while they waited for Kate Kendall to come back with Danny Elder.

Now I like you. After what he had been through, the words were healing.

Kate Kendall marched Danny into the station from her car, sat him in front of her desk, and glowered at him. He wore a shirt now, along with the soiled jeans and shabby sneakers.

With the atmosphere established to her liking, Kate proceeded to tell the youth what he had done.

"You didn't go to the Woodlins' to fix any pipe, did you? And it wasn't your old station wagon Miss Barton saw there. They sent for you to get rid of Miss Reeves's car. Told you to dispose of it in the quarry. But you just left it there, planning to go back for it when things cooled down. That's it, isn't it, Danny?"

The boy's long blond hair swished as he shook his head in vehement denial. "No, Miz Kendall, it ain't!"

"All right, then. Suppose you tell me what did happen."

He leaned toward her, talking partly with his hands. "Ma'am, it's true I never used my own car that night. But you got the rest all wrong. What happened, I was on my way over to Miz Woodlin's to fix the pipe—"

"On foot, I suppose you mean."

"Yeah, on foot. I cut through the woods to save time, and found the station wagon in there at the quarry with the key in it, like whoever left it there only meant to walk around or somethin', but never came back. Like maybe, you know, they fell in the water and drowned."

Kate's craggy face was a thundercloud.

"Go on."

"Well, I hung around and nobody showed up, so I—well, I just got in the car and drove it off. I drove it to Miz Woodlin's and parked it out front where Miz Barton here says she seen it. But when I was leavin', the Woodlins asked whose car it was, and told me to take it back or folks would say I stole it."

This time Kate said nothing. Mark could see she was shaken by the apparent logic of Danny's tale.

"So that's what I done," the youth concluded. "I took the car back there and left it where I found it."

"Where you found it," Kate repeated.

"Yeah. And I ain't seen it since. Honest."

It seemed to Mark the silence in the room would endure forever, but Kate finally said, "All right, Danny, I'll take you back." To Mark and Kim she added unhappily, "Just goes to show, doesn't it, how things can seem to be what they're not."

She opened the door and Danny slouched out, grinning in triumph—though maybe the grin, Mark thought, was something else that seemed to be what it was not. Kate closed the door behind them, leaving Mark to drive Kim home.

On the way Kim said, "Danny was lying, wasn't he?"

"I think so. His story seemed pretty thin in places."

"Such as?"

"If all he did was find the car and drive it to the Woodlins', why did they insist it was never there? Telling the truth wouldn't have hurt them or Danny."

"But by lying they were hindering you in finding your sister."

For a time they rode in silence.

"Furthermore," Kim said, "the only people Prue came in contact with, that we know of, are those at the Woodlin house. I'll keep my eyes and ears open, Mark."

"Be careful. If they think you're onto something—"

"I won't do anything foolish."

With an uneasy feeling that he had better come up with some answers quickly or she might risk her life to help him, Mark glumly watched her get out of the car and disappear into the house.

In the morning, confiding in no one, Mark drove alone to Danny Elder's. It seemed a peaceful enough place in its rustic setting, nothing in its dusty somnolence indicating that Kate Kendall had caused any consternation by her interrogation of Danny. As he turned into the yard he looked apprehensively for the dog Kate had warned about, but saw no sign of it.

Danny's old station wagon was gone.

The back door opened as he reached it, and a woman about Sarah Woodlin's age squinted out at him. Danny's grandmother, he guessed.

"Is Danny at home, Mrs. Elder?"

She shook her head. "Nor Clay, neither. Only me."

Should he try to talk to her? What he had come for was to confront the boy with certain probing questions that Kate had neglected to ask. He didn't think the old woman could answer them.

"Do you know when he might be here, Mrs. Elder?"

"Uh-uh. No idea."

"Well, thanks." He started back to his car, but something on the ground caught his eyes. Bending over, he picked up a shiny steel ball.

Danny's grandmother was still in the doorway when he turned. Walking back, he extended his hand with the missile in his palm. "This looks like a bearing. Has Danny been working on his car?"

"Since Tuesday mornin', but that ain't from the car. He was out here practicin' this mornin' with his slingshot." She snorted. "Stones ain't good enough. He has to waste his money on those things."

Since Tuesday morning. So Danny *had* gone to the Woodlins' on foot that night and *could* have found Prue's car at the quarry. But he had also taken part in the ambush.

On his way to the car Mark idly tossed the ball into the air a few times and caught it. Perhaps his show of indifference would persuade the old lady there was nothing to his keeping the thing, and she would not report it to Danny.

Should he go to the police station and tell Kate

what he had learned? No. For one thing, she might not be there and he would only be wasting precious time. For another, with her gullible acceptance of Danny's story, he had lost some of his respect for her.

He began, instead, a stakeout of the Elder house.

It was not easy. To observe without being seen, he had to park in the woods on the other side of the road. From there he could see only the ruts leading into the yard.

In about an hour Danny and his father returned in Danny's green station wagon. But neither reappeared. At dark Mark had to abandon his surveillance.

But he was back the next morning, and at nine fifteen the old car rattled out of the Elders' yard with Danny alone in it. When it was a safe distance down the road, Mark pulled out of hiding and followed.

Several miles of back roads later, Danny turned in at an abandoned farm on a dirt road. Only the fieldstone foundation remained of what must have been the house. But an ancient barn still struggled to stand, and its twin doors wore a padlock.

Danny's car vanished behind the barn, but a moment later the boy appeared on foot and put a key to the padlock. Then, dragging one of the heavy doors partly open, he slipped inside and pulled it shut after him.

Mark drove on past, stopping where his car could not be seen from the barn. Walking back, he found beside the road a broken stone wall that would hide him while he watched.

The sun climbed the morning sky and insects hummed in the heated air. A pair of gray squirrels played tag on the old house foundation. It was nearly noon. Then the barn door shuddered open again and Danny reappeared. After relocking the door, he went around back for his car and drove away.

Mark waited until the station wagon was out of sight, then hurried forward through the knee-high grass. He could not force the padlock, he saw at once;

it was almost new. Slowly he walked around the barn seeking another means of entry.

There were many half-rotted boards. At the back he found two together that looked decayed enough to be broken off. Bracing himself, he hauled on them until they snapped. After a check of the road to be sure he was still alone, he wriggled through the opening.

The barn was an eerie place, semi-dark, with dust motes dancing in thin beams of sunlight from gaps in roof and walls. An old tractor stood rusting. A wheelless buggy with rotting top rested on blocks of wood. Spiders had spun webs everywhere, and small live creatures made rustling sounds in accumulations of trash as he advanced.

The thing he sought stood just inside the big twin doors. Prue's car, which he had last seen at the quarry.

Parts of it were missing now. Some of the body had been stripped off—and disposed of too, apparently, since the pieces were nowhere to be seen. The engine, lifted out with a chain hoist that still hung from an overhead beam, lay on the floor with a box of tools beside it.

Danny must now be arrested and questioned again. This time, questioned properly.

Crouching, he squeezed through the opening where he had broken the boards out. Or part way through. When something slammed into his forearm and sent a shock-wave of pain to his shoulder, he hastily drew back.

After striking him, the missile fell to the ground outside the aperture and, dully shining, lay there in the sunlight. Another of the steel balls Danny Elder used for ammunition. Even as he stared at it, a second one barely missed him as it flashed into the barn's gloom.

The pain in his forearm slowly subsided, leaving only a dull ache. The arm had saved him, he realized.

In groping through the opening he had thrust it out in front of him just in time to keep the missile from smashing his face. Danny was a good shot.

He looked for something to use as a weapon. A jackstraw pile of old lumber lay nearby. Darting to it, he jerked out an arm-long piece of two-by-four and ran back to the wall.

He must be very quiet. Danny must be led to think the slingshot pellets had done their job.

Scarcely breathing, he held the two-by-four above his head and waited, like a batter awaiting a pitch. Time crawled.

Five minutes must have passed before he sensed that the one stalking him was just outside. Even then he was aware of nothing more, really, than a whisper of grass moving and a faint change in the quality of the light shining through the aperture.

Drawing in a deep, silent breath, he braced himself.

A hand appeared at the edge of the opening. A blond head intruded, eyes straining to probe the barn's dimness. The two-by-four descended.

With a grunt Danny Elder slumped to the ground and lay still, half in and half out of the gap. As Mark dragged him fully into the barn, he saw that one hand still gripped a slingshot.

But in a moment the boy's eyes flickered open. Gazing up into Mark's face, he made a sudden panicky effort to escape.

Pinning him down, Mark said grimly, "Don't try it."

"You got nothin' on me!"

"Only a stolen car and two attacks with a slingshot. And perhaps a murder." Twisting the weapon out of Danny's fingers, Mark thrust it into his pocket.

Still gripping the two-by-four in one hand, he hauled the youth erect. "Let's go. You first."

But it would not be easy, he realized. Though Danny was groggy he was not really hurt, and it was a long way to the car. And even if he were able to get Danny to the car, what then? A tough, resourceful kid like this was going to sit placidly beside him while he drove to the police station?

Moreover, his arm was beginning to stiffen. The steel ball must have bruised it, perhaps even cracked a bone. He was out of his depth here. And now Danny was aware of it. Derision curled the boy's mouth.

"Out to the road," Mark said.

"Sure, mister."

"You make one wrong move and I'll use this club again."

"Yeah."

Suddenly, without warning, Danny Elder burst into a run. But at the edge of the road toward which he ran, a familiar figure stepped from behind a screen of bushes.

Danny frantically changed direction. The figure halted, took aim with a revolver, and shouted, "Stop right there, Danny Elder, or I'll shoot!"

Danny stopped. And Kate Kendall, briskly advancing through the tall grass, halted ten feet from him. "Now you walk out to the road ahead of me, and don't try to be smart. Mr. Reeves, are you all right?"

"Yes, but glad to see you," Mark said wryly.

"I expect you are."

She marched Danny to where Mark had left his car. Her car was there, too. "Guess we'd better use yours," she said, "so you can do the driving while I keep a rein on this boy. We can come back for mine later."

Mark got behind the wheel. Prodding Danny onto the seat behind him, Kate got in and sat facing him, still holding the gun. "We'll just go to the station," she said. And as Mark put the car in motion: "Is your sister's station wagon back there in that barn, Mr. Reeves?"

"Yes."

"I thought so. How'd you find it?"

"I was convinced he had it, so I watched his house."

"H'm," Kate said. "Well, I was convinced he had it, too. Only difference is, I made a list of the places I thought he might have hidden it, and went looking. That old barn was number four on my list. Saw your car, though, before I got to it. You want to tell me what happened?"

He did, and she said to Danny, "What brought you back to the barn on foot after you drove away?"

"I come for some tools," Danny said sullenly.

"Tools?"

"My car quit on me down the road a ways."

"Well, well," Kate said. "Now isn't that ironical?"

At the police station Kate displayed a tenacity that made Mark wonder how he ever could have thought her incompetent. At first Danny Elder, handcuffed and ordered to "sit there and tell the truth for a change," would only say, "I ain't talkin'!" But Kate persisted. For forty-five minutes she thundered accusations, hissed questions, lashed him with words as though they were whips.

In the end she reduced him from a tough, sneering adult to a sniveling teenager who wanted only an end to his torment. That done, Kate removed the cuffs.

"Now suppose we begin at the beginning," she said then. "All this talk about you going to the Woodlins' that night to fix a pipe *was* just a coverup, wasn't it?"

He nodded.

"They phoned you to come? Real late?"

Again a nod.

"And when you got there, what did you find?"

"The blue station wagon was there in the driveway. I was to drive it to the quarry and get rid of it."

"Who told you to do that?"

"Miz Daphne."

"But you didn't do it, did you?"

He jerked his head from side to side.

"I was right when I talked to you before, wasn't I?

You just couldn't waste that lovely station wagon, so you left it there at the quarry and meant to go back for it. Then Mr. Reeves here began to dig too deep into what was going on, and you decided he had to be kept quiet."

"Not me," Danny said. "Miz Daphne."

"Daphne again?"

"We couldn't have you and Mr. Reeves snoopin' around so much, she said. Then she give me the note for Mr. Reeves and told me what I had to do when he showed up at the quarry."

"And what was that?"

"Get him with my slingshot, then put him in the car and push it into the water where no one would ever find it."

Mark said, repressing a shudder, "There was a man with you at the quarry when you tried to ambush me. Who was he? Your father?"

"Uh-uh. My old man don't know nothin' about any of this. It was Mr. Mayne."

After a moment of silence Kate said, "What do you know about this man's missing sister, Danny?"

"Nothin', Miz Kendall. I swear! I don't know nothin'!"

"You'd better not be lying again. What happened when Mr. Reeves got away from you at the quarry? What did Sarah and the others do then?"

"Mr. Mayne told me to get the car and hide it someplace."

"So you drove it to the old Layden barn to dismantle it. And what were you planning to do with the pieces, may I ask? Except those you meant to keep for yourself, of course."

The phone on Kate's desk rang but she ignored it, waiting for Danny's reply. Danny said, "I planned to bury 'em in the field there."

Kate plucked the phone from its cradle. "Police. Kate Kendall here." As she listened, her face filled with frown lines.

The caller was a woman, Mark guessed from the sound of the voice. But suddenly the voice fell silent and Kate, looking alarmed, said sharply, "Kim? Kim! What's wrong?"

With real fear in her eyes she looked at Mark. "She made a gasping sound, then someone slammed the phone down. She was telling me—" Kate shot to her feet. "Never mind! Come on!"

In her rush to the door she paused to glare at Danny. "You stay right here, Danny Elder, or you'll be sorry. You hear?" Then with Mark at her heels she was outside, running to Mark's car.

"The Woodlin place! Fast!"

When the car was out of the yard, racing down the road, Mark said fearfully, "What was Kim telling you?"

"She said, 'Kate, I'm at the Woodlins'. Kate, I've just found something terribly important. I think I've discovered *why* Mark's sister disappeared.' " Glancing at the trees flying by, Kate winced. "Slow down, will you? I didn't mean for you to kill us."

Mark cut the speed only a little. When he made the now familiar turn onto Mill Brook Road, the car swayed dangerously. He didn't care. If anything happened to Kim Barton, his life would lose all the meaning that had suddenly, wonderfully, come into it.

When they reached the old house he was racing up the piazza steps before Kate could get out of the car. Ignoring the bell, he tried to thrust the door open, but it was locked. He had to tug at the bell knob and wait, fuming, until someone came. His apprehension made the waiting an eternity.

It was the old lady who opened the door. Blinking in apparent surprise, she said, "Mr. Reeves? I didn't know we were expecting you today."

"We're coming in, Sarah," Kate Kendall snapped.

With a childish pout the old lady stepped back, allowing them to pass her. She was not wearing the purple velvet this time. Her attire was an ordinary housedress. She wore the band of purple around her neck, though, and nervously fingered the bow at her throat.

Kate went on into the first of the two living rooms, with Mark trailing. The older daughter, doing needlepoint, looked up.

"Leila," Kate said, "we're looking for Kim Barton."

"I don't believe she's here."

"Where is she?"

"Why, I'm afraid I can't say, Miss Kendall. We went to Salem to do some shopping, and only just got back."

"Where's your sister and her husband?"

"I'll try to find them for you." Putting the needlepoint aside, Leila stood up. "Just a moment, please."

She hurried into the adjoining room and Mark heard her calling, "Daphne! Victor! Where are you?" But he had no intention of waiting around just to be lied to by more members of the Woodlin clan. With a curt "I'll be back" to Kate, he made for the rear of the house.

He had not been in that part of the house before, but all he wanted was a back door. Finding one, he jerked it open.

There between house and barn, where she had said she always kept it, was Kim's car. A second car, older and bigger, evidently belonged to the Woodlins.

Returning to the front of the house, he ran up the stairs. Kim had said her room was over the front living room. Its door was closed, but when he turned the knob it opened.

She was not there. But she had not left the house, either—or if she had, she had gone without her handbag, which lay on the bureau. Impatiently he turned it upside down and spilled its contents onto the bed.

Would Kim have left her car keys and more than forty dollars in an unlocked room? In *this* house?

Fearing the worst, he hurried back downstairs. Sarah, her two daughters, and Victor Mayne sat in the front living room like silent judges at some ancient trial. He felt his skin crawl as he passed through.

Kate was in the other living room, frowning at a telephone on a Governor Winthrop desk. "Sarah says Kim went out about ten minutes ago," she told him. "The others say she was not here when they returned from Salem just before *we* got here."

"I think they're lying. Her bag is in her room with car keys and money in it. Her car is in the yard." He frowned at the desk. "Is this the phone she was using?"

"There's only the one. She must have been standing—" Kate suddenly looked down at the carpet, then knelt to examine it. It was an old Axminster, threadbare and faded. "Here! Look here!" she said triumphantly.

Hunkering down beside her, Mark saw she was pointing at two dark spots.

"Blood," Kate said. "At least, I think it is." Her fingers darted beyond the spots to snatch at something else. "And see this! And this! Bits of a broken vase!"

Mark could only nod.

She rose with the fragments of pottery clutched in her hand. "Kim was standing here talking to me, and someone came up behind—" Turning, she peered at a door beyond the desk. "Uh-huh. There used to be a gray vase on that little table. Someone came through that door, caught her phoning me, picked up the vase, and—" The music for marching was at full volume now, and Kate's eyes glittered. "Here!" Snatching her revolver from its holster, she pressed it into Mark's hand. "Keep an eye on those people while I look around!"

With a feeling he was being sucked into the vortex of a nightmare, Mark walked woodenly into the adjoining room and stood against the wall. The Woodlins censured him with their eyes. Not a word was spoken.

Kate, returning in five minutes, marched into the

room and planted herself before Sarah Woodlin's chair. Into Sarah's lap she dropped half a dozen pieces of a shattered gray vase.

"This is what you hit her with while she was phoning me. Now where is she?"

"I don't know what in the world you're talking about."

"You should have buried this broken vase, Sarah, but there wasn't time, was there? So, being a creature of habit, you threw it in the trash barrel on the back porch."

"Really, Kate!"

"I found your purple dress, too. Knew you must've been wearing it because you've still got the band around your neck. You should've got rid of that, too, instead of dropping it into the dirty-clothes hamper. Shall I get it and show you the spots of blood on it, Sarah? Or are you going to tell us where Kim is?"

"I'll tell you nothing, Kate Kendall!"

"Where is she, Sarah? What have you done with her?"

The old lady pressed her lips together and gazed into space.

"All right, then." Kate shot a glance at Victor Mayne and the two daughters, but apparently decided it would be a waste of time to shift her attack to them. She turned to Mark. "Guard them. I'm going to really search this house. *And* the barn." Spinning on one foot, she ran like a sprinter from the room.

Anger seethed in Mark as he glared at the four persons seated before him. "Mrs. Woodlin," he heard himself saying in the voice of a stranger, "if you've hurt my sister and Kim Barton, I—"

"You'll do what?" Sarah defiantly challenged.

"I won't stop until I see you rotting in prison!" In a fury he swung on the drab man who was married to Daphne. "Mayne, for God's sake can't *you* make her talk?"

"I don't cut any ice around here, mister."

"You helped Danny Elder ambush me at the quarry, damn you!"

Mayne recoiled as though struck, and suddenly Mark regretted having spoken. Before, Mayne had appeared to be no more than a spectator in the struggle with Sarah. Now his face was concrete-hard and his eyes were cold with menace.

How long would it take Kate to search the premises? Perhaps a long time. This old house had many rooms, a cellar, an attic. The barn was big, too. Meanwhile, Mayne's gaze chilled him with its intensity, and old Sarah, clapping her hands, giggled to herself like a delighted child.

Time crawled until Kate returned.

"Nothing in the house," she said. "But there's a trap door in the floor of that barn, and a root cellar under it. And I found a half-empty bowl of food there, and a pail somebody's been using for a toilet. I suspect your sister was imprisoned there until Kim created a problem with her phone call."

"My dear," Sarah said sweetly, "you're just wasting everybody's time and patience. Why don't you go home and leave us in peace?"

Kate ignored her. "Kim's here somewhere, Mark. Maybe Prudence, too. There wasn't time to carry out any elaborate scheme for disposing of them. Mark, there could be a built-in hiding place in this house. Lots of these old houses had them. Aren't you an architect?"

He nodded.

"Then can't you find it by measuring walls and things? Sarah!" Kate swung on the old lady. "Get me a tape measure!"

"Get your own."

Mark said quickly, "I've a tape in my car," and handed Kate the revolver. He was back in a moment. When he hesitated, trying to decide where to begin, Kate said, "Start here. If these others did go shopping, Sarah was alone here, and she couldn't have carried Kim up or down stairs by herself."

"Yes, start here!" Sarah clapped her hands. "Maybe we'll find a secret treasure!" Gleefully she bounced to her feet.

Her daughters and Victor Mayne remained seated, like a group of woodenly stiff figures in a bad painting.

The old lady trailed Mark about, watching his every move as he swiftly made measurements and jotted his findings in a notebook. She was hugely enjoying herself. Time and again he had to push her away as she pressed against him to see what he was writing.

He wondered why Kate did not order her to desist. But Kate, also trailing him about, made no comment.

Finding nothing in the room where Kim had been struck down, he hurried into the hall. There his gaze touched the main staircase, and a feeling of frustration all but crushed him.

The house was so big! Even with the search limited to the ground floor, the task could take hours. And if Kate were wrong—if the old lady *had* had help in dragging Kim up those stairs or down into the cellar . . .

In haste he measured the base of the staircase and yanked open the door of an under-stairs closet. A door-controlled light flashed on. Garments of various kinds hung there on a wooden rod. He shoved them aside. The floor was littered with overshoes, rubbers, bundles of old newspapers. He kicked them out behind him. The rear of the closet's plastered ceiling sloped to the floor at the angle of the staircase above it.

Nothing. He was wasting time. Impatiently he turned away.

But as he did so, a bell jangled in his mind and an inner voice crackled, "Hold it! That closet isn't deep enough!"

At the same moment Kate Kendall, peering at Sarah Woodlin, said crisply over her shoulder, "You're onto something, Mark. Her face says so! Look in there again!"

He glanced at Sarah's face and realized why Kate had let the old lady follow him around. Fear had replaced the mockery.

He plunged into the closet again. That ceiling at the rear, sloping down to the floor, had to be the answer. With the closet shorter than the base of the staircase above, there had to be a space behind it. His knuckles beat a tattoo and the sound was hollow.

His hands, gliding over the plaster, became those of a blind man reading an unseen face.

Suddenly there was a sharp click, and a section of the back wall dropped onto his fingertips. He lowered it to the floor, exposing a wedge of space under the foot of the stairs.

"Kim!"

But the dungeon held *two* women, both so immobilized they could not stir. His sister Prue was gagged with a towel and bound with rope. Kim Barton lay beside her with a trickle of blood on her forehead, entangled in a web of plastic clothesline and gagged with strips of bedsheet. Some papers lay scattered on the floor.

Mark cracked a shoulder on the underside of the staircase as he went to his knees, but in his agony of foreboding he felt little. Kim's eyes were closed. It might be too late.

But when he touched her, her eyes flickered open. Gently he drew her out of the secret compartment into the hall, then returned for his sister. In the hall the usually stern face of Kate Kendall wore an expression of profound relief. Sarah Woodlin leaned against the wall, staring at the floor.

It took him a few minutes to remove the gags and bonds from the rescued women. His sister embraced him; Kim reached for his hands. Kate said, "Maybe you should help Kim wash that blood from her face, Mark."

He did so, and Kate was in the front living room with the others when the two of them returned. His sister was saying to Kate, "I wasn't under the stairs long. They had me tied up in a root cellar under the barn—after knocking me out with something in a cup of tea, I mean. It wasn't very pleasant, I can tell you."

"I've seen that cellar," Kate said. "I can imagine."

"I guess they didn't know what to do with me. Then this evening they dragged me up out of there and put me under the stairs with this other girl—to get rid of both of us together, I suppose." Prue finally broke under the strain. "Oh, my God, they're terrible people! Especially that one!" She stabbed a finger at Sarah. "Even the others are afraid of *her*!"

"Because they don't know how to handle her," Kate said crisply. "But I do. And I'm going to, now that I've got enough to make it stick."

Mark had become aware that one person was missing. "Where's Mayne?"

Kate glared at the two daughters. "These two let him walk out while we were in the hall."

"What happened wasn't his fault," Daphne wailed. "He never wanted to be involved!"

Kate looked at Mark and shrugged. "Victor just announced he'd had enough and walked out, they say. It seems he and the two ladies here *were* shopping in Salem today and only did get back just before we arrived."

Kim said, "They weren't here when I phoned you. Only Sarah."

"And she caught you phoning."

"I thought she was in her room upstairs."

"I'd better use the phone myself," Kate said, "to make sure friend Victor doesn't get too far."

Victor's wife, Daphne, stopped sniveling and plucked at Kate's sleeve. "Please, Kate! He was only trying to help us!"

"Like he helped your mother keep this poor woman in the root cellar for a week?" Kate swung on the old lady. "Come to think of it, Sarah, just how did you get her out of that cellar if you were here alone?"

"She wasn't alone then," Prue said. "The others had returned."

Kate glared at the daughters again. "What did you have in mind to *do* with Prudence, anyway? Just keep her down there till she died of terror?"

"It was Mother's doing, Kate. Please!"

"And you covered up for her. All you had to do was pick up the phone, or speak out when I came here."

The daughters of Sarah Woodlin hung their heads.

"Furthermore," Kate grimly went on, "your Victor was party to an attempt on Mr. Reeves's life at the quarry. Remember *that.*"

The daughters looked accusingly at Sarah, and suddenly Victor Mayne's wife burst into uncontrollable sobbing. The other said in a dead voice, "Now see what you've done, Mother. Now we've *both* lost our husbands."

Sarah, with a toss of her head, walked away and sat down.

Returning from the telephone, Kate said, "I looked out back and the car is still there, so he must have gone on foot, still afraid to drive. He won't get far. I asked for assistance here, too." She touched Kim on the hand. "While we're waiting, why don't you tell us what happened?"

"I was hoping to find the answer to Prue's disappearance," Kim said. "I managed to get that Governor Winthrop desk open with a hairpin—she's always kept it locked—and I found some papers about the Reeveses and a diary in it."

"Where are they now?"

"Still there, I suppose. I just looked at them and put them back. Then I phoned you."

"I'll have a look," Kate said, and left the room. But she returned shaking her head. "She must have moved them. Destroyed them, probably, if she had the time."

"Of course I destroyed them!" Sarah said triumphantly. "You don't think I'm crazy, do you?"

"I think you're crazy, yes. But not all the time."

"Well, you won't find my diary. Or any papers, either. They're gone forever."

Kim said, "The papers appeared to be some kind of report she had prepared for Prue, tracing the Reeves family back to the old days in Salem. The diary was the shocker. There were half a dozen entries about Prue, leading up to a revelation that—"

"Hold on a minute," Mark interrupted. "Wait." Striding into the hall, he hurried to the niche under the stairs and gathered up the papers he had seen on the floor there. Obviously Kim hadn't noticed them when she was rescued and had been unaware of them before because she'd been unconscious when dragged in there. There was a notebook among them. When he re-entered the living room with his find, Sarah Woodlin closed her eyes in defeat.

He handed Kim the diary, and she fingered its pages. "Listen to this: 'Today I answered a letter I found in a magazine, from a woman named Reeves who thinks she may be descended from the Reeveses of Salem. Now wouldn't it be the answer to my lifelong prayers if she *is*.' "

Again Kim turned pages. "And this: 'Today I received another letter from Prudence Reeves, with more information. She *is* descended from the Salem Reeveses, I am certain.' "

Again the rustling of the pages was the only sound. "And now just listen to *this* entry, dated the day before Prue arrived here," Kim said. " 'Yesterday I finished my investigation, and now I know for sure that Prudence is a direct descendant of the Reeves woman who testified against *my* poor ancestor, Sarah Abbott, causing Sarah to be hanged as a witch. And tomorrow she will be here! At long last, after all these years, the score can be settled and my Sarah Abbott can rest in peace.' "

Closing the book, Kim handed it to Kate Kendall, who gazed stonily in accusing silence at Sarah Woodlin.

"I suppose you'll put me in prison now," Sarah said.

"You'll certainly be put somewhere."

With a toss of her head the old lady looked at her daughters. "Well, that ought to make *you* two happy. You'll have the house to yourselves at last."

"Sarah," Kate said, "don't you realize you meant to murder someone?"

"Of course I do. And she'd have deserved it."

It was all over, Mark realized. Victor Mayne might be caught or might not be; it made no difference. If he had a bad heart, he might not even live to be caught. Danny Elder would be punished somehow. This was the end.

He looked at Kim and knew that, for him, it might also be a beginning.

A YOUNG MAN CALLED SMITH

by Patricia Moyes

Of course, the whole thing was my fault. I admit that. All the same, even though my husband Tom says that I'm the daffiest, most scatterbrained woman that ever walked, I maintain that it was the sort of mistake anybody might have made.

It happened last summer, when Tom decided that since he was going to Paris for the International Plastics Exhibition, he might as well take a quick flip around his clients in Zurich, Vienna, Milan, and Lisbon while he was about it. That's one of the disadvantages of being married to a tycoon. Half the time you see him only before breakfast and after dinner, and the rest of the time you don't see him at all. However, there are compensations, like a flat in town and a rambling country house near the Sussex coast and a well-stocked wardrobe and a bank manager who sees you personally to the door, bowing all the way. I wouldn't like you to think I was complaining, especially as I happen to have the best and sweetest husband in the world thrown in as a sort of bonus.

Tom's quite a bit older than I am, and I think maybe that's why he worries about having to leave me alone when he goes off on these trips. This time, I must admit that I was really quite upset when he broke the bad news. You see, we were all set to go down to Meadowcroft—that's the Sussex house—for a couple of weeks' peace and quiet.

"Never mind, Margie love," he said. "You go on down to Meadowcroft, and I'll join you when I can."

"I don't like being there alone," I objected. We don't have any help living-in at Meadowcroft, just a woman who comes in two mornings a week.

Then Tom had an inspiration. "I know. Why don't you take Sister Susie down there with you? She's on holiday, isn't she? She'd probably enjoy it, and she'll be company for you. You can take it in turns to guard my stamps."

This last was a bit of a family joke. Tom's passion in life, next to the plastics business, is stamp collecting. He's been at it ever since he was a schoolboy, and by now—with money to spend and plenty of know-how—he's accumulated a collection worth several thousand pounds. As he keeps on pointing out to me, stamps are just about the easiest things for a thief to smuggle out of the country, and he's so scared of his collection's being burgled that it travels everywhere with us, in a sort of tin trunk. There are only two keys, one on Tom's key ring and the other in a special drawer in whichever house we're in: Tom says he wouldn't trust it to my handbag, and I dare say he's right. Mind you, it's not that he couldn't afford to replace the whole collection over and over again: it's the time and trouble he's put into those stamps that make them so precious to him.

Well, my young sister Sue jumped at the idea of coming to Meadowcroft with me. She was teaching at a primary school in South London at the time, and, having blued all her available cash on a skiing holiday in January, she was faced with the prospect of spending the long summer vacation either doing a temporary job, or moping in her dismal bedsitter in Clapham. As we drove down to Sussex, Sue confided to me that my invitation had been especially welcome because she had just parted forever from the latest of a long line of boyfriends.

"Not that I'm moping for him, Margie, don't think

that. He turned out to be a complete birdbrain. But I'd sort of got used to having him around."

This seemed to give me an opportunity of bringing up a subject that I'd had on my mind for some time.

"I do think, Sue," I said, "that you ought to think seriously about your future." I tried to sound as mature and parental as I could, which wasn't very, considering that Sue's twenty-three and I'm only five years older: but since our parents died ten years ago, I've had to do quite a bit of mothering vis-à-vis young Sue, and she generally took it very well when I lectured her.

This time, however, she seemed to sense what was coming, and shut up like a clam. "I don't know what you mean," she said. She closed her mouth very tight and looked out of the car window.

"Look, honey," I said. "Let's face it. You and I have only one asset in this world—our looks. There's no getting away from it."

"I happen to think that other things matter," said Sue, stubbornly.

"Of course they do," I said. "It's just that we don't happen to be well endowed with the other things. I admit you're ten times as clever as I am, but that still doesn't put you in the Einstein class, does it? You may like to think of yourself as a great intellect, but in fact you're an overworked, badly paid school teacher, and likely to remain so, if you don't get a grip on yourself."

"And do what?"

"Now where looks are concerned," I went on, ignoring her interruption, "you're in the number one, A level, super first class. You begin where Helen of Troy left off."

This wasn't such an exaggeration, either. As I've hinted, we're both quite personable, but whereas I tend to be the small, fluffy, blonde type, Sue is sort of statuesque. I don't mean in her measurements. I mean in the sort of dignity and elegance she has. She's got corn-colored hair and green eyes the size of gob-stoppers and a honey and peaches skin, and when she smiles it's as though some goddess or archangel had dropped in to make sure that all's well with the world. My objection was that she insisted on wasting these riches on penniless art students and would-be poets—the whole tribe of washouts that Tom had christened "Sue's bearded weirdies." I put this point of view to her now.

"I'm not suggesting," I said, "that you should sell yourself for filthy lucre, so stop looking at me like that. I'm just saying that if you'd only take the trouble to meet a few people who are . . . well . . . getting on in the world, as it were . . . then it's almost a dead cert that you'll fall in love with one of them. Look at Tom and me. You don't think I married him for his money, do you?"

"Of course not, Margie." Sue sounded shocked by the idea. "You were just terribly lucky."

"Lucky *and* sensible," I pointed out. "I found Tom simply because I decided to exclude from my circle of acquaintances any man whose income fell below a certain level. And sure enough, after a bit, along came Tom. Set your sights in the upper brackets, my girl—there are some nice fellows up there, you know."

Sue sighed. "I *do* get a bit bored with being broke," she admitted. "The trouble is, all the rich men I've ever met are so stupid. They're shallow, ill-informed, and fatuous."

"That's because you haven't explored far enough," I said. I could tell I was making headway because Sue fell into a thoughtful meditation, quite unlike her earlier hostile silence.

At last she said, "All right. I'll give it a try. You introduce me to all the rich men you can find while we're at Meadowcroft, and I'll be prepared to consider them."

"That's my girl," I said.

As it turned out, the laugh was on me because when

we got to Sussex I found that any of our neighbors who fell into the right category were away sunning themselves in Elba or Sardinia. In England, the weather was idyllic. The sun shone, and Sue and I had tea in the garden: but we had it alone. She never said a word about our conversation in the car, but I couldn't help feeling that she was laughing at me, just a little.

After a week, I began to get worried in case she was bored, and fretting for the banished boyfriend. So I was pleased when, around teatime on the second Tuesday, I looked up from my gardening to see a battered red sports car making its way noisily up the drive. It looked and sounded as though it had been constructed out of a do-it-yourself kit with several vital parts missing, but as it roared to a shuddering halt outside the front door, I saw that it contained a young man. Rather a good-looking young man. I stepped out of the herbaceous border, beaming welcome.

"Good afternoon," I said.

The young man jumped out of the car and came towards me. "Oh," he said. "You must be . . . I mean . . . are you Mrs. Westlake?"

"I am."

"My name's Smith. Bobby Smith. I work for Amalgamated Plastics. I met your husband at the Paris Exhibition last week, Mrs. Westlake, and when he heard I was planning to holiday in Shinglesea, he suggested I should look you up. I hope you don't mind."

"Not at all," I said. I didn't try to make it sound too convincing. A closer look at Mr. Smith had decided me that Sue and I could well do without him. He was wearing a dirty duffel coat and crumpled grey flannels, and his brown hair looked as though it hadn't been combed for a week. In fact, he looked too much like a bearded weirdie for comfort, and I hoped that he would take the hint from my chilly tone, and leave.

But not a bit of it. "So I thought I'd—" he began. And then suddenly his eyes seemed to grow larger, and to protrude as though pushed from within, and his face turned a dull puce. He emitted a sound which can best be transcribed as "glug." What had happened, of course, was that Sue had come out of the house.

"This is my sister, Sue Davidson," I said. "Sue, meet Bobby Smith, a friend of Tom's."

"How do you do?" gurgled Smith. "Delighted to meet you. Not really a friend of Mr. Westlake's, you know . . . just met at the Paris show . . ."

He had got hold of Sue's hand by this time, and was pumping it up and down as though he expected thereby to induce water to gush from her mouth. Sue looked at him with, I was pleased to note, no enthusiasm at all.

"How are you?" she said distantly, like a goddess making conversation with some of the less desirable elements of the underworld. There was an awkward pause.

I was aware of mixed emotions. Much as I wanted to be rid of the young man, he had been invited by Tom to call on us, and hospitality is hospitality. I didn't feel I could send him packing without the elementary courtesy of a cup of tea. This I offered, and he accepted with alacrity. I left him in the drawing room with Sue while I went to boil the kettle.

When I came back, Sue was sitting on the sofa, with Bobby Smith as close beside her as it was possible for him to be without actually constituting the basis for a complaint. Every time Sue edged away from him, he shifted towards her to close the gap, and by now he had her pretty well pinioned in the corner. He was talking about the insides of racing cars. He continued to talk while we had our tea, and afterwards asked to be shown Tom's stamp collection, about which he had heard so much. Reluctantly, I unlocked it, and, by making him walk over to the display case to see it, succeeded momentarily in relieving the pressure on Sue.

As soon as the stamps had been inspected, admired, and locked up again, Bobby reverted to the subject of cars, and began to press Sue to come for what he called "a spin in my old bus." Now, Sue is a gently nurtured girl and finds it difficult to dish out a plain, discourteous refusal. Having made it obvious in at least six different ways that she did not want to go, she eventually agreed to a short ride, but only on condition that I came, too.

It was purgatory. There was, strictly speaking, no back seat—just a sort of bench covered with a filthy, moth-eaten rug. We scorched and snarled our way to the nearest village where Bobby stopped at the inn and bought us each a disgusting bottle of livid-green fizzy lemonade and a petrified sausage roll. We eventually arrived home at half-past six; I was aching in every muscle and bone, and it was with horror that I realized that Bobby had no intention of departing. He settled himself comfortably in the drawing room with the drink which I had felt in duty bound to offer him.

When I went out to the kitchen to fetch more ice, Sue followed me. As soon as the door was shut behind her, she let fly. "Margie, it's too *awful*! You *must* get rid of him! He'll be here all night at this rate, and he keeps trying to *paw* me . . . it's *disgusting*. Can't you *do* something?"

"Don't worry, honey," I said. "Leave him to me."

I went back to the drawing room and said, with a cold smile, "Well, Mr. Smith, I'm so sorry I can't ask you to stay any longer, but my sister and I are due at a cocktail party at seven, and we have to change. So—"

"Oh, that's all right," replied the wretched youth airily. "I'll wait for you down here, and drive you over to your party."

"And how," inquired Sue icily, "do we get back again?"

"I'll wait for you," he said, cheerfully. "I'd be glad to come in with you, but I'm not really dressed for a social evening, and these country houses are so hideously bourgeois. It'll be up to you to slip away pretty smartly, and we'll all go out to dinner together."

Sue shot me a look of utter despair, but I was able to take this one in my stride. "I'm sorry, Mr. Smith," I said, "this isn't the sort of party that we want to slip away from, and we're invited to stay on for dinner afterwards."

"Oh, I say," he said. "What frightfully bad luck." You could tell he was really sorry for us, missing the treat of dining with him. "Anyhow, I'll wait till you leave, and speed you on your way."

There was nothing for it. Sue and I had to go upstairs and solemnly change into cocktail rig, and get the car out. Even then I didn't think we'd get rid of him. He insisted on writing down for Sue the address of the third-rate boarding house in Shinglesea which had the bad luck to have drawn his custom, and he assured us that he'd be calling again very soon. Our spirits lifted a little when he said that he was breaking his holiday the following day to visit an aunt in Norfolk, but they sank again when he urged us not to worry, as he'd be back by the weekend.

When we finally got into the car and drove off, he followed us for several miles until I finally shook him off by superior local knowledge. It was then, speeding recklessly up a leafy lane, that Sue and I both began to laugh hysterically. By the time we got home, however, our mood had hardened: and the last straw came when I found, on the drawing room sofa, the gold propelling pencil which Bobby had produced from his pocket to write his address for Sue. It bore the engraved initials *R.S.*

"He did it on purpose!" exploded Sue. "He deliberately left it behind so that he'd have an excuse to come back. Well, he's got another think coming. We've got his address, so you can send it back to him, Margie, with a note telling him to go and jump off the cliff."

"I can't very well do that," I said, "but I can write

and tell him that you've had to go back to London. He won't come here for the pleasure of *my* company."

"Good idea," said Sue. "And the next time an unidentified car comes up this drive, Margie, you and I are going to dive into the nearest haystack and stay there until the all-clear sounds."

She was wrong, of course. It was just after four next afternoon, and I was in the pantry arranging some flowers that I'd cut from the garden, when I heard the gentle purring of an expensive motor car in the drive. For a moment, I had a panicky fear that it might be the unspeakable Smith returned unexpectedly from Norfolk—but the well-bred murmur of the engine reassured me. I went to the drawing room window and looked out.

In the drive stood a grey E-type Jaguar, and beside it stood a young man who might have stepped straight into a women's magazine illustration, no questions asked. He was tall and slim, with straight, shining fair hair, and he wore a beautifully cut sports jacket and a crisp white shirt with a silk scarf in the neck of it. You could tell at a glance that he didn't suffer from halitosis, B.O., or dandruff. He was sunburnt, and even from the drawing room I could see that his hands were as lean and sensitive a couple as ever caressed a steering wheel. Then he turned his head towards me, and I saw that his eyes were dark cornflower blue, thus giving him a score of ten out of ten. The reason he had turned was that Sue had seen him from her swing chair on the lawn, and was walking over to investigate.

By the time I got there, Sue was standing beside the Jaguar, gazing at its proprietor with a sort of stunned expression. She did not actually say "glug," but it was implicit in her whole demeanor.

"Margie," she said, in a faint voice, "this is Robin Smith. He's a friend of Tom's. Mr. Smith, this is my sister, Mrs. Westlake."

"How very nice to meet you." The apparition

turned to me, giving me the full benefit of the dark blue eyes, together with a smile which made even my matronly heart beat a little faster. "I ran into your husband in Paris, and he suggested I might look you up. I'm holidaying in Shinglesea for a week or two."

"You will come in and have some tea, won't you?" Sue asked anxiously, with half an eye on me. I think she was afraid that I might not have grasped that this was the exception that proved the rule.

"If you're sure I'm not disturbing you," said Robin. "I only meant to stay a moment . . ." We fairly hustled him indoors.

I went off to get tea. When I came back, Sue was sitting—if that's the right word—on the sofa, displaying a length of exquisite leg, like a goddess who has heard that Apollo will be along at any moment and is anxious not to miss him. Robin was sitting on a small and rather uncomfortable chair on the far side of the room, talking about the implications of pop art. This seemed almost too good to be true. When, over the cucumber sandwiches and thin bread and butter, he went on to discuss twelfth-century stained glass and the influence of Ezra Pound on modern poetry and the correct method of preparing *coq au vin*, I could barely contain myself for delight.

The effect on Sue was apparent. By the time we got to Ezra Pound, she had stopped draping herself over the sofa, and was taking a lively part in the conversation—which is more than I was, but that didn't matter. The important thing was that the two of them were striking sparks off each other.

Eventually, we got round to the subject of cars, and Sue dropped a couple of mammoth hints about how she's always wondered what it would be like to ride in a *really* fast car. Robin simply said that he'd wondered the same thing himself, and hoped that a friend of his might let him try a couple of laps at Silverstone in a Lotus one of these days. Then he looked down at his watch, and said that he really must be going.

Sue was looking at me in a dumb, pleading sort of way, but I couldn't detain the man by force. I did my best to prolong the conversation by asking where in Shinglesea he was staying.

"Just outside the town," he said. "The Shinglesea Towers. Do you know it?"

"I do indeed," I said. It was one of the most exclusive and expensive seaside hotels in Britain.

"It's not bad," he said. "Quite reasonable food, taken all in all, and of course everything tastes better when eaten on a terrace on a warm, moonlit night."

"Like tonight," said Sue, brazenly. (I felt quite ashamed of her.)

After that the poor man could hardly fail to invite us to dine with him. He did it beautifully, though—exactly as though it was a brilliant idea which had just occurred to him.

I tried to keep some semblance of dignity, but the way Sue said, "Oh, yes, *please*," ruined any effect it might have had. We both went up to change, and I lent her my coffee-colored Balmain chiffon, my mutation mink stole, and some diamond clips and a bracelet. I must say she looked good enough to eat.

It was arranged that Sue and Robin should go ahead in the Jaguar, and that I should follow on in the little runabout we keep in the country. The two of them were in the lounge when I arrived, and Robin provided us with cocktails and then went off to change. One doesn't dine in a sports jacket at the Shinglesea Towers. A few minutes later he came back in a dark suit, looking more like an advertisement for gracious living than ever, and we made our way through the dining room and out onto the terrace.

Though I say it myself, we were quite a sensational-looking trio, and we caused a stir. Waiters were fairly tripping over each other for the privilege of showing us to our table, and I was aware of knives and forks freezing into immobility all over the room as a hundred heads turned to watch our progress. I sneaked a quick look at Sue, and was delighted to see that she was carrying it off superbly. A goddess moving graciously among her humble, earthly devotees. (I felt proud of her.)

It was an enchanted evening. We ate *fois gras* and *homard a l'Américaine* and fresh peaches, and we drank champagne. Sue and Robin danced together with as much ease and expertise as if they'd been rehearsing for weeks, and in the intervals of dancing, they talked about every subject under the sun. Most of the conversation was miles above my head, but I was perfectly happy just to sit and listen. It seemed to me that I was seeing my sister in her natural element for the first time. She was never meant to live in a bedsitter and teach English to pudding-faced kids, and it pleased me to think that Sue was obviously coming to the same conclusion herself.

It seemed no time at all before the witching hour arrived. The band played the last waltz, the dancers and diners dispersed, and Sue and I found ourselves on the front steps of the hotel, shaking hands with Robin and thanking him for a marvelous evening. Then we got into the car, and I waved a last goodbye to Robin and drove off. At once, Sue burst into tears.

"Take it easy, honey," I said. "I know you're excited and—"

"I've . . . I've n-never had such a b-b-beautiful evening in all my life . . ." sobbed Sue.

"I know," I said, soothingly. "But you'll have plenty more."

This produced a despairing wail. "I w-won't! I'll never see him again!"

"That's just nonsense," I said. "He's obviously crazy about you."

"Then why d-didn't he say a s-single word about meeting again?" sniffed Sue. "He's only here till next week, and he didn't even ask for my address in London, or give me his. I may as well face it, Margie," she went on, in a fresh burst of misery, "I b-bore him stiff. I'm not pretty enough or clever enough or—"

"My dear young idiot," I said firmly, "pull yourself together. Robin Smith is a very correct and well-mannered young man. When you come to think of it, he thrust his company on us this evening—"

"He didn't!"

"I'm looking at it from his point of view. He turned up uninvited. Then he asked us to dinner, and we accepted—but for all he knows, it may have been just politeness on our part. What I'm driving at is that the next move is up to us. Up to me, to be precise."

"Is it?" Sue still sounded doubtful.

"Of course it is. I shall write to Robin tomorrow, and ask him to . . . to . . . I know! To spend the weekend at Meadowcroft."

"Margie, you're an angel!" squeaked Sue, and nearly put us into the ditch by flinging her arms round my neck just as I was taking a tricky bend. She sang happily to herself the rest of the way home.

The next morning, when I went to my desk to write to Robin, I found myself face to face with that horrible gold propelling pencil, and decided to write both letters while I was about it. It was even more important, now, to keep the unspeakable Bobby away from the house.

I spent some time composing the letters, and when I had finished I felt quite pleased with them. I took them to Sue for her to read.

The first one went as follows:

Dear Mr. Smith,

After your visit, I found the enclosed pencil, which I think belongs to you. I am sending it back to save you the trouble of calling here for it.

My sister has asked me to tell you that she has had to return to London unexpectedly. I do not expect to see her again for some time.

Yours sincerely,
Margaret Westlake

"Pretty chilling, I think you'll agree," I said to Sue, with satisfaction. She was for making it even ruder, but I protested that only a rhinoceros would fail to get the message. I then showed her the second letter.

Dear Mr. Smith,

Neither Sue nor I feel that we thanked you enough for entertaining us so regally. It was a splendid evening, with superb food, drink, and company—and Sue is still talking about her ride in your fabulous car.

It occurred to me that, if you feel you have had enough of hotel life for the time being, you might like to spend this coming weekend with us here at Meadowcroft. It would give us such pleasure—do say you'll come, and make it Friday evening if you can.

Very sincerely,
Margie Westlake

I had to drive into Shinglesea to do some shopping, so I decided to drop the letters in by hand, to avoid delay. The two envelopes were lying on my desk—one addressed to "R. Smith, Esq., Shinglesea Towers Hotel," and the other to "R. Smith, Esq., Ocean View, Pebble Road, Shinglesea." I wrapped the appropriate letter round the propelling pencil, and then slipped both letters into the envelopes and sealed them. One I delivered to the immaculate receptionist at the Shinglesea Towers, and the other to the sleazy landlady of Ocean View. I expect you'll have guessed by now what happened, and I still maintain that anybody might have made the same mistake.

Disaster struck with the arrival of the post on Friday morning. At first, I was pleased to see a letter with the monogram of Shinglesea Towers embossed on the envelope, but when I picked it up and felt the long, thin, solid object inside, my heart did an unpleasant somersault. I tore open the envelope. Out fell the propelling pencil. Trembling, I opened the letter, which was written in a handsome Italian hand.

Dear Mrs. Westlake,
I am returning the pencil, as I am afraid that, despite the similarity of initials, it is not mine.
I am sorry to hear that your sister has had to leave so suddenly.

Yours sincerely,
Robin Smith

Of course, I had to confess to Sue. She began to wail like a banshee, declaring that her life had been ruined and that she might as well sign on for the nearest convent straight away. This brought me to my senses.

"There's no point just sitting there snivelling," I said. "Fortunately, no great harm has been done. I shall ring Robin straight away and explain that there's been a mistake."

I contacted Robin at the Shinglesea Towers without any difficulty, and although he sounded a bit standoffish at first—and no wonder, after that letter—he soon melted, and said that he was delighted to hear that Sue hadn't had to go to London after all, and that nothing would please him more than to spend the weekend with us. In fact, he said, he'd been on the point of going back to London because he found hotels desperately boring after a few days. Such was our rejoicing at this, and so pressing was the planning of menus, and the shopping, and the deciding of what clothes to wear, that the darker side of the picture remained completely forgotten until after lunch.

It was only then, when Sue was up in my room trying on everything in my wardrobe to see what suited her best, that the awful truth hit me. If Robin had received the chilly letter, then the unspeakable Bobby had received a gushing invitation to spend the weekend with us. An ordinary person, I reflected, reading that letter with its references to superb food and drink and a fabulous car, would realize immediately that there'd been a mistake, but Bobby Smith was perfectly capable of construing it as a legitimate description of our hellish jaunt to the local pub. I fairly ran to the telephone.

"Ocean View," said the flat, unpleasant voice that I recognized as belonging to the landlady.

"I want to speak to Mr. Robert Smith."

"He's left."

"Yes, I know. But he's back again, isn't he? I mean, he said he was coming back today."

"He's left and come back and left again. Not half an hour ago. No consideration, some people haven't."

"You mean—he's gone for good?"

"That's what he said. Without so much as by-your-leave. The room was reserved till Sunday." The voice took on a menacing note.

"Do you know where he went?"

"I do not. To stay with friends in the neighborhood, he said. A likely story, I don't think. Hadn't got the money to pay till Sunday, more like."

"You don't happen to know if he . . . I mean, I left a note for him this morning and I wondered whether he'd received it . . ."

"If it was left in, it'll have been handed to him," said the voice huffily.

"Thank you," I said, and rang off.

As I came out into the hall, I met Sue careering down the stairs. She was still wearing the gold lamé evening dress that she'd been trying on when I went to telephone. She clutched my arm.

"Margie! Coming up the drive! He's here!"

"I thought as much," I said, gloomily.

"You've got to get rid of him!"

"My dear Sue, I'll do my best, but I can't work miracles. You'd better go up and change into something more suitable. And for heaven's sake, behave yourself."

It was plain that Sue would have liked to express herself at some length, doubtless on the ruined-life motif, but the angry snarl of the home-made red car put an end to further conversation. Sue gave me a look into which she managed to pack a couple of tirades, a tragic renunciation of all future happiness, and a raspberry. She then gathered up the gold lamé and scudded up the stairs like a goddess surprised by a satyr, just as Bobby Smith walked in through the front door. He did not even bother to ring.

"Ah, Margie! Here I am," he announced unnecessarily. "Good idea of yours, having me here for the weekend. Shinglesea was becoming tedious."

"As a matter of fact—" I began, feebly.

"Shan't be a moment. Just get my things out of the car."

I followed him to the front door. The red menace was standing steaming in the drive, and from its noisome interior Bobby began producing an assortment of articles, as a conjuror will from a top hat. First came three battered suitcases, and a kind of wickerwork basket tied up with string. Then a tennis racket, a snorkel mask, a pair of ice skates, binoculars, a bagful of golf clubs, an inflatable air bed, and a string bag full of paperback thrillers.

"Never know how the holiday's going to turn out, do you?" remarked Bobby, as he assembled this collection in the porch. "If you'll just show me my room, I'll take this lot up, and then come back for the rest."

"The rest?"

"Oh, just my cameras and transistor radio and tape recorder. I don't like leaving valuable equipment in an open car. You never know who's skulking in the shrubbery, do you?" He laughed loudly.

"No," I said. "You don't."

"Well . . ." He was festooned with baggage by this time. "Lead on, MacDuff. I'm right behind you. But quick, woman, before I drop the lot."

It was all too much for me. Meekly, I led the way to the smaller of the two spare rooms.

When the last load of gear had been safely stowed away, Bobby strolled into the drawing room, flopped onto the sofa and put his feet up, and remarked, "Where's young Sue?"

"She's changing," I said. I knew that Sue, from behind her bedroom door, must have observed what had happened, and I knew she wouldn't appear until she had to.

"Changing?" Bobby smiled, with repellent smugness. "She needn't have bothered to dress up just for me."

"She isn't," I assured him.

"What do you mean?"

"Just that we're expecting another house guest. He should be here any moment."

Bobby looked really annoyed. "Oh, lord," he said. "Couldn't you have put him off? We don't want anybody else."

There was a pretty solid statuette of the Goddess of Plenty in pink jade on a small table near my right hand, and I came within an ace of grabbing it and beaning the wretched youth. My hand was stayed, however, by the whisper of tires in the drive: through the window, I saw the Jaguar pulling up.

"There he is now," I said, and hurried out.

Robin had only one suitcase ("No point in getting the rest of the stuff out of the car," he said). I took him up to the best spare room, where Sue had lovingly arranged a big bowl of red roses. I showed him the guest bathroom, and told him that drinks would be ready downstairs whenever he was. When I came into the drawing room with the tray of glasses, Bobby and Robin were both sitting there, eyeing each other with mutual suspicion.

"Have you two introduced yourselves?" I asked, with a ghastly attempt at gaiety. "Mr. Smith, meet Mr. Smith. Robin, this is Bobby. Bobby—Robin."

They smirked halfheartedly at each other, in the manner of small boys forced to shake hands politely but only waiting for the schoolmaster's back to be turned for the rough stuff to begin.

"I thought perhaps you might know each other already," I went on, "since you both met Tom at the Plastics Exhibition in Paris." This produced no reaction. I blundered on. "Bobby's in plastics, I know—Amalgamated, isn't it?" Bobby nodded. "I suppose you're in the same line of country, Robin."

"In a way," said Robin. There was another endless pause.

"Well," I said, "what about a drink?"

I poured the drinks, and we sat there in clammy silence. I offered a tour of the garden, which both young men declined. Their attention was fixed unswervingly on the door through which Sue might be expected to appear.

At last I stood up and said, "Well, if I don't get things going in the kitchen, we'll have no supper. Do help yourselves to drinks. I'll see if I can find that sister of mine to entertain you."

I ran upstairs and into Sue's room. She had changed into a simple brown linen dress and was lying on her bed, reading a detective story.

"Sue!" I said. I wanted to shout, but I had to make do with a sort of stage whisper. "For heaven's sake! You've got to come down and help me!"

"I won't come down while that man's in the house."

"Don't be childish! You simply can't leave me to cope by myself."

"It was all your fault in the first place," Sue pointed out. "And anyway, I don't know what you're complaining about. You're not being pursued by that . . . that gargoyle."

"But—"

"Get him out of the house, and I'll come down. Otherwise, I stay here."

"I can't simply throw him out! He's got about fifty suitcases, and he's just unpacked."

Sue was sensible enough to see the logic of this. She relented a little. "All right. Get him out of the place for an hour or so, to give me a chance of seeing Robin alone . . . please, Margie . . . I promise I'll behave if I can have just an hour . . ."

Well, there was only one way to do it. I went downstairs again and begged Bobby to take me for another ride in his gorgeous motor car.

I was gratified to see that I had judged him correctly. Nothing else would have got him out of the house. As it was, I could see the inner struggle that was going on, and I quickly tipped the balance by enthusing in a nauseating way over the vile machine, and asking endless questions. We were all three out in the drive by then, admiring the scarlet brute. The grey Jaguar stood quietly aloof, looking aristocratic and unamused. Bobby had already dismissed it with a quick glance and a scathing, "I see you've got one of those reliable old ladies. Too run-of-the-mill for my taste, I'm afraid." This had done nothing to endear him to Robin.

At last we set out, bumping and roaring across the countryside, with Bobby humming tunelessly to himself, and me clutching the solider portions of the vehicle and praying for a quick release. After about two hundred years, we stopped at the same pub, and this time I insisted on a double gin. After all, I wasn't driving, and the mere sight of that green lemonade made me feel sick.

To my surprise, Bobby started talking about Robin. Wanted to know how long I'd known him, where I'd met him, and so on. Most impertinent, I considered, but it's difficult to refuse outright to answer a question. By the time the catechism was over, I was uncomfortably aware that I had revealed that I knew nothing whatsoever about Robin. "Any more than I do about you," I added, pointedly. "If you knew my husband better, you'd understand. He's a tremendously friendly soul, and he's continually issuing invitations to total strangers. I'm quite used to it."

What I didn't add was that, while it's true that Tom does scatter invitations, his scattering is usually very selective. He sums people up in a flash, and has a way of finding out their entire life history in the time that it takes most people to shake hands and comment on the weather. Robin was just the sort of person who would appeal to Tom, but I couldn't understand how he had come to fraternize with a character like Bobby Smith. I'd never known Tom to pick a dud before, and it bothered me.

We got home eventually, to find that Sue and Robin had gone off in the Jaguar. This made me very cross, and since Bobby obviously felt the same way, a bond of a kind was created between us. I must say that he was very useful in the kitchen, too. When, between us, we'd prepared a delicious mixed grill and green salad and there was still no sign of the others, we decided to go ahead and eat. I opened a bottle of Tom's Volnay, and by the time it was half empty, I had decided that Bobby Smith might be almost tolerable if only he'd get the engine-oil out of his fingernails and try not to be so conceited.

Robin and Sue came back at half-past eight, sparkling and laughing and hoping that we hadn't waited dinner for them. I'm afraid I was pretty terse with them both. Apart from anything else, Bobby had succeeded in planting nasty little wisps of suspicion in my mind. I became increasingly aware that I knew nothing whatsoever about either of these two young men. I should never have invited one, let alone both, to stay in the house. Sue and I were quite defenseless, several miles from the nearest village, and with Tom's stamp collection—let alone my jewelry—simply asking to be burgled. Later on in the evening, when Sue actually suggested getting the stamps out to show them to Robin, I could have screamed. Since by now both our visitors knew where the key was normally kept, I decided to slip it into my handbag and take it up to my room for the night.

I slept hardly at all. I lay awake for hours, wishing that Tom were at home or that I could contact him. As it was, I didn't even know what country he was in. Next morning I was up and about by seven, making myself a cup of tea. And when the postman dropped a letter in Tom's handwriting through the letter box, it seemed like a direct answer to prayer. I rushed to open it.

Tom's not much of a letter writer. This was a typical scrawl, written in the middle of a busy day from a hotel in Milan. All was going well, he said. He was just off to Lisbon, and couldn't possibly say when he'd be home, but I could be sure it would be as soon as ever he could make it. Paris had been magic, business-wise, and he'd bought me a little present. The letter ended with his reassurances that I was the only girl in the world as far as he was concerned, and sketched out a rough program of what he planned to do the moment he got home. That was all. Then I noticed the small letters P.T.O. at the bottom. I turned the page over and read—

> *P.S. You may get a visit from a young man called Smith. Met him in Paris. A very bright lad, and could be important, so be specially nice to him, will you, angel? Thought he might be amusing company for Sister Sue.*

I read the P.S. three times, and each time it made me feel sicker. Of course. What an idiot I'd been. It was too much even for the long arm of coincidence that Tom should have met *two* young men in Paris, both called Smith, both in plastics, and should have invited them both to visit us. The letter clinched it. *A* young man, it said. Not two young men. No, I had to face it. One of them was an impostor—an adventurer, probably a criminal, who had overheard Tom's invitation to the genuine Smith, and taken a chance on cashing in on it. The question was—which was the real Smith, and which was the phony? There seemed no way of finding out.

I was sitting miserably in the kitchen, reading Tom's P.S. for the tenth time, when the door began to edge open slowly. My nerves were so taut by then that I wouldn't have been surprised to see a Thing from Outer Space creeping round the door. I let out a small scream. What did, in fact, creep round the door was Bobby Smith. He was wearing an ancient camel-hair dressing gown, and he looked like a Thing from Outer Space that has left its comb and razor on a neighboring planet.

He appeared as surprised to see me as I was to see him. For a moment, we goggled at each other. Then he gave a sort of gulp, and said, "Oh. Good morning, Mrs. Westlake."

"Good morning," I said.

"I see you're up."

"Yes."

"I . . . er . . . I woke early, and I thought I . . . that is . . . a cup of tea, you know . . ."

"Help yourself," I said. "I've just made it."

"Oh. Thanks very much."

He sat down at the table opposite me and poured himself a beaker. Then he said, "As a matter of fact, I'm glad to have an opportunity of talking to you, Mrs. Westlake."

"Really?"

"Yes. It's about . . . well . . . it's rather awkward, really. It's about Smith."

"Robin Smith?"

"That's right. It's been worrying me ever since yesterday. You see, I was positive I'd seen him before somewhere. And this morning, lying in bed, it suddenly came to me."

"What did?"

"Where I'd seen him. It was last week in Paris, at the Exhibition."

"Well, of course it was." I was in no mood for banalities, and I suppose I must have spoken sharply because Bobby looked at me in a surprised way. Then he said, in a patronizing drawl, "I'm afraid you don't quite understand, Mrs. Westlake. Events like the Plastics Show . . . well, they attract the best people in the business from all over the world . . . people like your husband, for example . . ."

"I know that."

He leant forward, and took another gulp of tea. "They also attract a crowd of hangers-on. The nastiest sort, who skulk around in the bars on the off-chance of getting an introduction to somebody important. All of them are shady characters, and some are downright crooks." He paused impressively. "And your Robin Smith was one of them!"

"How can you be so sure?" I felt cold with fear, thinking of Sue.

"I remember now. It was the day I met Mr. Westlake. I noticed this crowd of suspicious-looking shysters hanging round the bar where we lunched. Robin Smith was one of them."

"How curious," I said, "that it's taken you so long to recognize him."

This did not disconcert Bobby. "It's the clothes, you see. And the beard."

"The what?"

"The clothes, the car, the whole setup . . . he had me fooled for a bit, I admit that. You see, when I saw him in Paris, he was as scruffy as the rest of them. And he wore a beard. A disguise, I presume."

"Bobby," I said, faintly, "I think you must be making a mistake."

"I hope I am, for your sake," said the young wretch. "I suppose it just might be one of those cases of doubles or identical twins that one reads about, but I doubt it. I doubt it very much. So if you've got any valuables in the house, I'd advise you to keep them under lock and key."

"I shall go and have a bath," I said.

By the time I had bathed and dressed and come downstairs again, Bobby had gone. My dear, comforting Mrs. Waters had arrived and was clucking round the kitchen like a plump Sussex hen. Coffee was brewing, and a clutch of boiled eggs nestled under a tea cosy, beside a rackful of toast. In the dining room, Robin—devastating as ever in a silk dressing gown—was reading the morning paper. He jumped up as I came in.

"Good morning, Mrs. Westlake. What can I get you? Coffee, tea, eggs?"

"I'll serve myself, thank you, Robin," I said.

He sat down again. When I had helped myself, he took a quick glance round, as though to make sure we were alone, and then said, "I'm afraid I owe you an apology for yesterday evening."

"Oh, for heaven's sake, it doesn't matter," I said. "If you and Sue wanted to—"

"No, no. You don't understand." Again the furtive look round. "You see, the reason we were so long over our drive was that Sue was telling me about . . ." He hesitated. "About the *other* Mr. Smith."

"Bobby, you mean?"

"Yes. Now, I don't want to alarm you, Mrs. Westlake, but just how long have you known him? Have you checked up on his background and his credentials? I was in Paris myself last week, and I know the sort of undesirables who hang around international shows in the hope of meeting a big man like your husband. Sue is distinctly worried about Smith, and I don't blame her."

"Sue has taken a personal dislike to him," I said. "That doesn't make him a criminal."

"Of course it doesn't. I'm not accusing anybody of anything," said Robin, rather hastily. "But I understand that he has shown a suspicious interest in your husband's stamp collection. Not to mention Sue's diamonds."

"Sue's—?" I began, astonished, and then I remembered our dinner in Shinglesea. Of course Robin thought the jewels were hers. "He asked to see Tom's stamps, that's all," I said.

"Exactly. Now, what I'm going to suggest is that you'd be easier in your mind if you turned the keys of the stamp collection and the jewel cases over to me. It's a man's responsibility to look after valuables like that. Sue absolutely agrees with me."

"Certainly not!" I had blurted out the words before I could stop myself. I gulped a bit, and then went on, more calmly, "I do appreciate your offer, Robin, but I'm quite used to standing on my own feet, you know."

"Well, at least tell me where the keys are, so that I can keep an eye on them. I noticed you didn't put the stamp collection key back in its usual place last night."

"The keys are quite safe, thank you," I said, hoping I sounded more confident than I felt. "I think it's better for all of us that nobody but myself should know where they are." Actually, they were in my sponge bag.

"If you really feel like that . . ." said Robin, shaking his head regretfully. And at that moment Sue appeared, looking ravishing in the orange silk trousers and lilac shirt that I brought back from Italy in the spring.

"Margie, darling," she cried, "has Robin told you what I—"

Fortunately, before she could get any further, Bobby came in, rubbing his hands and enthusing about the weather. We all had breakfast.

While I was eating, I was also making a plan. I know I'm a constitutional dimwit, so I dare say my strategy wasn't up to much. Napoleon or Alexander the Great would have done better. However, after intensive brooding over two boiled eggs, I came to these conclusions:

1) One of the Smiths was an impostor.
2) I could see no way of ascertaining which.
3) The object of the impostor was robbery.
4) The object of the robbery was in the house, viz. Tom's stamps or my diamonds or both.
5) Nobody can steal a thing while separated from it by several miles of Sussex.
6) We would therefore spend the day picnicking on the beach.

"I have decided," I said, "that we will spend the day picnicking on the beach."

I didn't exactly expect the others to fall over themselves with delight at the idea, but I did think they might have shown a little more polite enthusiasm. However, my determination to keep both Smiths away from Meadowcroft for as long as possible far outweighed any sensitive feelings I might have had. I went ahead with my preparations regardless, and by eleven o'clock we were rolling towards the coast—Sue and Robin in the Jaguar, Bobby and myself in the runabout. I couldn't have faced the scarlet horror again to save my life. In the car Bobby made an attempt to bring up the subject of Robin and his unreliability, but I was firm.

"I want to hear no more of that," I said. "We've come out for a jolly picnic, and a jolly picnic we're jolly well going to have. So shut up."

Well, it wasn't all that jolly, but it might have been worse. The sun shone, and the sea was smooth and blue, and the seagulls fooled about catching crumbs in a distinctly diverting manner. We all swam and sunbathed, and then I opened the vacuum flask and dished out ice-cold martinis, and the atmosphere grew a little more relaxed.

Not for long, alas. Young Sue, in a euphorious state

of mind and a minuscule black bikini, had rashly decided to include even Bobby in the sunshine of her smile. This, of course, revived all the miserable young man's ardor, with the result that he immediately tried to muscle in between Robin and Sue. The effect of my carefully prepared picnic lunch was quite spoiled by the fact that the two men were sniping at each other verbally the whole time, as well as physically jockeying for position, which made the whole party a bit restless. Afterwards, I managed to persuade them both to go off for another swim while Sue and I took a nap. At least that was the proposed program, but in fact I started pouring my heart out to Sue the moment the men were out of earshot.

I told her about Tom's letter, with its sinister P.S.; I told her about Bobby's suspicions and Robin's sinister offer to look after the keys. I appealed to her to help me. Useless, of course. She was absolutely furious.

"If anybody's an impostor, it's that frightful Bobby!" she said. "How exactly like him, trying to blacken Robin's character behind his back! Of all the filthy, snide, low-down tricks . . . You wait. By the time I've finished with that young man, he'll wish he'd gone to Devil's Island for his holiday!"

"Do be reasonable, Sue," I begged—but it was no good. However, by pretty rigorous questioning, I was able to elicit some interesting information—not from her replies, but from her stubborn silences. It appeared that, in spite of all the time they had spent together, she knew as little about Robin as when she first met him. He had not told her where he worked, or what his job was. She did not know his address, or even where he lived, although she had gathered that it was somewhere in London. He had made no mention of parents, sisters, or brothers. The only thing she had learned was that he did a lot of traveling, both in England and on the continent—and this fact brought me no comfort.

By the time we got home, we were all fairly exhausted, what with the fresh air, the hot sunshine, and the highly charged emotional atmosphere. So it was not surprising that we all voted to call it a day quite soon after supper and departed to our respective bedrooms.

I strung the keys of the stamp cabinet and my jewel case on a ribbon round my neck, climbed into bed, and fell asleep almost at once. But a couple of hours later I was awake again, tossing and turning and brooding. I wasn't really worried about the diamonds. I could see the outline of the jewel case on my dressing table, faintly silhouetted against the uncurtained window. Anyway, the diamonds were mine, and they were well insured. Tom's stamps, on the other hand, were quite a different matter. A competent burglar could very easily pick the lock, and some of the rarer specimens were virtually irreplaceable. I heard the hall clock strike midnight, and then the half hour, and I could bear it no longer. After all, I was responsible. I'd told Tom I would look after his stamps, and I didn't mean to let him down. I decided to go downstairs, taking the jewel case with me, and sleep on the sofa beside the precious collection.

The house was dark and sleeping as I tiptoed out of my room. I slipped down the back stairs so as not to disturb the others, and for the same reason I did not switch on any lights. I made my way through the kitchen to the drawing room, groped my way to the sofa, stowed the jewel box on the floor, and was about to settle down when a small, insistent noise made me sit bolt upright, frozen with fright. I listened again. There was no doubt about it. Someone was coming slowly and stealthily down the main staircase and across the hall.

It was very dark in the drawing room, for the heavy damask curtains were closely drawn. My eyes had become somewhat accustomed to the gloom, but even so I could distinguish no more than the anonymous figure of a man as he came slipping silently through the half-open doorway. I sat rigid, not breathing. The man moved rather clumsily across the room towards me, groping among the chairs and tables.

And then something else happened. More footsteps—louder this time—and a second figure creeping in through the half-open door. A moment of darkness and stillness. Then a step, a sudden crash as a table overturned, and a man's voice shouted, "Got you!"

All bedlam broke loose then. The dark room seemed full of flailing arms and legs, snorts and grunts and shouts, the thud of falling furniture and the tinkle of breaking ornaments. There was nothing for it but swift action.

With my superior local knowledge, it was quite easy for me to make my way to the door that led to the main hall, and neither of the combatants was in any state to notice my movement. Once at the door, I flung it open and switched on the light, as though I had just arrived from upstairs. At the same moment, Sue came flying down the stairs like a fugitive naiad in her pale green chiffon negligée. We stood together in the doorway, watching with interest and apprehension as our two Mr. Smiths rolled about on the floor, evidently bent on mutual destruction.

It was all over quite quickly. Robin was the stronger and fitter of the two, and soon he had his rival securely pinioned, arms behind him, and was sitting astride Bobby's angrily writhing body.

"Well, Mrs. Westlake," said Robin, only slightly out of breath, "what did I tell you? I don't think he'll give you any more trouble. I suggest that you ring the police at once."

"Oh, Robin, you are wonderful," said Sue.

"Mrs. Westlake," came an indignant mutter from the floor. Bobby was finding some difficulty in speaking through a mouthful of carpet. "Mrs. Westlake! It's all a mistake! I can explain—"

"Now, you two," I said with as much authority as I could muster, "will you kindly get up off the floor and sit down like reasonable human beings and tell me what happened."

Robin looked doubtful. "Is it safe to let him go?" he asked.

"I'll take the responsibility," I said. "Get up."

The two of them climbed to their feet and dusted themselves off. Fortunately Bobby was none the worse for his trouncing, and soon we were all sitting round in armchairs, like a ghastly travesty of an ordinary late-night party.

"Now," I said, "I want both your stories. You first, Robin."

"Very simple," said Robin. "I was lying awake in bed when I heard somebody moving about down here, and so I came down to investigate. The room was pitch dark, but I could hear somebody breathing, and I hadn't been in here more than a few seconds before he attacked me. Smith—*if* that is his name, which I doubt—obviously decided that attack was the best form of defense."

"A pack of lies!" shouted Bobby. "I've told you my suspicions already, Mrs. Westlake, and I thought it probable that Smith—*if* that is his name, which I doubt—would make an attempt at burglary tonight. So instead of going to bed, I put out my light and kept watch from my room. My door was very slightly ajar, and I could see his door. Sure enough, soon after half past twelve I saw him come out and sneak downstairs. So I followed him, and caught him in here, red-handed. The police should be informed at once."

It was at that moment that Robin spotted the jewel case on the floor.

"That settles it," he shouted. "Do you see? He'd already taken the jewel case from upstairs!"

"I hadn't! It was you—!"

"How could Robin have taken the jewel case," Sue chimed in, "if you watched him come out of his room and go downstairs?"

"Exactly!" said Robin, triumphantly. "Mrs. Westlake, I really advise you to call the police."

"So do I," said Sue.

"And so do I," said Bobby.

They were all looking at me. There was a terrible silence—and then it was broken by the loveliest sound I've ever heard in my life. The banging of the front door, heavy steps in the hall, and Tom's voice calling, "Hey, Margie! Are you still up?"

I was out into the hall like a rocketing pheasant, and the next moment my arms were round Tom's neck and my nose firmly embedded in his shirt front. He seemed surprised.

"Here, I say, no need to overdo it, old girl," he said, laughing. "Yes, I got through in Lisbon by five o'clock, grabbed a plane at eight, picked up my car at London Airport, and here I am."

I didn't say a word. I just propelled him into the drawing room. The two young men were both on their feet, and I couldn't help noticing that Robin had gone very pale. Sue must have noticed it, too, because she had edged over and was standing beside him in a protective sort of way, like a tigress with a brood of cubs.

"Hello, young Sue," said Tom, cheerfully. "Having a good holiday?" He turned to Bobby. "Ah, my young friend from Amalgamated Plastics. So you found your way here. I hope Margie's been looking after you."

"Mrs. Westlake has been very kind," said Bobby, with a nasty emphasis.

Tom turned to me. "Young Bobby Smith," he said, "is a future captain of the plastics industry, and I'd say the same even if his father weren't the chairman and owner of Amalgamated Plastics. The boy's starting at the bottom and working up, and a very good thing, too. Your father tells me you're living on your salary," he added, to Bobby.

"That's right, sir."

"Most creditable," said Tom, "for a young fellow

who must be a millionaire in his own right already, eh?"

I closed my eyes. I heard Sue give a sort of strangled gasp. And then I opened my eyes again, and saw that Tom had turned to look at Robin. That young man was standing very upright and swaying slightly, as though facing a firing squad.

"Well," said Tom, cheerfully, "and who's this? Margie, aren't you going to introduce me—?" Then, suddenly, he stopped dead. And began to laugh. "Good lord," he said. "If it isn't Robin." He slapped Robin affectionately on the back. "Why the fancy dress, eh? Come into money, or something?" Robin went from white to pink and back again, but said nothing. Tom said to me, "Didn't recognize the young scamp for a moment. Last time I saw him in Paris, he was wearing dirty jeans, a shirt covered in paint, and a rather offensive beard. His usual rig."

"So . . . you do know him . . . ?" I began.

"Certainly I do. Known him for years. Son of one of my oldest friends. You remember Valentine Smith."

"The artist!" gasped Sue.

"That's right. Could have been a big businessman, old Val, but chucked it all to go beachcombing and painting. And Robin's followed in his footsteps. How's the old man, Robin? Still stony broke and enjoying it?"

"Yes, sir," said Robin, in a small voice.

"Well," Tom went on, "I'll be frank with you, old lad, I'm glad to see you smartening yourself up a bit. Life in a garret on bread and cheese is all very well, but . . . So you've got yourself a steady job at last, have you?"

"Of course he has," said Sue. She was almost shouting. "He's got an E-type Jag and he stays in the best hotels and—"

"Please, Sue," said Robin. He sounded as though he had a fishbone stuck in his throat. "I think . . . I'd better explain . . ."

"Explain what?"

"I haven't got a job. I haven't got any money. The Jag isn't mine—I borrowed it. You see, last week I won five hundred pounds with a Premium Bond, and—"

"A Premium Bond?" said Sue, as if she'd never heard of the things.

"That's right. And a pal of mine bet me I couldn't carry it off for a week—staying in a snob hotel, and everything. So I borrowed the car, bought some clothes, and came down here—"

"Why down here?" Sue was ominously quiet.

"Well, I knew my father's old friend Tom Westlake had his country house here—"

I could keep silent no longer. "I see," I said. "I see it all very clearly. You met Tom in Paris, and he told you that I would be here with my sister. You reckoned that Tom's sister-in-law would be a good catch. You came here deliberately fortune-hunting—"

"Don't say that," pleaded Robin. "It sounds so terrible. It was just a joke. I'd never met a rich, beautiful, spoilt girl, dripping in diamonds, and I thought it would be a bit of fun to find one, and lead her on, and then tell her I was only a penniless artist after all. I never reckoned that she'd be a person like Sue—"

"Well," I said, with triumph, "your plan misfired, didn't it? Because it may interest you to know that the diamonds and the mink and everything else are mine. Sue teaches English in a primary school in Clapham, and lives in a bedsitter, and—"

There didn't seem much point in going on because I had lost my audience. Sue and Robin were looking at each other in a starry-eyed sort of way, and the next thing I knew they were locked in the sort of embrace that was obviously going to go on for a very long time. There didn't seem anything for it but to melt tactfully into the kitchen and prepare drinks all round.

I'd hustled Tom and Bobby out of the room, and was just leaving myself, when Sue looked at me over Robin's shoulder. "You see, Margie darling," she said, "I *knew* he was too nice to be rich!"

THE DRESSING TABLE MURDER

by C. M. Chan

"Come to lunch, Jack," said Phillip Bethancourt.

Detective Sergeant Jack Gibbons cradled the phone against his shoulder and cast a cautious glance at the clock on the nightstand. The hands pointed to eleven thirty and he lay back on his pillows with a sigh.

"When?" he asked suspiciously.

A note of amusement crept into Bethancourt's voice. "Why, Jack," he said, "did you tie one on last night? You sound a bit foggy."

"I am a bit foggy," admitted Gibbons. "In fact, you woke me up."

"Well, rise and shine. It's a beautiful, sunny Sunday—probably the last we'll have, and it's no good wasting it in bed. Marla and I have planned lunch in Kew Gardens. She's got one of her model friends coming along, and we want to make it a foursome. We'll pick you up in half an hour."

Gibbons thought that the sun, while undoubtedly bright, would hardly be warming enough for a trip to the Gardens and said so.

"Nonsense," replied Bethancourt. "I tell you, we're having a heat wave. We'll be round at twelve."

Gibbons started to protest and found himself doing so to a dial tone. Cursing, he peeled back the covers and made for the bathroom.

In half an hour, he had showered, shaved, and drunk two cups of coffee. He was not yet dressed, but that hardly mattered. Phillip Bethancourt was never on time for anything and when accompanied by his girlfriend, Marla Tate, he was always twice as late as usual. Marla, one of the top fashion models in England, was punctual at work, but that seemed to put such a strain on her that she found it impossible to be punctual for anything else. What Gibbons, who was never late himself, couldn't understand was why they were always later when together.

Thus, he was not really surprised to hear the phone ring at twelve fifteen, heralding, he supposed, an announcement of a further delayed arrival.

This, however, was not the case. The voice at the other end was not the voice of Bethancourt but the voice of Scotland Yard, reminding him that he was on call.

Mrs. Delia MacGruder had been murdered. Under suspicious circumstances. Would Detective Gibbons please go over to her townhouse immediately.

Gibbons sighed and said he would.

In ten more minutes, the doorbell rang and Gibbons opened the door to admit a young man unremarkable in appearance. He was a little over average height, fairish and slender, with good, if somewhat delicate, features and mischievously bright eyes behind tortoiseshell glasses. He was accompanied and utterly eclipsed by a tall, slender woman with an abundance of copper-colored hair, flawless, creamy skin, and a face of undeniable beauty. High cheekbones slanted down to full, rosy lips, the nose was straight and fine, and above all reigned enormous jade-green eyes.

Behind them followed by far the most dignified member of the party: a large Russian wolfhound.

"I'm sorry," said Gibbons. "I tried to call, but you'd already left. I can't go."

"Not even," said Marla, smiling enticingly, "to meet Janet?"

Gibbons shook his head. "I'm afraid not. The Yard called and I have to go look at a murder. Wealthy woman apparently poisoned in her townhouse. It's a bloody nuisance."

"It sounds rather interesting," said Bethancourt, who was an amateur sleuth. "Who was it?"

"Delia MacGruder."

"Don't know her." He shook his head regretfully. "Still, it sounds intriguing. Look, we'll run you over there—"

"Phillip," said Marla sharply, "we still have to pick Janet up."

"Damn, that's right. Look here, darling, you take the car and get Janet and go on ahead. Jack and I will take a cab and meet you as soon as we're done."

Marla's look was frosty. "You can't just cancel on lunch like that."

"But I'm not cancelling, Marla, I'm merely running a little late. Now you go ahead, and Jack and I will catch you up in no time. Here are the keys. Come, we'll all go down together."

Marla, splendidly arctic in her anger, stalked from the flat. Downstairs, she gave Bethancourt a look that boded him no good when she did see him again, climbed into the grey Jaguar, and drove off at something approaching the speed of light.

"My," said Gibbons, who never failed to be impressed by Marla's fits of temper. Then, "She's left you with the dog."

"That's all right," said Bethancourt. "Cerberus is quite well-trained. He'll wait outside for us. Come on, let's find a cab."

Bethancourt and Gibbons had been at Oxford together, where they had had a nodding acquaintance, but a chance meeting in a London pub a year or two after they had come down was the real basis of their friendship. On a typical raw November night they had come across each other, Bethancourt gloomy over a girl who had just shown him the door, Gibbons even gloomier over a difficult murder case at the Yard. His superiors could make nothing of it and as a result were pressing their subordinate, who could make nothing of it either and who was the more distressed as he felt that this was his opportunity to distinguish himself. Over the whiskies, Bethancourt found himself forgetting about girls as he became fascinated by the tangled threads of the case, which seemed, on the face of it, almost impossible to unravel. Gibbons, for his part, discovered it made his own ideas clearer to talk the thing out with someone divorced from the Yard. The next day Bethancourt rang Gibbons, deprecatingly putting out a few thoughts which Gibbons found very illuminating indeed. It was not long before the case was solved and Gibbons was promoted to detective sergeant on the strength of it. The celebration attendant on this glorious event had cemented their friendship, and the whole episode had given Bethancourt a new hobby.

So they came now to the scene of this latest crime without having to explain Bethancourt's presence and without Gibbons' having to warn him to stay out of the way and keep quiet.

The dead woman's dressing room was small, but very nicely appointed. Beside the single window was a dressing table and a stool. The police photographer was pressed against the opposite wall in an attempt to get a full view of the scene.

Delia MacGruder had been seated at the dressing table, applying makeup after apparently taking a bath. She had been clad in a bathrobe, a small, slight woman of about fifty—still attractive of face, if one was to judge by the picture in a silver frame on the table. The face of the body was too contorted from its death throes to judge anything of the kind. The drawer of the dressing table was slightly open, and scattered over the top were various bottles and compacts. To one side stood a cold cup of coffee, half-drunk, with the cream congealing on the top. On the thick carpet by the dead woman lay an ornate handmirror and another compact—open—apparently dropped by the victim.

The body lay sprawled by the stool, the face contorted and blue. Bethancourt shuddered as he inspected it, then hastily backed away. The doctor looked up at him and grinned. Bethancourt, incapable at the moment of smiling back, stopped and began to peer beneath the dressing table.

"What are you looking for?" asked Gibbons, coming up on his other side.

"That," replied Bethancourt, pointing to a small, slender brush lying neglected against the wall. "She must have dropped it when she died. Or she might have knocked it from the table."

"What is it?"

"An eyeliner brush. That's the eyeliner on the floor over there. Her face is awfully discolored, but as far as I could make out, she'd actually put on all the stuff that's on the table. And she'd started on the eyeliner. Mascara, rouge, and lipstick are missing, so I presume they're in the drawer."

Gibbons walked over to the drawer and opened it farther. Within was a jumble of boxes, pencils, and small bottles. He looked at Bethancourt.

"There," said that young man, pointing. "Mascara, rouge, and a plethora of lipsticks." He grinned. "Going out with a fashion model does give one an edge in these situations."

"Gibbons!"

"Yes, sir?"

Chief Inspector Carmichael came up from where he had been talking to the doctor. "Hello, Phillip," he said genially, as was appropriate to the son of an intimate friend of the head of Scotland Yard. "Following the footprints with us again, are you?"

"I thought I'd just come and have a look, sir, since Jack here did me out of lunch."

"Well, splendid to see you. Gibbons, the doctor definitely says poison. Put the coffee in for analysis and anything else you can find around here that's edible. You might check the bathroom as well."

Gibbons nodded and turned to give orders for the coffee to be preserved. Bethancourt drifted away, wandering out of the room and into the bedroom. The bed was unmade, but otherwise the room was in perfect order. Finding nothing of interest, he wandered farther, into the next room, which was a gentleman's dressing room. Here a closet door stood open and a sweater had been thrown negligently over an armchair. Bethancourt peered into the closet, turned back, and eased open a bureau drawer, where he found an orderly array of socks. The next drawer held shirts.

"There you are." Gibbons stood in the doorway. "Looking for anything in particular?"

"No. Just being nosy." Bethancourt poked under the shirts.

"I'm going downstairs to interview the maid. I thought you'd like to come."

"Of course. Wait a moment—what's this?"

He withdrew his hand from beneath the shirts and held up a photograph of a girl. A very beautiful girl in a revealing dress.

"My," said Bethancourt. "Oh, my America, my new-found land."

"Let's have a look." Gibbons took the photo, gave a low whistle.

Bethancourt grinned. "It's amazing," he said, "how quickly one's mind can revert to the baser instincts."

"Still," said Gibbons regretfully, "it doesn't necessarily mean anything. Lots of men have mistresses and don't murder their wives."

"True," said Bethancourt. "Or it could be even more innocent than that—a niece or what have you. Well, let's see what the maid has to say."

The maid, a plump woman of about forty, was in tears. The policeman who was with her gave her name for her and it was with great difficulty that Gibbons succeeded in eliciting the information that she had worked for the MacGruders for five years. Bethancourt sat beside her and patted her hand.

"Now, now," he said soothingly, "you must try to be brave. You must try to help Detective Gibbons here so he can find out who did this dreadful thing."

The maid hiccupped, choked out that it was indeed a dreadful thing and she just couldn't believe it had happened, that poor Mrs. MacGruder was gone all in an instant, just like that. She didn't see how a body was to bear it. Bethancourt patted her hand again and looked helplessly at Gibbons.

"Now, Mrs. Andrews," said that young man, "my men tell me that you say Mr. MacGruder left the house this morning at nine. Was anyone else in the house after that besides yourself and Mrs. MacGruder?"

Mrs. Andrews shook her head vehemently and sobbed.

"Does anyone else usually reside here?"

Another shake of the head.

"No? The MacGruders had no children then?"

Mrs. Andrews sniffed and hiccuped. "Mrs. MacGruder had two sons by her first marriage," she managed. Apparently the thought of these two now motherless boys was more than she could bear, for she burst into fresh sobbing, adding that the sons did not live in the house.

"Very well, that's very good," said Gibbons encouragingly. "They don't live here. Just so. Where do they live?"

The response was nearly unintelligible.

"I think," said Bethancourt, "she said Cirencester."

"Well, at any rate they don't seem to be in the immediate neighborhood." Gibbons returned his attention to Mrs. Andrews. "Now then," he said, "I'm going to ask you to be very brave and remember about this morning."

Mrs. Andrews' sobs acquired renewed vigor.

It was at this point that Bethancourt sat up and said, "Tea!" in a very firm manner. Both Gibbons and the policeman stared at him. Even Mrs. Andrews cast him a startled glance. Bethancourt, ignoring them all, leapt from the sofa and strode out of the room.

Gibbons shook his head and sighed. "Now, Mrs. Andrews," he began again.

Ten minutes later he had gleaned the bare information that Mr. MacGruder had left the house at nine to catch a train to the suburbs and play golf with some friends who apparently were also a business connection. Mrs. Andrews was dabbing ineffectually at her tears with a tissue when Bethancourt returned, bearing a tray.

"Here we go," he said in an unnaturally cheerful voice. "Here's some nice hot tea for you, Mrs. Andrews. Now you blow your nose and have a sip of this—it'll put you right in a moment. Milk or sugar?"

Mrs. Andrews looked at him gratefully and said she'd like milk. "You're a nice lad," she added.

"You mustn't flatter me, Mrs. Andrews," said Bethancourt, beaming as if the queen had just announced the intention of knighting him. "And don't forget to blow your nose—it's a very important part of the process. Now, doesn't that feel better? Good. Now when did Mr. MacGruder leave the house?"

The tea had an almost magical effect. Mrs. Andrews, although still sniffling and dabbing her eyes, now managed to give a coherent account of the morning. Delia MacGruder, having seen her husband off, had remained in the dining room reading the paper. At about ten thirty she had gone upstairs to bathe and change prior to taking the twelve sixteen train to meet her husband and his friends for lunch. At about eleven she had come down for more coffee and returned upstairs. Mrs. Andrews had heard a thud from upstairs some twenty minutes later, but just assumed Mrs. MacGruder had dropped something.

"I was vacuuming," she said tearfully, "just doing the living room once over lightly, when I noticed it was a bit past twelve and I thought to myself, Mrs.

MacGruder will miss that train if she don't hurry. And then I thought I'd just step up and remind her, thinking maybe she'd got the time mixed up, though that's not like her—always very punctual she was, thinking it rude to keep people waiting. So I go up and knock on her door, but there's no answer, and then I get scared, but I open the door anyhow and there she was, oh, what a horrible sight . . ."

"Very horrible," agreed Bethancourt, with some feeling. "So you ran out and called the ambulance? Or did you go in, try to revive her?"

"I should have done," wailed the woman. "But she looked so awful, like something out of one of those horror films, I just ran straight downstairs with my heart in my throat. I was all a-tremble, just shaking like a leaf, so bad as I could hardly dial the phone . . ."

Here she burst into sobs again. Bethancourt patted her hand and Gibbons murmured that she needn't answer any more questions just now. Then he and Bethancourt withdrew.

"They've removed the body, sir," said a policeman who was waiting for them in the hall. "And we've gotten hold of the husband—he's on his way back. Should be here any minute."

"Have they finished upstairs?"

"Just about, sir. The fingerprint men are packing up, and the chief says we're to seal the room once they've gone. He said he'd be down to meet the husband and you should wait for him here."

"Very well. I'll be here if Mr. MacGruder arrives before the chief comes down."

The policeman nodded and moved off. Gibbons looked round for Bethancourt, found him across the hall in the study, rifling the drawers of the desk. There was a hard look in his eyes behind the glasses.

"There's a back door in the kitchen," he said. "But it's locked and bolted."

"I know," said Gibbons. "My men checked it out."

"Then you realize that, if the poison was in the coffee, only the maid could have put it there? To get upstairs from the kitchen, you have to pass through the dining room and the living room, where Mrs. Andrews was cleaning. There's no back stair."

"No," said Gibbons, "I hadn't realized." Then he added, "But we don't know there was anything in the coffee."

"That's true." Bethancourt paused, withdrew a handful of letters from the desk. "Here we are," he said. "Letters addressed to 'Dear Mum,' signed by 'Tom.' Return address in Cirencester, last name is Follet. And here's another one, different street, but still Cirencester, signed 'Bill and Annie.' "

"Probably a wife," said Gibbons. "Well, we'll have to find out if they were in Cirencester this morning. There—that must be Mr. MacGruder arriving."

David MacGruder was a well-preserved man of something over forty. He was very pale and held himself in total control. He was accompanied by his wife's solicitor, with whom he had been playing golf. The solicitor was an older man in a pair of highly regrettable plaid trousers.

Gibbons spoke with them briefly, saying the chief inspector would be down presently and would Mr. MacGruder wait for him in the living room? He explained that the body had been taken away and that he had sealed up the dressing room and was leaving a man there. MacGruder nodded dully, accepting everything without question.

Gibbons found Bethancourt outside, sitting on the front stoop with the dog, Cerberus.

"All done?"

Gibbons nodded.

Bethancourt glanced at his watch. "Quarter to three. I guess we'd better run up and find the girls," he said, without much enthusiasm.

"You'd better," retorted Gibbons. "I've got to go to the office and write a report. I've got to put in the coffee for analysis and see that it's marked down for first thing in the morning. I've got to put someone on the track of those two sons in Cirencester. There are dozens of things I've got to do and somewhere in between them all I may find time for a ham sandwich."

"See here," said Bethancourt, "you can't leave me to face Marla's wrath alone."

Gibbons grinned ruthlessly. "Oh, can't I?" he said. "Anyway, it's your own fault. You knew she'd be angry when you insisted on coming with me."

"Ah, well, I thought it would be worth it. And it has been. It's a very interesting problem and I'm going to enjoy working it out for you. Come, Cerberus," he added, ignoring his friend's protests. "It seems we are being deserted in the face of the enemy. Into the breach, old fellow."

Jack Gibbons, having had a very long and busy day, leaned comfortably back in one of Phillip Bethancourt's roomy armchairs, planted his feet on one of the several coffee tables in the room, and took a deep swallow of single malt whisky. Bethancourt occupied a spacious and very comfortable flat, if a trifle oddly furnished. It had been decorated solely by its owner, who had money enough but a very eccentric taste. He was very fond of coffee tables.

He emerged now from the kitchen, a cigarette between his lips.

"The lasagna is in the oven," he said. "It should take about half an hour." He turned to the bar to replenish his drink.

"I would have thought," ventured Gibbons, "that you would have been busy with Marla tonight. After yesterday, I mean."

Bethancourt made a face. "She's madder than I gave her credit for," he admitted, seating himself on the edge of a black lacquer coffee table. "She didn't go to the Gardens yesterday— she took the car all the way to Brighton just to make sure I wouldn't find her and would spend a lot of time looking. We had a beautiful row last night," he concluded glumly.

"Appalling."

"Yes, it was, rather." Bethancourt shrugged and turned to other things. "What did the postmortem find?" he asked.

"Delia MacGruder died of cyanide poisoning."

"In the coffee?"

"There was nothing in the coffee but cream. Neither was there anything in the pot, which figures, as the maid had also been drinking out of it."

"But it would be very easy to poison one cup and then, once it had done its work, take it away, wash it out, and fill it with fresh coffee."

"It would only be easy if you were the maid, as you pointed out yesterday. And if she really did do it, why should she claim to have been in the living room, making it impossible for anyone else to get to the coffee? She could just as well have been cleaning the study or the bathroom or anywhere in the house."

"She could be shielding someone else," suggested Bethancourt. "Possibly she let someone into the house."

"Possibly. It's also perfectly possible that someone else came in through the front door."

"What about MacGruder?"

Gibbons shook his head regretfully. "He would be a beautiful suspect, but his alibi has been confirmed. He left the house at nine and caught the nine eighteen from Victoria. We know this because the solicitor met him at the station. They proceeded directly to the golf course, where they met a third man and went out to the course. They finished at about twelve thirty and went to the clubhouse to meet their wives for lunch. Instead they met a policeman who informed them of Mrs. MacGruder's death."

"Well, he's out then."

"Yes, and it's a pity because he's the only one so far with a motive. In fact, it's classic. Mrs. MacGruder's first husband was a wealthy man with a thriving business. He died eight years ago in a car accident, leaving everything to his wife. Mrs. MacGruder, who already had money of her own, met and married David MacGruder almost six years ago. Prior to that he had been a businessman earning a good salary, but by no means a spectacular one. He retired after his marriage. And he's eight years younger than his wife was."

"But he couldn't have done it."

"No. Nor could anyone except the maid. Who else could walk in on her while she was getting dressed and not be immediately challenged?"

Phillip leaned back. "A lover," he suggested, "or her sons. Or another woman."

"Well, we haven't finished checking the sons' movements yet. And I suppose they might have had keys to the townhouse. Another woman would have had trouble getting in."

Bethancourt lit a cigarette and sipped his whisky. "Not if she had a key," he said. "And it's really amazing how many people do have keys to other people's flats. A neighbor, for instance, who was asked to look in occasionally when last the MacGruders were traveling. But by far the easiest solution is the maid."

"No," said Gibbons, "it doesn't feel right to me. Where would she get cyanide to begin with? And if she did get it, why wouldn't she put all she had in the coffee? Mrs. MacGruder had taken a very small dose—that's all it takes, of course, but most people don't know that. In nine out of ten poison cases, you get an overdose. Moreover, why would she do it at all?"

Bethancourt waved a hand. "A million reasons. A deep-seated hatred of her employer. Maybe Mrs. MacGruder left her a fortune in her will. But I will grant you that it's not likely. Unfortunately, if you do away with the maid, you also do away with the idea the poison was in the coffee. And that leaves us with another problem."

"Which is?"

"That someone popped in on her while she was in the middle of dressing and making up, just after breakfast and not anywhere near lunch or even elevenses, and got her to eat something. I mean, what does one say?"

"One says, 'Hullo, I can see I'm interrupting, but I just wanted you to taste these marvelous chocolates.' "

"Possibly," admitted Bethancourt grudgingly. "But think about what happens then. Mrs. MacGruder puts down her mirror and makeup and eats a chocolate or whatever. It kills her and in falling, she knocks the handmirror and the makeup she was just using off the table, but nothing else."

"Perhaps she had put them down on a different part of the table."

"Why should she? She put everything else as she finished with it right above the drawer. Habit is very strong, Jack. I invariably put the shaving cream down on the top of the sink. It's routine—I always do it. When interrupted in the act of using it, habit takes over and I still put it on top of the sink. But it has to be something really important to interrupt me at all. Haven't you ever noticed how women hate to be interrupted in the middle of putting on makeup? They look silly half madeup and they know it. What would you do if someone popped in on you while you were shaving?"

"I'd say, 'Excuse me—you don't mind if I just finish up here?' "

"Exactly."

"That's all very well, Phillip, but it must have happened that way. Maybe Mrs. MacGruder had an overpowering passion for chocolates."

"No," said Bethancourt. "It just means that there's something about it we haven't figured out yet."

"Not to mention who it was that fed it to her."

"There is that. Anyone else on your list of suspects?"

"The family seems the best bet. After all, she did have money to leave, and ten to one she left it to her husband and sons. But we don't know about that yet. Otherwise, we haven't uncovered anyone else with a motive."

"What about the girl in the photograph?"

Gibbons grinned. "I asked about that. Mr. MacGruder claims she's an old friend of the family's. I said in that case, there was no reason we shouldn't have her address and he more or less had to give it to me. Her name's Sarah Duncan and she says Mr. MacGruder is just a friend with whom she dines occasionally."

Bethancourt reached for the bottle and topped up both glasses. "Does she have an alibi?" he asked.

"Not exactly. She's an actress. She was at an audition that morning, but it was a cattle call and she didn't get onstage until one. She was definitely seen there, but the times are hazy. She could have slipped out and come back. But, obviously, if she was MacGruder's mistress, she wouldn't have known his wife. If she had suddenly appeared in the dressing room, it's hardly likely that Mrs. MacGruder would have stopped to eat anything she gave her. Besides, it would be a bit awkward, what?"

"Just a bit, I should imagine. Still, it might be worth looking into. I'll do that, if you like. As soon as I make up with Marla."

"What do you mean?"

"What budding actress wouldn't jump at the chance to become friends with Marla Tate? Marla runs in the right and very elite circles."

"That's true. All right then. And meanwhile, I'll find out about the sons. After all, it's only been twenty-four hours. Tomorrow may turn up a lot."

"Tomorrow may turn up a lot for you," retorted Bethancourt. "I've got to spend the day making up to

Marla and, if there's any time left after that, there's that article that should have been finished last Tuesday."

Gibbons grinned. Sixty years ago, a young man possessed of as much family money as Bethancourt would have been expected to do very little beyond upholding the title of "gentleman." Now, however, society dictated that one should not be idle, and various projects had been suggested to Phillip by his parents upon completion of his education. None of these had had any great success, Bethancourt being disinclined toward organization and regular schedules. No compromise was reached until he wrote an article for a periodical and was pleasantly surprised to find it accepted for publication. He immediately sent copies to all his relatives, wrote a second piece which was also published, and thereupon called himself a writer, turning out articles with just enough frequency to appease his parents. Gibbons, who had to work for a living, was not in the least sympathetic toward the problems of this so-called career.

"You'll get it out all right," he said now, draining his glass. "And if you don't, it won't matter much." Bethancourt glared at him and he laughed. "Oh, come," he said, "you know for all your complaining nothing catastrophic ever happens."

"I think," said Bethancourt, with a great deal of wounded dignity, "that it's time I got the lasagna out of the oven." He moved off to the kitchen while Gibbons chuckled.

Phillip Bethancourt lay propped up in bed two mornings later, a cup of coffee balanced on his stomach. Marla had been appeased for his neglect and now he was leisurely watching her put on makeup. He had never really followed the whole process before. In a moment or two, Marla noticed his watchful gaze and looked up from her mirror.

"Is there something wrong?" she asked.

"No, no," he assured her. He had an idea. Setting

aside the coffee, he rolled out of bed and went to the kitchen. In a moment he returned, munching on a piece of cheese.

"Mmm," he said, as casually as he could. "Really delicious, this."

Marla threw him a startled glance. "Cheese?" she said. "First thing in the morning?"

"This is something special," he assured her. "Have a taste?"

"In a minute, darling." She drew a pencil line along her lid, smudged it expertly with a finger.

Bethancourt wandered back to the bed, absently laying the cheese on the nightstand. Of course, Marla never ate anything in the morning. Still, she liked cheese. And Delia MacGruder had just finished breakfast. Even if one really liked something, would one be quite so eager for it directly after a meal? Still, people were odd about food. Mrs. MacGruder had been slender; perhaps she was on a perennial diet . . .

Marla set aside her mirror and rose. "Aren't you ever going to get up?" she asked as she moved toward the bathroom.

Bethancourt shrugged for answer. Then there was the matter of the keys. He no longer had keys to his own parents' house; then again, they had moved since he had left home.

"Marla," he called, "do you have keys to your parents' house?"

She emerged, drying her hands, and gazed curiously at him. "They live in Yorkshire," she said. "Why on earth should I have keys to a house in Yorkshire?"

"Just wondering."

She shook her head and left the room.

Marla had keys to his apartment; so did the couple downstairs and the cleaning lady. Probably if someone wanted his keys it would not be too difficult to abscond with a set long enough to make copies. No, keys were not the problem.

"Phillip," said Marla from the doorway, an exasperated look on her face, "what on earth is wrong with you this morning? That cheese in the kitchen is the same stuff we were eating two nights ago when you said you knew a place we could get better."

The phone rang that evening as Bethancourt, true to form, was emerging from the bath some ten minutes after he had been appointed to leave the flat.

"I've been to Cirencester," said Gibbons cheerfully. "The sons are shaping up nicely. As you so cleverly deduced, one of them is married—the younger one, although they're much of an age: twenty five and twenty-six. The younger one is William and is married to Annie. Tom, the elder, lives alone and I think he's gay."

"That," said Bethancourt dryly, "does not mean he's a murderer."

"True," said Gibbons cheerfully, "but listen to this: he's got his own small antique shop, which he runs with the help of an assistant. He was not there on Sunday morning."

"Why on earth should he be?" asked Bethancourt. "Does he break the Sabbath by having his shop open on Sundays?"

"No, but evidently he usually spends Sunday mornings there to go over inventory, leaving around eleven to have brunch with his brother and his wife. Last Sunday, however, he drove to Windsor to have a look at some antiques a gentleman there was selling."

"And did he indeed arrive in Windsor?"

"Oh, yes, dead on time for his appointment at one thirty. He had plenty of time, especially since a neighbor says she saw his car leaving at about eight."

"Eight?" mused Bethancourt. "That's pretty early to be starting for a one thirty appointment. It's about an hour and a half or so to Windsor from Cirencester."

"He says he stopped by the shop, just to look in and make sure everything was all right. No one saw him, however. He also claims to have stopped at a pub for an early lunch before keeping his appointment, but no one at the pub remembers him either. We're in the midst of looking into his finances to see if he was in need of money. Antiques is not a cheap business, you know."

"So I do. What about the other brother?"

"Bill was at home with his wife. They had brunch alone, since Tom wasn't coming, and were having a perfectly normal, uneventful Sunday until they heard the news from MacGruder. Bill works with an investment firm in Bristol. Oh, and his wife is pregnant."

"Life and death," commented Bethancourt. "How poignant."

"Well," said Gibbons, ignoring this, "I think that's the crop. Except that neither brother thought much of their stepfather. They'd heard rumors that he cheated on their mother."

"Virtuous man that I am," said Bethancourt, "I am just about to venture out and either prove or disprove that rumor. Sarah Duncan is performing in a disreputable little showcase in——, to which Marla has ungraciously agreed to go."

"In return, no doubt, for some favor on your part. Really, Phillip, sometimes I wonder why you put up with her."

"Take a good look at her next time you're 'round," retorted Bethancourt. "The answer should be fairly obvious. I'll report tomorrow."

"That," said Marla, as they emerged from the theater, "was dreadful. And that little girl was particularly dreadful. I really don't see why I should make up to her."

"You should make up to her," answered Bethancourt, "because I, the beloved object in your life, have asked you to. Besides, I've promised you that necklace you've taken a fancy to if you do. Come on, the pub should be just around here."

"Don't be silly," said Marla, "we can't go to the pub yet—they'll all still be at the theater, changing. If we're to do this properly, we have to make an entrance."

"Oh. Quite right, my love." Bethancourt looked about. The weather was still remarkably mild, but a fine rain was falling. "There," he said, "that restaurant looks fairly expensive—too expensive for anyone in that play to be in. We'll go there."

Accordingly, they made their way across the street, re-emerging some forty-five minutes later to proceed to the pub frequented by the cast and crew of *Doing the Bunk*.

Marla's presence in the audience had been duly noted by both these parties, who were avidly discussing it when she swept in, shaking the rain from her famous coppery hair. She regarded the assembled group with something of the attitude of a queen surveying a not very promising group of peasants until Bethancourt poked her in the ribs. Suddenly she smiled.

"Ah!" she exclaimed. "Look, Phillip, we've stumbled on the cast of that delightful little play." Then she waded into them, effusively commenting on the play and their performances in it.

This, naturally, was well-received. Bethancourt steered her steadily toward Sarah Duncan, who had changed her rather skimpy excuse for a costume (in Bethancourt's opinion the sole highlight of the play) for a black jumper and skirt. Marla did her part magnificently, complimenting the girl and initiating a conversation about acting and the difficulties of getting started. It was all going quite well until Bethancourt noticed the danger signs: Marla was getting bored and there were three young men bearing down on her other side, vying for her attention. In no time at all she had abandoned her escort and Sarah Duncan and was happily exchanging quips with her circle of admirers.

"She's marvelous," said Sarah with a sigh. "Even more beautiful than her photographs." She looked at Bethancourt. "Do you think she'd mind if I asked her how she got started? I've tried to do some modeling, but you need really good pictures before they'll even look at you."

"Marla always had the best pictures she could get," lied Bethancourt. "But, you see, she also had me."

Sarah looked at him questioningly.

"Well," he said modestly, hoping fervently that Marla was not listening, "I happen to have a bit of money, you see. Having a sponsor," he added, "always helps. But a pretty girl like you shouldn't find that much of a problem."

"No," she answered, considering. Then, in a burst of confidentiality, "Of course, I do have someone and he's been helpful here and there. But he's not really connected to any theater people."

Bethancourt laughed. "Neither was I," he said. "I learned quick enough. You should have him take you round to the right places, buy a few drinks for people."

She frowned. "Well, that's not always possible."

"Ah," said Bethancourt, with quick understanding. "Married, is he?"

"Well, yes."

"Here, let me get you another. Bartender, two pints of bitter here."

Sarah drank deeply.

"Married men are difficult," went on Bethancourt sympathetically. "Or so I've heard. I've never been one, myself."

She giggled a little at that and then sobered, frowning again. She looked up at Bethancourt. "Actually," she said, "I'm in a bit of a pickle with my married man. You see, he isn't married any more. His wife died just the other day—rather horrible it was really. But you see my problem is that—supposing he asks me to marry him now? I mean, I like him well enough, and he's been very helpful with money and things, but he's a bit older than me and, well, I don't really think I want to marry him."

"That's difficult," said Bethancourt, trying hard not

to gloat. "But, of course, the sea is full of fish, don't you know. And he'll have to wait a while anyway, if his wife's just died. Did she go suddenly?"

"Oh, very. In fact," she said, lowering her voice, "they say it was murder."

"How dreadful!" exclaimed Bethancourt, feigning astonishment. He was forming another appropriate question when Marla suddenly noticed that if several men were paying court to her, Phillip had become involved in a tete-a-tete with a woman whose breasts were far too perfect to be safe. Marla's own breasts were on the small side and she was correspondingly sensitive to the size and shape of breasts that might be superior to her own. Sarah's endowments had been rather prominently featured in the play and Marla had no doubts about them or the rest of the girl's features: far too pretty for Phillip to be trusted with. She cut in on their conversation like a buzz saw into a tree trunk.

"Darling," she said, expertly wrapping herself around him, apparently overcome with affection, "I've finished my drink. Don't you think it's time we were going?"

Bethancourt considered rapidly. There was very little more, he was convinced, to be gotten out of Sarah Duncan and he had only just made up with Marla yesterday. To risk another bout with her mercurial temper could be dangerous. "Absolutely, beloved," he answered.

Bethancourt found Gibbons in his office the next afternoon surrounded by photographs of the scene of the crime and various reports.

"Usefully employed, as always," said Bethancourt cheerfully, shedding his Burberry and slumping into a chair. Cerberus followed his master in and arranged himself elegantly at his feet.

His friend shot him a harried look. "Carmichael's been in twice this morning to ask how it's going," he said with a groan. "The press is having a field day, and MacGruder, now he's over the shock, is making a fuss. And I'm more confused than ever."

"Oh?" asked Bethancourt, lighting a cigarette, unmoved by this panoply of catastrophes. "I thought the sons were shaping up nicely."

"I've got the preliminary report on their finances back," said Gibbons, searching amid the mass of papers on his desk. "And it's exactly the opposite of what would make me happy. To top it off, we haven't had an ounce of luck in tracing cyanide to anyone."

"What's wrong with their finances?" asked Bethancourt, lifting a sheaf of reports in search of an ashtray.

"Tom, son number one, has a hefty bank account. He's invested wisely and his antiques business is booming. He buys nothing he can't afford and sells everything at a goodly markup. However, over the past few months there have been fairly hefty withdrawals."

"Aha!" said Bethancourt with satisfaction. "Blackmail, perhaps?"

"Not unless it's his brother who's been blackmailing him," said Gibbons. "The withdrawals are all in the form of checks made out to his brother. So my man looked into Bill's affairs as well and found son number two has made some very risky investments and is presently almost broke. He's been borrowing from his brother to meet his household expenses and there are still outstanding bills. Big ones."

"Well, there's a motive for you, at any rate," said Bethancourt. "It could be he'd appealed to his mother for money and she'd said no. Possibly his brother was cutting him off as well."

"Don't flick your ashes in the wastebasket: it's full of paper."

"You've buried your ashtray so deep a gravedigger couldn't find it."

"It's right there, fathead."

"Where? Oh, I see, under the desk. Of course, how

silly of me." Bethancourt retrieved the ashtray and returned to the subject at hand. "There," he said, "all right and proper. So, suspicion lifts itself from Tom and fastens itself firmly on Bill."

"That's just what it doesn't do," said Gibbons gloomily. "Bill, as you will remember, was at home on Sunday morning with his wife."

"The pregnant one," supplied Bethancourt. "I remember perfectly. But husbands and wives have been known to become accomplices before."

"Not when they're sitting at home. Their neighbor spent the morning washing his car in his driveway. It took him a couple of hours all told, and he swears that from ten to twelve Bill's car was sitting empty in the drive."

"That's rather difficult," said Bethancourt slowly. "I don't really see, if brother Tom was no longer willing to lend him money, that he would be willing to murder their mother for Bill."

"Not bloody likely. Anyway, they're reading the will at four o'clock and I'm going down to hear it and talk to Bill about his financial problems afterward."

"Then you'd better hurry," said Bethancourt. "It's a quarter to now."

"Good Lord, really?" said Gibbons, springing up.

"Here," said Bethancourt, "I'll go with you. We'll take a taxi and I can tell you all about Sarah Duncan on the way."

"Oh, right, I'd forgotten about her," said Gibbons, flinging his overcoat around him. "What did you find?"

"She was definitely having an affair with MacGruder," answered Bethancourt, following him. "But she doesn't want to marry him. I think she was telling the truth. She didn't do it. Cerberus, watch your tail."

Gibbons shook his head.

"It's a funny case," he said. "All our leads seem to just peter out."

"Because we haven't got hold of the right one yet," said Bethancourt, ushering him out the door.

Delia MacGruder had left a bequest of one hundred thousand pounds to each of her sons. There was a small bequest of five hundred pounds to the maid, Mrs. Andrews. The rest of the estate, including investments and real estate, was left to her husband. Nobody in the solicitor's office seemed surprised or upset by the will. They were all dressed somberly, as befitted the occasion: MacGruder and his stepson Bill in charcoal grey suits and dark ties, Annie and Mrs. Andrews in black dresses; Tom was not present. Bethancourt had an instant of wishing he was not wearing a tweed jacket and khakis.

The reading of the will did not take long. The family expressed thanks to the solicitor, who had abandoned his plaid trousers for a dark blue pinstripe. He explained that of course probate would be held up while the police concluded their investigation into this tragic occurrence. Everyone seemed united in ignoring the presence of the police in the room. Gibbons finally approached the solicitor and asked if there was a room where he could ask Bill and his wife a few questions.

"That's ridiculous!" snapped MacGruder, before the solicitor could respond. "Perhaps if the police would stop plaguing my family, you'd be able to concentrate on finding my wife's murderer."

Gibbons shot him a cool stare, but, "Just doing my duty, sir," was all he said.

"We're happy to help," said Annie quietly, but firmly. She was six or seven months pregnant and her paleness was emphasized by the black of her dress.

MacGruder snorted. "It's stupid to think you had anything to do with it," he said belligerently. "And I resent it, I resent it very much."

"It seems to me," said Bill with a glint in his eyes, "that it's for us to resent, not you."

"You can use the conference room," interrupted the solicitor hurriedly. "My secretary will show you."

MacGruder stormed out and the others followed him more quietly.

They settled at one end of the oval oak table, Gibbons introducing Bethancourt as his colleague.

"What a beautiful dog," said Annie, holding out a hand to Cerberus who deigned to sniff it politely.

"Thank you," said Bethancourt. "His name's Cerberus."

She shot him a startled glance.

"I'm sorry to have to trouble you again," said Gibbons, "but there are just a few things that want clearing up. I understand, Mr. Follet, that you had been borrowing heavily from your brother to cover your debts."

"What?" Abandoning Cerberus, Annie sat up straight and stared at her husband. "What does he mean, Bill? What debts?"

Follet turned to her with a miserable look in his eyes. "I'm sorry," he said hopelessly. "I—I didn't want you to know. Really, sergeant, couldn't you have asked me in private?" he demanded, turning to Gibbons.

"I'm very sorry, sir," said Gibbons, somewhat taken aback. "I had no idea your wife didn't know of your financial affairs."

"But what's wrong?" asked Annie. "We were doing so well—you said so when we—when we planned the baby."

"I'm sorry," said Follet again. "It was the Conglomerated options. It—it looked like such a good thing, Annie. You know I told you about it—"

"I remember," she said, a little dazedly. "You sold off some of our other investments to go into it. But it was doing well, Bill. You said it was."

Follet gulped. "I'm afraid I lied. It was totally unexpected, but, well, I lost everything I put into it. Everybody did. And now I owe on the options. And, Annie, I put our savings into it as well."

Her eyes widened. "Our savings?" she whispered. "Bill, how could you?"

"Oh, I didn't use all of it. But the rest went when I had to pay on the options. God," he shook his head, "I should have known. I've said it to myself a hundred times. I should have known. But everyone at the office seemed so sure . . ."

Gibbons coughed diplomatically. "I'm very sorry, ma'am, to have to have been the cause of this news."

"No," she said softly. "It was better that I should know." She was staring dully at her stomach, one hand resting on the bulge, while her husband gazed helplessly at her.

"We'll be all right," he said reassuringly. "I'm afraid I haven't been any too smart with the money I've borrowed from Tom, but with mother's inheritance I can at least replace our savings and use the rest to get us back on our feet."

"Yes, of course," she said, not looking up. Cerberus sniffed and gently put his nose in her lap. She smiled a little at him and rested one hand on his head.

"Good boy," muttered Bethancourt under his breath.

Gibbons was coughing again. "Your brother wasn't here today, Mr. Follet?" he asked.

"What?" Follet turned his attention back to the detective. "No, he wasn't. His assistant had an accident this morning—broke his arm falling off a ladder—and had to go to hospital. Tom didn't want to close the shop and, anyway, we all knew what was in the will. This was really just a formality. I said I'd give him a full report."

"I see," said Gibbons. "Now, about this money, sir. Your brother had full knowledge of what had happened?"

"Yes, of course. Tom's careful; he wouldn't have lent me that kind of money if I hadn't explained."

"He did not himself lose any in this investment?"

Follet gave a dry laugh. "Not a penny. He wouldn't touch it. He's a very conservative sort of man with money, sergeant. I suppose I would have done well to follow his example."

"And had you applied to your mother or stepfather for help as well?"

Follet looked surprised. "Of course not. I think I told you, sergeant, that I don't much care for David MacGruder. And I didn't want Mother to know any more than I wanted Annie to. Mother was so proud of me. Of both Tom and me. Tom's always been her favorite, I suppose, but she was proud of me, too. I couldn't bear to let her know how I'd mucked up."

"I understand, sir. You said just now that your mother's inheritance would help you over the bad times. What, may I ask, did you plan to do before her death occurred?"

"Borrow more from Tom, I suppose. There wasn't much else I could do. He'd have given it to me, but the devil of it was, I couldn't see my way to paying him back. I mean, with the baby coming and all, there just wasn't much chance I would have any extra money for years."

"Your brother understood this?"

"Oh, yes. He wasn't too pleased, mind. Talked to me pretty sharply the last time I had to ask him for more. Said if I was going to borrow any more, he wanted to see to it that I didn't invest in anything foolish. I couldn't very well argue with him."

"Naturally not," agreed Gibbons. "Just one other thing, sir. I noticed your car when I visited you before. A Ford Fiesta, I believe. Do you have a second car for your wife?"

Follet looked puzzled. "Yes," he answered. "A Mini. It's rather elderly; we bought it when we were first married."

"But it wasn't there on Monday when I visited you."

"No," broke in Annie. "It was in the garage. Don't

you remember, Bill? It broke down on me on Saturday. We didn't get it back till Wednesday."

"I see," said Gibbons. "What garage do you use?"

"Gleason's on the corner of our lane and the Chedworth road. But what on earth does that have to do with anything?"

"We just like to verify everything, sir. You know the police—everything has to be confirmed," Gibbons smiled.

"But I don't understand. Is there something wrong with the car? They said at the shop the alternator bolt had sheared."

"Ah, was that it? That'll stop a car dead, sure enough," said Gibbons. "Well, thank you very much for your time. And, again, I'm very sorry to have been indiscreet."

He and Bethancourt extricated themselves with some difficulty, emerging eventually into the street with the dog at their heels.

"Well," said Gibbons, "that was worse than expected. And now I've got to run all the way over to Cirencester and talk to the mechanic and the brother again. And I might as well see that neighbor while I'm about it." He glanced at his companion. "I don't suppose," he suggested, "that you would want to give me a lift?"

"To Cirencester?" Bethancourt considered. He was really more the armchair sort of detective; he greatly preferred to let Gibbons collect all the information and deliver it so that he could put the pieces of the puzzle together in his head. Still, he had to admit that meeting the people concerned often helped. And Tom Follet was still the prime suspect. "I suppose I could," he said.

"It could provide the only bright spot in my day if you would," said Gibbons persuasively.

"By all means then. Every day should have a bright spot." He hailed a passing taxi. "We'll have to go round to the garage. MacGruder's quite the obnoxious one, isn't he?"

Gibbons grunted as he got into the cab and made room for Bethancourt beside him. "I've talked to some of the MacGruders' friends," he said. "They all seem agreed that the marriage was a happy one, and that MacGruder is a charming fellow."

"Really?"

"Yes, he evidently got on with almost everyone except the stepsons. Still, I suppose having your wife murdered is something that could adversely affect your temperament."

"I suppose," said Bethancourt thoughtfully.

Gleason was just closing up shop for the day when they arrived, but he appeared willing enough to answer their questions. Yes, the Mini had been towed in on Saturday and put in the lot. Yes, of course he locked the lot when he left for the night. Well, no, he hadn't got a chance to look at it on Saturday. In fact, he hadn't done anything with it till Monday afternoon—he was a busy man. But there wasn't much wrong, really. The alternator bolt had sheared and dropped out, and that meant the alternator had begun to drop, and *that* meant the connections had come loose and there was no electricity. Can't run a car without electricity. He had started to fix it on Tuesday, but then there was that Mercedes come in and what with that and another thing, he didn't get the job finished till Wednesday morning. No, of course he didn't work on Sundays. Well, he supposed someone could have come in on Sunday, but they would have had to pick the lock on the gates and it had looked all right to him when he opened up on Monday. Yes, someone might have borrowed the Mini, or any other car for that matter, but they would have had to fix it first. It stood to reason he didn't have running cars here—people didn't bring in cars that worked all right.

"But you don't know for certain that there was anything wrong with the Mini before Monday afternoon?" asked Gibbons.

Gleason snorted. "Of *course* there was something wrong with it," he said. "It died, didn't it? George had a look at it when he went to tow it and if it had been a little fiddling thing, he would have put it right on the spot."

"I see. Well, thank you very much, Mr. Gleason."

"Where to now?" asked Bethancourt, once they were back in the Jaguar.

"I guess we'd better go see if Tom Follet's still at his shop. Take a right at the corner."

Bethancourt eased the car out into the traffic and followed directions: "Well," he said, "it doesn't look too promising, does it? I somehow doubt that a well-brought-up Englishman like Bill Follet knows how to pick locks."

"No, and it doesn't seem as if he could have gotten a copy of a key either," Gibbons sighed.

"Cheer up," said Bethancourt. "You've still got one son who doesn't have an alibi and who was in the neighborhood of the murder."

"And who apparently has no motive."

"One hundred thousand pounds is plenty of motive," replied Bethancourt. "Oh, I know he was doing well enough, but he's in antiques. Supposing there was a particularly juicy piece he desperately wanted? Something really magnificent that costs a bundle. He could have developed a mania or what have you for it. People have done murder for less."

"I guess so," said Gibbons gloomily.

Follet's Antiques was a small shop, but very well appointed, with every piece set off advantageously. There was a goodly mixture of styles and periods, but none of it seemed to clash. Bethancourt peered closely at an exquisite Chinese vase.

"That's the best piece in the shop," said a voice. "Good afternoon, Sergeant Gibbons."

Tom Follet was a tall, thin young man who looked very different from his brother. He was much darker in complexion and his face was longer. He smiled at them.

"I take it," he said, "that I inherited enough today to make me an even better suspect?"

"Yes," said Gibbons frankly, "if only there was some evidence that you needed it."

Follet shook his head. "If I had needed it, she would have given it to me. My mother was a generous woman and I loved her deeply. She was really a rare person. Everyone who knew her loved her—except, of course, for my stepfather."

"Why not him?" asked Bethancourt curiously. "He married her and it seems the marriage was a happy one."

"He married her for her money and he cheated on her," said Follet shortly. "She knew he had other women, too, but she wouldn't listen to a word about it. Said she was getting on and she knew he loved her. She'd just never run into someone who didn't love her before, that was all."

"But they were happy?" persisted Bethancourt.

"I suppose they were. Why shouldn't they be? He had the money he wanted and she had him. He was very charming and she loved him. And, really, Bill and I never made much of a fuss about it. She was desolate when our father died and I think we both felt that she deserved what happiness she could find. So long as she remained deluded about MacGruder, what was the harm? And he'd never leave the money."

"But you don't think he killed her?"

Follet's face darkened. "How could he have?" he asked. "He was miles away, playing golf, wasn't he?"

"Yes," said Gibbons, "I'm afraid his alibi is confirmed in every particular. But I really came today to ask you about your brother."

"Bill? I hope you're not suspecting him now. He was with Annie all day anyhow."

"That's true," said Gibbons. "No, it's another matter. I understand you made several checks for rather large sums out to him over the past four months. Why was that?"

"He needed money," answered Follet promptly. "He'd made some very foolish investments and overextended himself as well. I warned him against it at the time. Frankly, I would have been inclined to lend him very little, as a lesson to him. But there was Annie and the baby to consider."

"Did she ask you for money, too?"

"Oh, no, she knew nothing about it. Bill was quite anxious lest she find out—he didn't want her to be disappointed in him. I told him it would be better to let her know what had happened, but he would have none of it."

"Do you know if he applied to his mother for loans as well?"

"No, he didn't. The same went for her as went for Annie. I said he was silly. Mother had enough to completely restore his losses, and she would have given it to him if it took all she had. But he couldn't bear the thought of her knowing what a fool he'd been, so I helped him out as best I could." He grinned. "I suppose I was just as silly. I could have told Mother I'd spent a lot on a fake and had her give me the money to give to Bill. But I didn't want her thinking less of me any more than Bill did. It's not that she would have complained, or been anything but sympathetic, mind. But there it is. We wanted her to be proud of us."

"And of course," said Bethancourt, "there was no reason that she should be disappointed in you. It's hard to lie about something like that."

"Yes, it is."

"This is a delicate question, Mr. Follet, but I do need to ask it. Was your mother aware that you are gay?"

"Yes," answered Follet unemotionally. "She knew."

"And how did she feel about that?"

"We didn't discuss it much. Naturally she was displeased, but my mother was good with unpleasant facts. Like David's infidelity. If there was nothing to be done about it, she just left it alone."

"I see."

There was a pause and then Gibbons asked suddenly, "What do you do if you find a piece you can't afford but would like to have?"

"I don't buy it," answered Follet. "Everything in the shop is for sale, sergeant. If I had a hankering after, say, a Fabergé egg, it would be pointless to go into debt for it just to sell it to someone else."

"But if you wanted it for yourself?"

"That," said Follet seriously, "would have been more foolish than Bill and his investments."

The Foxes lived next door to Bill and Annie Follet. Mrs. Fox, a woman of about sixty, opened the door to them.

"No," she said when asked, "Jim isn't back yet. Don't get home for another half hour or so."

"We just wanted to go over what he told the other policeman the other day," explained Gibbons.

"Oh, about the car," she said. "Well, he was washing and polishing for a solid two hours, I can tell you that. I brought him out some tea once, and a beer a little later when he was almost done."

"And when would that have been, Mrs. Fox?"

"He went out straight after breakfast. We have it late on Sundays, so it might have been ten o'clock when he started. Maybe about ten thirty I came out with the tea. And then I did up the kitchen and went up to make the bed and have my bath. It was when I came down and found him still at it that I brought out the beer. Must have been getting on for noon. Yes, it was, because I asked him, would he be done in time for lunch and he said yes."

"And the Follets' car was parked in their drive both times when you came out?"

"His car was. The red one. I don't remember seeing her car."

"Thank you very much, Mrs. Fox. Do you know the Follets well?"

"I see them often enough, but we don't have them over, nor them us. We're a bit elderly for them."

"Have you ever seen Mrs. MacGruder, Mr. Follet's mother?"

"She's been down once or twice. A very nice woman, and I was awful sorry to hear about her being killed like that. Annie spoke of her often—always said what a wonderful person she was. Really fond of her, she seemed, and that's not always the case with mothers and daughters-in-law. In fact, I think on Sunday as ever was, Annie said her mother-in-law would be coming down when the baby was born, and how glad she was about it."

"You saw Annie on Sunday?"

"Oh, yes, I went out back after breakfast to feed the dog and they were both out there in the garden, looking at their herbs. I waved and we just passed the time of day for a minute or two."

"What time would this have been, Mrs. Fox?"

"Well, let's see. It was before I took Jim the tea, so it must have been around ten fifteen, maybe a little later."

"Ten fifteen? Well, thank you very much, Mrs. Fox. You've been a very great help."

"Isn't that just the way of it?" grumbled Gibbons when they were back in the car. "If I'd gone to see her first, I needn't have bothered with Gleason at all. Or if the bloody police out here had thought to talk to her as well as her husband."

"Yes," said Bethancourt absently. "You know, Jack, I think we've got the wrong end of this case altogether. Look at what we've got so far: a dead woman with three people who stood to gain by her death. Two of them couldn't possibly have murdered her, the third could have, but has no motive. I suppose you asked the solicitor whether she had had any intention of changing her will?"

"I did. She didn't, at least not so far as he knew."

"I think it's time we had another talk with Mr. MacGruder."

MacGruder did not look at all pleased to see them but, when pressed, invited them in. He led the way to the living room, but did not offer them seats.

"Well?" he demanded. "What is it now?"

"We wanted to ask you some questions about your stepson Tom," said Gibbons.

"Still harping on the family? Well, go ahead."

"Did your wife know that he was a homosexual?"

"Of course," grunted MacGruder. "There was no secret about it."

"Did they ever quarrel about it? Or about anything to your knowledge."

"Well," said MacGruder thoughtfully, "there was some kind of a row that last time he visited."

"When would that have been?"

"A month ago, maybe. I don't know what it was about. I know she had been worried about him—all this AIDS going around, you know. She might have said something that set him off. Anyway, she was pretty upset after he left. Said he was unreasonable and he had better get over it."

"Did she suggest she might want to change her will?"

"Change it?" MacGruder looked startled. "Never. Oh, you mean Tom. No, she never said anything, although she might not have. It would be like her to take care of it herself and then tell me afterwards."

"She didn't see Tom again before she died?"

"No. She went down to Cirencester about a week before she was killed, but Tom had gone to an auction that day and wasn't around. She was back for dinner that night, as I recollect."

"But you didn't hear what the argument was about?"

"No," said MacGruder irritably. "Didn't I just say I hadn't?"

"Just so," said Gibbons soothingly. "Well, thank you very much, Mr. MacGruder. We won't take up any more of your time."

"That's the first decent bit of information I've had in a long time," said Gibbons. "Can you drop me by the Yard? I'd like to call the brothers again and get some corroboration, if any."

"His times are right."

"What? Oh, yes, you mean about the visits. Yes, that all works out well enough. And it's fortunate that Bill and Annie saw her after Tom. She may have said something to them about the argument."

"They may not be very willing to tell you, if she did," said Bethancourt. "I imagine their loyalties lie with Tom rather than with MacGruder."

"Well, I have to ask, don't I? If they won't say anything, perhaps one of her friends will—there's that widow she was such great friends with. I'll also be interested to see what explanation Tom Follet gives for the row."

"Yes," said Bethancourt. "I'll be interested in that, too."

Marla was asleep. Bethancourt slipped out of the bed and stood a moment looking down at her. They had had another fight that evening when they had returned home to find a message from Gibbons on the machine and Bethancourt had insisted on ringing him back. They had made up, more or less, but she was sure to be sulky in the morning.

He turned and, wrapping a heavy silk robe about himself, crept from the room. In the study, he switched on the lamp and poured himself a scotch. He could not sleep. Cerberus, wakened by the absence of his master, padded quietly into the room and sat at Bethancourt's knee. Bethancourt fondled his ears and then picked up one of the police photos provided by Gibbons. There was something wrong about this case. Gibbons had reported that the Follets were united in denying that Tom had had any kind of argument with his mother before her death. That could mean only one thing, but Bethancourt was at a loss to explain it. He stared at the photograph. It was all there: the body sprawled on the floor, obviously fallen from the stool; the handmirror and eyeliner compact to one side, the brush cast to the other side against the wall. The dressing table itself, otherwise undisturbed. The larger mirror on the wall, a small clock to one side of the table with the cup of coffee next to it, and a picture of the MacGruders in a silver gilt frame on the other side. In the space between lay a small bottle of foundation, two cases of eyeshadow, and a brown pencil, all set out in an orderly fashion.

Bethancourt sighed. There was something missing, he could feel it in his bones. But he could not think of what it was.

"Really," said Marla, "every time one of these cases comes along, you become totally preoccupied. It's worse than when you're writing. At least then you admit that you're preoccupied."

Bethancourt shifted uncomfortably behind the steering wheel. Marla had many virtues, but he had often had cause to wish that her temper was more restrained. He apologized, knowing it would do him no good, and it did not. She went on about his disgraceful behavior the evening before until he pulled up outside the studio where she was working that day. There was a parking space out front so he pulled into it and offered to come up for a few minutes—another conciliatory action and one which Marla accepted in better spirit. With Marla, actions spoke louder than words.

The studio was a bustle of activity. Marla was whisked away almost immediately to be fussed over by the fashion editor and the makeup man. Jim, the photographer, who knew and liked Bethancourt, found a few minutes to chat, but was then appealed to by several people to "come and look at this." Left alone, Bethancourt cast an eye over the clothes and accessories (hastily being arranged by the editor) to be shot, idly watched a harried assistant setting up another light, and finally wandered over to where Marla was having her face administered to by the makeup man.

"I may push off now," he announced. "What time shall I pick you up?"

Marla cast a jade green eye up at him, started to reply and was promptly hushed by the makeup man. Obediently, she closed her eyes and held a finger up to Bethancourt. The makeup man didn't spare him a glance. Expertly, he added color to Marla's lids, licked a finger to smudge the edges, smeared a line of color beneath her eyes, and turned momentarily back to his paraphernalia.

"I have to stop by the office tonight," said Marla. "How about meeting me there at six?"

"Six it is."

"Hold still," said the makeup man, taking her chin in one hand.

Marla touched a finger to her lips in the motion of blowing a kiss and then closed her eyes again. Bethancourt started to turn away and then paused to watch the makeup man draw the moistened brush along Marla's lashes, leaving a thin black line behind. He dunked the brush in a cup of water, dabbed it in the liner, and repeated the performance on the other eye.

Bethancourt forced himself to turn away, thinking, that's what Delia MacGruder was doing when someone came in and murdered her. She had painted one line on her right eye and was about to do the left when she stopped. She stopped to eat or drink something someone handed her, and she died.

He proceeded to have coffee with his agent in an attempt to pacify the man, who was irate about deadlines and Bethancourt's failure to meet them. Bethancourt reflected that everyone was releasing their frustrations this morning by yelling at him. He went home, ostensibly to write an article, actually to sit in an armchair and stare out at nothing until the telephone rang.

"If she had a fight with her son, she didn't tell anybody," said Gibbons gloomily.

"Then maybe she didn't have one."

"But why would MacGruder lie?"

"Maybe he killed her. He did have the most to gain."

"Don't be silly, Phillip," said Gibbons, irritably. "He was playing golf with two other men when she died."

"That's true," said Bethancourt meditatively.

"I hate it when you're calm like this," said Gibbons. "Here I am, practically foaming at the mouth and you're sitting at home in perfect peace. Why is that?"

"Because you have ambition and I don't," replied Bethancourt. "You have a job and you want to do it well and rise up through the ranks. Whereas I would like to be able to discover who killed Delia MacGruder, but if I don't, I figure someone like you will. It's true that you have to work for a living and I don't, but you enjoy your work and take pride in it, while I don't take pride in much of anything."

"That's not true, Phillip," said Gibbons. "What you do, you do very well. And you do and know about a lot more different things than I do. You just don't care particularly what anybody else thinks of you. I have to care. At least, I have to care what Carmichael thinks."

"How is he today?"

"Ready to roast me. Well, that's not entirely true. He did allow as how I had followed up all leads admirably, only he wants to know why they don't go anywhere. God knows I don't know why."

"I do," said Bethancourt. "I told you: we've got

hold of the wrong angle somehow. Go back to the beginning, Jack. That's where we went wrong. There was something odd about the dressing room, and I'd give a hundred pounds if I could just remember what it was."

"So would I," said Gibbons, "and a hundred pounds is more to me than it is to you. Look, I've got to go console Carmichael with today's agenda. Call me if you have any new thoughts."

"All right."

He hung up the receiver and found Cerberus at his side.

"Time for your walk, old fellow? All right, let me get my coat."

Cerberus followed him to the door in a dignified manner that managed to convey a discreet pleasure in the coming outing, but no particular anxiety. They were in the meadows of Hyde Park and were turning for home when the answer suddenly came to Bethancourt. He stopped dead and the dog looked round curiously at him. He saw with crystal clarity every minute action of the makeup man that morning. He saw the contorted face of the dead woman and the complete inventory of the dressing room. And he saw what was missing.

He took Cerberus home at a run. He hardly needed to consult the police photo for confirmation, but he did so anyway. Then, jubilant, anxious, full of the news, he dialed Scotland Yard. But Jack Gibbons was out to lunch.

Gibbons was enjoying the cottage pie in a pub two blocks from his office. His cohort, Chris O'Leary, was having sausage. Between bites and sips of beer, they discussed the MacGruder murder and their superior's eccentricities. It was with some surprise, therefore, that Gibbons felt his shoulder taken in a strong grip and heard a familiar voice saying, "Jack! Thank God I've found you—I've been to three pubs already. Tell me—what did you take away from the dressing room?"

"Take away?" asked the detective in surprise, setting down his fork.

"Yes, yes," replied Bethancourt impatiently. "Take away, impound as evidence. The coffee, of course, but what else?"

"Oh." Understanding dawned. "Not much. Just the makeup on the table—"

"Including the eyeliner?"

"Yes, that and the handmirror and the brush."

"Thank God!" Bethancourt sank down on a stool with relief.

"Look here, Phillip, what's this all about? Have you had an idea?"

"I've figured it out," Bethancourt announced, taking off his glasses and polishing them on his pants leg. "The cyanide was in the eyeliner."

Both Gibbons and O'Leary frowned. "But that's much slower," said Gibbons. "And I think it would have blinded her first—"

"No, no," broke in Bethancourt. "You don't understand. That sort of eyeliner needs water to be applied. You have to wet the brush first. But there was no water on the dressing table. Therefore," he paused significantly, "she must have licked the brush to wet it. And the brush; of course, had cyanide all over it by then."

Back at Scotland Yard, Bethancourt repeated his explanation twice—once with pantomime—while the eyeliner was analyzed and found to contain cyanide.

"The eyeliner is bung full of it," said the chemist with satisfaction. "And the brush is covered, too. Only about twenty milligrams, but that's all it would take for someone as small as she was."

"That leaves little doubt," said Gibbons. "It had to be the husband. Who else would know that she habitually licked the brush?"

"That's a point," mused Bethancourt. "It will still be tough going in court. Any decent defense counsel will manage to explain why twenty other people would know."

"And would have the opportunity between one morning and the next?" said Gibbons. "And it will be cinched if we can trace cyanide to his possession. We've not done much about that—thinking, you see, since he had an alibi, there wasn't much use in it. We've a good chance of turning something up. After all, cyanide isn't an easy thing to get hold of."

"If you can do that, the case is sewn up. As it is, it's not bad—not with that motive tacked on."

Gibbons grinned. "You've been brilliant, Phillip. As usual."

"It came to me watching Marla being made up this morning," Bethancourt began and then he stopped with an anxious expression. "My God, what time is it?"

"Just on six."

"Lord!" Bethancourt leapt from his chair. "If I hurry I can manage being only ten minutes late. Damn rush hour traffic! No, bless it, I can tell her I got caught in a jam. Call you later, Jack. Come, Cerberus."

Gibbons, with an amused grin, watched his friend careen out the door and down the hall.

Some weeks later, Jack Gibbons shed his overcoat in Bethancourt's hallway and proceeded to the living room, where he was met by the agreeable sight of both Cerberus and Marla curled up together before a roaring fire.

"Whisky?" suggested Bethancourt, and Gibbons nodded and followed him to the bar.

"They got a conviction this afternoon, you know," said Gibbons in an undertone.

"I heard on the radio," said Bethancourt, pouring. "I wanted to be there, but Marla only just got back from that ski shoot this morning and she didn't want to go."

Gibbons glanced back at the girl beside the dog and at the firelight glinting in her hair.

"They said on the radio the jury didn't take long."

"No, once we had traced the cyanide to his possession, it was pretty clear-cut. They were back inside of two hours."

"Then here's to us."

"We make a good team," nodded Gibbons, knocking his glass gently against Bethancourt's.

A MATTER OF TASTE

by Dorothy L. Sayers

Halte-là! . . . attention! . . . F—e!"

The young man in the gray suit pushed his way through the protesting porters and leaped nimbly for the footboard of the guard's van as the Paris-Evreux express steamed out of the Invalides. The guard, with an eye to a tip, fielded him adroitly from among the detaining hands.

"It is happy for monsieur that he is so agile," he remarked. "Monsieur is in a hurry?"

"Somewhat. Thank you. I can get through by the corridor?"

"But certainly. The *premières* are two coaches away, beyond the luggage van."

The young man rewarded his rescuer, and made his way forward, mopping his face. As he passed the piled-up luggage, something caught his eye, and he stopped to investigate. It was a suitcase, nearly new, of expensive-looking leather, labeled conspicuously:

LORD PETER WIMSEY,
Hôtel Saumon d'Or,
Verneuil-sur-Eure.

and bore witness to its itinerary thus:

LONDON-PARIS
(Waterloo) (Gare St. Lazare)
via Southampton-Havre.
PARIS-VERNEUIL
(Ch. de Fer de l'Ouest)

The young man whistled, and sat down on a trunk to think it out.

Somewhere there had been a leakage, and they were on his trail. Nor did they care who knew it. There were hundreds of people in London and Paris who would know the name of Wimsey, not counting the police of both countries. In addition to belonging to one of the oldest ducal families in England, Lord Peter had made himself conspicuous by his meddling with crime detection. A label like this was a gratuitous advertisement.

But the amazing thing was that the pursuers were not troubling to hide themselves from the pursued. That argued very great confidence. That he should have got into the guard's van was, of course, an accident, but, even so, he might have seen it on the platform, or anywhere.

An accident? It occurred to him—not for the first time, but definitely now, and without doubt—that it was indeed an accident for them that he was here. The series of maddening delays that had held him up between London and the Invalides presented itself to him with an air of prearrangement. The preposterous accusation, for instance, of the woman who had accosted him in Piccadilly, and the slow process of extricating himself at Marlborough Street. It was easy to hold a man up on some trumped-up charge till an important plan had matured.

Then there was the lavatory door at Waterloo, which had so ludicrously locked itself upon him. Being athletic, he had climbed over the partition, to find the attendant mysteriously absent. And, in Paris, was it by chance that he had had a deaf taxi driver, who mistook the direction "Quai d'Orléans" for "Gare de Lyon," and drove a mile and a half in the wrong direction before the shouts of his fare attracted his attention?

They were clever, the pursuers, and circumspect. They had accurate information; they would delay him, but without taking any overt step; they knew that, if only they could keep time on their side, they needed no other ally.

Did they know he was on the train? If not, he still kept the advantage, for they would travel in a false security, thinking him to be left, raging and helpless, in the Invalides. He decided to make a cautious reconnaissance.

The first step was to change his gray suit for another of inconspicuous navy-blue cloth, which he had in his small black bag. This he did in the privacy of the Men's Room, substituting for his gray soft hat a large traveling cap, which pulled well down over his eyes.

There was little difficulty in locating the man he was in search of. He found him seated in the inner corner of a first-class compartment, facing the engine, so that the watcher could approach unseen from behind. On the rack was a handsome dressing case, with the initials P.D.B.W. The young man was familiar with Wimsey's narrow, beaky face, flat yellow hair, and insolent dropped eyelids. He smiled a little grimly.

"He is confident," he thought, "and has regrettably made the mistake of underrating the enemy. Good! This is where I retire into a *seconde* and keep my eyes open. The next act of this melodrama will take place, I fancy, at Dreux."

It is a rule on the Chemin de Fer de l'Ouest that all Paris-Evreux trains, whether of Grande Vitesse or what Lord Peter Wimsey preferred to call Grande Paresse, shall halt for an interminable period at Dreux. The young man (now in navy-blue) watched his quarry safely into the refreshment room, and slipped unobtrusively out of the station.

In a quarter of an hour he was back—this time in a heavy motoring coat, helmet, and goggles, at the wheel of a powerful hired Peugeot. Coming quietly onto the platform, he took up his station behind the wall of the *lampisterie*, where he could keep an eye on the train and the buffet door. After fifteen minutes his patience was rewarded by the sight of his man again boarding the express, dressing case in hand.

The porters slammed the doors, crying, "Next stop Verneuil!" The engine panted and groaned; the long train of gray-green carriages clanked slowly away. The motorist drew a breath of satisfaction, and, hurrying past the barrier, started up the car. He knew that he had a good eighty miles an hour under his hood, and there is no speed limit in France.

Mon Souci, the seat of that eccentric and eremitical genius the Comte de Rueil, is situated three kilometers from Verneuil. It is a sorrowful and decayed château, desolate at the termination of its neglected avenue of pines. The mournful state of a nobility without an allegiance surrounds it. The stone nymphs droop greenly over their dry and moldering fountains. An occasional peasant creaks with a single wagonload of wood along the ill-forested glades. It has the atmosphere of sunset at all hours of the day. The woodwork is dry and gaping for lack of paint. Through the jalousies one sees the prim *salon*, with its beautiful and faded furniture. Even the last of its ill-dressed, ill-favored women has withered away from Mon Souci, with her in-bred, exaggerated features and her long white gloves.

But at the rear of the château a chimney smokes incessantly. It is the furnace of the laboratory, the only living and modern thing among the old and dying; the only place tended and loved, petted and spoiled, heir to the long solicitude which Counts of a more light-hearted day had given to stable and kennel, portrait gallery and ballroom. And below, in the cool cellar, lie row upon row the dusty bottles, each an enchanged glass coffin in which the Sleeping Beauty of the vine grows ever more ravishing.

As the Peugeot came to a standstill in the courtyard, the driver observed with considerable surprise that he was not the Count's only visitor. An immense super-Renault, like a *merveilleuse* of the Directoire, all hood and no body, had been drawn so ostentatiously across the entrance as to embarrass the approach of any new-comer. Its glittering panels were embellished with a coat of arms, and the Count's elderly servant was at that moment staggering beneath the weight of two large and elaborate suitcases, bearing in silver letters that could be read a mile away the legend: LORD PETER WIMSEY.

The Peugeot driver gazed with astonishment at this display, and grinned sardonically. "Lord Peter seems rather ubiquitous in this country," he observed to himself. Then, taking pen and paper from his bag, he busied himself with a little letter writing.

By the time that the suitcases had been carried in, and the Renault had purred its smooth way to the outbuildings, the document was complete and enclosed in an envelope addressed to the Comte de Rueil. "The hoist with his own petard touch," said the young man, and, stepping up to the door, presented the envelope to the manservant.

"I am the bearer of a letter of introduction to Monsieur le Comte," he said. "Will you have the obligingness to present it to him? My name is Bredon—Death Bredon."

The man bowed, and begged him to enter.

"If monsieur will have the goodness to seat himself in the hall for a few moments. Monsieur le Comte is engaged with another gentleman, but I will lose no time in making monsieur's arrival known."

The young man sat down and waited. The windows of the hall looked out upon the entrance, and it was not long before the château's sleep was disturbed by the hooting of yet another motor horn. A station taxi-cab came noisily up the avenue. The man from the first-class carriage and the luggage labeled P.D.B.W. were deposited on the doorstep. Lord Peter Wimsey dismissed the driver and rang the bell.

"Now," said Mr. Bredon, "the fun is going to begin." He effaced himself as far as possible in the shadow of a tall *armoire normande*.

"Good evening," said the newcomer to the manservant, in admirable French, "I am Lord Peter Wimsey. I arrive upon the invitation of Monsieur le Comte de Rueil. Monsieur le Comte is at liberty?"

"Milord Peter Wimsey? Pardon, monsieur, but I do not understand. Milord de Wimsey is already arrived and is with Monsieur le Comte at this moment."

"You surprise me," said the other, with complete imperturbability, "for certainly no one but myself has any right to that name. It seems as though some person more ingenious than honest has had the bright idea of impersonating me."

The servant was clearly at a loss.

"Perhaps," he suggested, "monsieur can show his *papiers d'identité*."

"Although it is somewhat unusual to produce one's credentials on the doorstep when paying a private visit," replied his lordship, with unaltered good humor, "I have not the slightest objection. Here is my passport, here is a *permis de séjour* granted to me in Paris, here my visiting card, and here a quantity of correspondence addressed to me at the Hôtel Meurice, Paris, at my flat in Piccadilly, London, at the Marlborough Club, London, and at my brother's house at King's Denver. Is that sufficiently in order?"

The servant perused the documents carefully, particularly impressed by the *permis de séjour*.

"It appears there is some mistake," he murmured dubiously. "If monsieur will follow me, I will acquaint Monsieur le Comte."

They disappeared through the folding doors at the back of the hall, and Bredon was left alone.

"Quite a little boom in Richmonds today," he observed, "each of us more unscrupulous than the last. The occasion obviously calls for a refined subtlety of method."

After what he judged to be a hectic ten minutes in the Count's library, the servant reappeared, searching for him.

"Monsieur le Comte's compliments, and would monsieur step this way?"

Bredon entered the room with a jaunty step. He had created for himself the mastery of this situation. The Count, a thin, elderly man, his fingers deeply stained with chemicals, sat, with a perturbed expression, at his desk. In two armchairs sat the two Wimseys.

Bredon noted that, while the Wimsey he had seen in the train (whom he mentally named Peter I) retained his unruffled smile, Peter II (he of the Renault) had the flushed and indignant air of an Englishman affronted. The two men were superficially alike—both fair, lean, and long-nosed, with the nondescript, inelastic face which predominates in any assembly of well-bred Anglo-Saxons.

"Mr. Bredon," said the Count, "I am charmed to have the pleasure of making your acquaintance, and regret that I must at once call upon you for a service as singular as it is important. You have presented to me a letter of introduction from your cousin, Lord Peter Wimsey. Will you now be good enough to inform me which of these gentlemen he is?"

Bredon let his glance pass slowly from the one claimant to the other, meditating what answer would best serve his own ends. One, at any rate, of the men in this room was a formidable intellect, trained in the detection of imposture.

"Well?" said Peter II. "Are you going to acknowledge me, Bredon "

Peter I extracted a cigarette from a silver case. "Your confederate does not seem very well up in his part," he remarked, with a quiet smile at Peter II.

"Monsieur le Comte," said Bredon, "I regret extremely that I cannot assist you in the matter. My acquaintance with my cousin, like your own, has been made and maintained entirely through correspondence on a subject of common interest. My profession," he added, "has made me unpopular with my family."

There was a very slight sigh of relief somewhere. The false Wimsey—whichever he was—had gained a respite. Bredon smiled.

"An excellent move, Mr. Bredon," said Peter I, "but it will hardly explain—allow me." He took the letter from the Count's hesitating hand. "It will hardly explain the fact that the ink of this letter of recommendation, dated three weeks ago, is even now scarcely dry—though I congratulate you on the very plausible imitation of my handwriting."

"If *you* can forge my handwriting," said Peter II, "so can this Mr. Bredon." He read the letter aloud over his double's shoulder.

" 'Monsieur le Comte—I have the honor to present to you my friend and cousin, Mr. Death Bredon, who, I understand, is to be traveling in your part of France next month. He is very anxious to view your interesting library. Although a journalist by profession, he really knows something about books.' I am delighted to learn for the first time that I have such a cousin. An interviewer's trick, I fancy. Monsieur le Comte, Fleet Street appears well informed about our family names. Possibly it is equally well informed about the object of my visit to Mon Souci?"

"If," said Bredon boldly, "you refer to the acquisition of the de Rueil formula for poison gas for the British Government, I can answer for my own knowledge, though possibly the rest of Fleet Street is less completely enlightened." He weighed his words carefully now, warned by his slip. The sharp eyes and detective ability of Peter II alarmed him far more than the caustic tongue of Peter I.

The Count uttered an exclamation of dismay.

"Gentlemen," he said, "one thing is obvious—that there has been somewhere a disastrous leakage of information. Which of you is the Lord Peter Wimsey to whom I should entrust the formula I do not know. Both of you are supplied with papers of identity; both appear completely instructed in this matter; both of your handwritings correspond with the letters I have previously received from Lord Peter, and both of you have offered me the sum agreed upon in Bank of England notes.

"In addition, this third gentleman arrives endowed with an equal facility in handwritings, an introductory letter surrounded by most suspicious circumstances, and a degree of acquaintance with this whole matter which alarms me. I can see but one solution. All of you must remain here at the château while I send to England for some elucidation of this mystery. To the genuine Lord Peter I offer my apologies, and assure him that I will endeavor to make his stay as agreeable as possible. Will this satisfy you? It will? I am delighted to hear it. My servants will show you to your bedrooms, and dinner will be at half-past seven."

"It is delightful to think," said Mr. Bredon, as he fingered his glass and passed it before his nostrils with the air of a connoisseur, "that whichever of these gentlemen has the right to the name he assumes is assured tonight of a truly Olympian satisfaction." His impudence had returned to him, and he challenged the company with an air. "Your cellars, Monsieur le Comte, are as well known among men endowed with a palate as your talents among men of science. No eloquence could say more."

The two Lord Peters murmured assent.

"I am the more pleased by your commendation," said the Count, "that it suggests to me a little test which, with your kind cooperation, will, I think, assist us very much in determining which of you gentlemen is Lord Peter Wimsey and which his talented impersonator. Is it not matter of common notoriety that Lord Peter has a palate for wine almost unequaled in Europe?"

"You flatter me, Monsieur le Comte," said Peter II modestly.

"I wouldn't like to say unequaled," said Peter I, chiming in like a well-trained duet; "let's call it fair to middling. Less liable to misconstruction and all that."

"Your lordship does yourself an injustice," said Bredon, addressing both men with impartial deference. "The bet which you won from Mr. Frederick Arbuthnot at the Egotists' Club, when he challenged you to name the vintage years of seventeen wines blindfold, received its due prominence in the *Evening Wire*."

"I was in extra form that night," said Peter I.

"A fluke," laughed Peter II.

"The test I propose, gentlemen, is on similar lines," pursued the Count, "though somewhat less strenuous. There are six courses ordered for dinner tonight. With each we will drink a different wine, which my butler shall bring in with the label concealed. You shall each in turn give me your opinion upon the vintage. By this means we shall perhaps arrive at something, since the most brilliant forger—of whom I gather I have at least two at my table tonight—can scarcely forge a palate for wine. If too hazardous a mixture of wines should produce a temporary incommodity in the morning, you will, I feel sure, suffer it gladly this once in the case of truth."

The two Wimseys bowed.

"*In vino veritàs*," said Mr. Bredon, with a laugh. He at least was well seasoned, and foresaw opportunities for himself.

"Accident, and my butler, having placed you at my right hand, monsieur," went on the Count, addressing Peter I, "I will ask you to begin by pronouncing, as accurately as may be, upon the wine which you have just drunk."

"That is scarcely a searching ordeal," said the other, with a smile. "I can say definitely that it is a very pleasant and well-matured Chablis Moutonne; and, since ten years is an excellent age for a Chablis—a real Chablis—I should vote for 1916, which was perhaps the best of the war vintages in that district."

"Have you anything to add to that opinion, monsieur?" inquired the Count deferentially of Peter II.

"I wouldn't like to be dogmatic to a year or so," said that gentleman critically, "but if I must commit myself, don't you know, I should say 1915—decidedly 1915."

The Count bowed, and turned to Bredon.

"Perhaps you, too, monsieur, would be interested to give an opinion," he suggested, with the exquisite courtesy always shown to the plain man in the society of experts.

"I'd rather not set a standard which I might not be able to live up to," replied Bredon a little maliciously. "I know that it is 1915, for I happened to see the label."

Peter II looked a little disconcerted.

"We will arrange matters better in future," said the Count. "Pardon me." He stepped apart for a few moments' conference with the butler, who presently advanced to remove the oysters and bring in the soup.

The next candidate for attention arrived swathed to the lip in damask.

"It is your turn to speak first, monsieur," said the Count to Peter II. "Permit me to offer you an olive to cleanse the palate. No haste, I beg. Even for the most excellent political ends, good wine must not be used with disrespect."

The rebuke was not unnecessary, for, after a preliminary sip, Peter II had taken a deep draft of the heady white richness. Under Peter I's quizzical eye he wilted quite visibly.

"It is—it is Sauterne," he began, and stopped. Then, gathering encouragement from Bredon's smile, he said, with more aplomb, "Château Yquem, 1911—ah! the queen of white wines, sir; as what's-his-name says." He drained his glass defiantly.

The Count's face was a study as he slowly detached his fascinated gaze from Peter II to fix it on Peter I.

"If I had to be impersonated by somebody," murmured the latter gently, "it would have been more flattering to have had it undertaken by a person to whom all white wines were *not* alike. Well, now, sir, this admirable vintage is, of course, a Montrachet of—let me see"—he rolled the wine delicately on his tongue—"of 1911. And a very attractive wine it is, though, with all due deference to yourself, Monsieur le Comte, I feel that it is perhaps slightly too sweet to occupy its present place in the menu. True, with this excellent *consommé marmite*, a sweetish wine is not altogether out of place, but, in my own humble opinion, it would have shown to better advantage with the *confitures*."

"There, now," said Bredon innocently, "it just shows how one may be misled. Had not I had the advantage of Lord Peter's expert opinion—for certainly nobody who could mistake Montrachet for Sauterne has any claim to the name of Wimsey—I should have pronounced this to be, not the Montrachet-Aîné, but the Chevalier-Montrachet of the same year, which is a trifle sweeter. But no doubt, as your lordship says, drinking it with the soup has caused it to appear sweeter to me than it actually is."

The Count looked sharply at him, but made no comment.

"Have another olive," said Peter I kindly. "You can't judge wine if your mind is on other flavors."

"Thanks frightfully," said Bredon. "And that reminds me—" He launched into a rather pointless story about olives, which lasted out the soup and bridged the interval to the entrance of an exquisitely cooked sole.

The Count's eye followed the pale amber wine rather thoughtfully as it trilled into the glasses. Bredon raised his in the approved manner to his nostrils, and his face flushed a little. With the first sip he turned excitedly to his host.

"Good God, sir—" he began.

The lifted hand cautioned him to silence.

Peter I sipped, inhaled, sipped again, and his brows clouded. Peter II had by this time apparently abandoned his pretensions. He drank thirstily, with a beaming smile and a lessening hold upon reality.

"Eh bien, monsieur?" inquired the Count gently.

"This," said Peter I, "is certainly hock, and the noblest hock I have ever tasted, but I must admit that for the moment I cannot precisely place it."

"No?" said Bredon. His voice was like bean-honey now; sweet and harsh together. "Nor the other gentleman? And yet I fancy I could place it within a couple of miles, though it is a wine I had hardly looked to find in a French cellar at this time. It is hock, as your lordship says, and at that it is Johannisberger. Not the plebeian cousin, but the *echter* Schloss Johannisberger from the castle vineyard itself. Your lordship must have missed it—to your great loss—during the war years. My father laid some down the year before he died, but it appears that the ducal cellars at Denver were less well furnished."

"I must set about remedying the omission," said the remaining Peter, with determination.

The *poulet* was served to the accompaniment of an argument over the Lafitte, his lordship placing it at 1878, Bredon maintaining it to be a relic of the glorious 'seventy-fives, slightly overmatured, but both agreeing as to its great age and noble pedigree.

As to the Clos-Vougeôt, on the other hand, there was complete agreement; after a tentative suggestion of 1915, it was pronounced finally by Peter I to belong to the equally admirable though slightly lighter 1911 crop. The *pré-salé* was removed and amid general applause, and the dessert was brought in.

"Is it necessary," asked Peter I, with a slight smile in the direction of Peter II—now happily murmuring,

"Damn good wine, damn good dinner, damn good show"—"is it necessary to prolong this farce any further?"

"Your lordship will not, surely, refuse to proceed with the discussion?" cried the Count.

"The point is sufficiently made, I fancy."

"But no one will surely ever refuse to discuss wine," said Bredon, "least of all your lordship, who is so great an authority."

"Not on this," said the other. "Frankly, it is a wine I do not care about. It is sweet and coarse, qualities that would damn any wine in the eyes—the mouth, rather—of a connoisseur. Did your excellent father have this laid down also, Mr. Bredon?"

Bredon shook his head.

"No," he said, "no. Genuine Imperial Tokay is beyond the opportunities of Grub Street, I fear. Though I agree with you that it is horribly overrated—with all due deference to yourself, Monsieur le Comte."

"In that case," said the Count, "we will pass at once to the liqueur. I admit that I had thought of puzzling these gentlemen with the local product, but, since one competitor seems to have scratched, it shall be brandy—the only fitting close to a good wine list."

In a slightly embarrassing silence the huge, round-bellied balloon glasses were set upon the table, and the few precious drops poured gently into each and set lightly swinging to release the bouquet.

"This," said Peter I, charmed again into amiability, "is, indeed, a wonderful old French brandy. Half a century old, I suppose."

"Your lordship's praise lacks warmth," replied Bredon. "This is *the* brandy—the brandy of brandies—the superb—the incomparable—the true Napoleon. It should be honored like the emperor it truly is."

He rose to his feet, his napkin in his hand.

"Sir," said the Count, turning to him, "I have on my right a most admirable judge of wine, but you are unique." He motioned to the butler, who solemnly brought forward the empty bottles, unswathed now, from the humble Chablis to the stately Napoleon, with the imperial seal blown in the glass. "Every time you have been correct as to growth and year. There cannot be six men in the world with such a palate as yours, and I thought that but one of them was an Englishman. Will you not favor us, this time, with your real name?"

"It doesn't matter what his name is," said Peter I. He rose. "Put up your hands, all of you. Count, the formula!"

Bredon's hands came up with a jerk, still clutching the napkin. The white folds spurted flame as his shot struck the other's revolver cleanly between trigger and barrel, exploding the charge, to the extreme detriment of the glass chandelier. Peter I stood shaking his paralyzed hand and cursing.

Bredon kept him covered while he cocked a wary eye at Peter II, who, his rosy visions scattered by the report, seemed struggling back to aggressiveness.

"Since the entertainment appears to be taking a lively turn," observed Bredon, "perhaps you would be so good, Count, as to search these gentlemen for further firearms. Thank you. Now, why should we not all sit down again and pass the bottle round?"

"You—*you* are—" growled Peter I.

"Oh, my name is Bredon all right," said the young man cheerfully. "I loathe aliases. Like another fellow's clothes, you know—never seem quite to fit. Peter Death Bredon Wimsey—a bit lengthy and all that, but handy when taken in installments. I've got a passport and all those things, too, but I didn't offer them, as their reputation here seems a little blown upon, so to speak.

"As regards the formula, I think I'd better give my personal check for it—all sorts of people seem able to go about flourishing Bank of England notes. Personally, I think all this secret diplomacy work is a mistake, but that's the War Office's pigeon. I suppose we all brought similar credentials. Yes, I thought so. Some bright person seems to have sold himself very successfully in two places at once. But you two must have been having a lively time, each of you thinking the other was me."

"My lord," said the Count heavily, "these two men are, or were, Englishmen, I suppose. I do not care to know what Governments have purchased their treachery. But where they stand, I, alas! stand too. To our venal and corrupt Republic I, as a Royalist, acknowledge no allegiance. But it is in my heart that I have agreed to sell my country to England because of my poverty. Go back to your War Office and say I will not give you the formula. If war should come between our countries—which may God avert!—I will be found on the side of France. That, my lord, is my last word."

Wimsey bowed.

"Sir," said he, "it appears that my mission has, after all, failed. I am glad of it. This trafficking in destruction is a dirty kind of business after all. Let us shut the door on these two, who are neither flesh nor fowl, and finish the brandy in the library."

ARRIE AND JASPER

by Amanda Cross

My aunt Kate Fansler doesn't care for children. I'm her niece, but I never really got to know her till we ran into each other when I was a student at Harvard. It's true my cousin Leo spent a summer with her, and lived with her a year or so when he was in high school, but he wasn't really a child in high school, and during that summer she had a hired companion for him and sent him to day camp besides. Kate always refused to become defensive about this. "I know it's an eccentric attitude," she admitted, "but not a dangerous one. The worst fate I've ever inflicted on any child is to avoid it. As it happens, however," she added, "I did once more or less solve a case for a child. Do you think that will serve to redeem me in the eyes of those with maternal instincts?"

Kate was in her office at the university, about to conclude that her office hour was over and the thought of a martini with Reed could be realistically contemplated, when she heard a timid knock. She looked through the glass in the top half of her door and saw a silhouette reaching only a few inches above where the glass began. She opened the door to find herself confronting a girl child wearing a school uniform, glasses, braces, and a frown. Kate stared at the child so long she asked if she might come in. Kate apologized and ushered her in, closing the door.

"Forgive me," Kate said. "I was just a bit startled.

You look rather young for graduate school. Or even for college, if it comes to that. Are you lost?"

"I've come to hire you as a detective," the child said. "I have money. My father says you probably couldn't find a herd of buffalo in a field covered with snow, but I figure if he doesn't like you you must be good."

"My dear young woman," Kate said, dropping back into the chair behind her desk, "I don't know which misapprehension to confront first. But, in the order in which you offered them, I'm not a detective, either private or police—they work at that job a lot harder than I do. I have detected from time to time, but I never take money, it might cloud the fine, careless rapture of the adventure. I don't know who your father is, and I'm somewhat concerned that you hold his opinion in such low regard."

You might think all this verbiage would have frightened the kid, but she held her ground admirably. "I hope I didn't offend you about the money," she said, returning her wallet to her pocket. "I would be very glad of your help."

"It doesn't sound to me as though your father would approve of your seeking my help, nor of my offering it. Who is your father? Someone I know?"

"His name is Professor Witherspoon," the child said, assured that his name was sufficient to establish his identity and credentials in Kate's eyes. She was quite right. Witherspoon was a member of Kate's department, and to say that he and Kate never saw eye to eye on anything was to put their relationship in its least emotional terms. Kate was frank to admit that she could never decide if he was a monster or a lunatic. The best that could be said on her side was that most of the department agreed with her. Kate eyed his progeny with some dismay.

"It sounds to me as though I'm the last person you should come to. Am I to gather that your dislike of your father is sufficient to recommend to you someone he despises?"

The girl had no trouble with this one, either, merely nodding. "I think he's the most awful man I know," she added. "I didn't come to you just for that reason, though. My sister took a class with you, and she considered you worthy of recommendation."

"Well," Kate said with some relief, "I'm glad to hear there is one member of your family that you like. But I can't say I ever remember having a Witherspoon in my class. I don't remember all my students' names, but I have a feeling I would have noticed hers."

"Roxanna has taken our mother's name—Albright. I'm going to do the same as soon as I can. I'll have to wait at least until I leave high school. My sister is a lot older than me. She's very smart and very beautiful; not like me."

"You look fine to me," Kate said. She meant it. Kate is the best disregarder of beauty in any conventional sense I've ever met, and if a person is glamorous or studiously well dressed, they have to go a long way to gain her trust.

"I don't look like my mother," the child said with evident regret. "Also I'm strabismic and have an overbite. Put differently," she added, "my eyes have difficulty focusing on the same object, and my upper and lower jaws fail to meet properly. I think it's because I was such a disappointment. I was unexpected, you see, but they hoped—that is, my father hoped—that at least I would be a boy. I wasn't," she added sadly, in case Kate had any doubt.

Had the kid but known it, she had picked the quickest way to Kate's sympathies. I think Kate asked her what she wanted in order to get her off the topic of her drawbacks.

"I want you to find my dog," she said.

About this time, I'm sure, Kate was beginning to think of that martini with something close to passion. "I wouldn't know how to begin to look for a lost dog in this city," she said. "I'm afraid it may have been snatched by someone, or else wandered off. Have you tried the ASPCA?"

"He wasn't lost, he was stolen. And not on the streets, out of the apartment. The doorman saw someone leaving with Jasper under his arm. And the apartment wasn't broken into. Which means it was an inside job."

Kate took the bull by the horns (the same bull, according to Witherspoon, which she would be capable of overlooking in a china shop). "Do you suspect your father?" she asked.

"I don't know who to suspect." The kid sighed. "But Jasper meant, means, an awful lot to me." And she began to cry. She raised her glasses and wiped her eyes on her sleeve.

"What kind of dog was he?" Kate asked for something to say. "I gather not a mastiff if someone could carry him out."

"He's a Jack Russell terrier. The breed isn't yet accepted by the American Kennel Club, though it is by the English. Jack Russell terriers are small, very low to the ground, white with brown faces and ears, and tough as anything. Don't you see, it had to be someone Jasper knew, someone he thought was taking him out. He loves to go out," she added, sniffing, "but he's a fierce watchdog with anyone he doesn't know."

"You haven't told me your name," Kate said.

"Arabella. It was my father's mother's name. She was a suffragette who chained herself to fences. My father hated her. People like my sister call me Arrie."

Of course it occurred to Kate that the kid needed a therapist, not a detective, and she also probably needed a new father and a new dog. "What about your mother?" she asked. "You haven't mentioned her."

"She's away trying to stop drinking. She's much younger than my father. She was a graduate student.

She's his second wife. We have two much older stepsisters from his first marriage. My father has never been able to produce a son, to his sorrow. I hope my mother gets better. The man where she is says the whole family ought to help, but my father hasn't the time. My sister and I went down there once." She trailed off.

Poor Kate didn't really know what to do. She wanted to help the kid, but there didn't seem to be any evident practical course of assistance. Arrie seemed to understand her dilemma. "You could think about it," she said. "My sister says you're very good at thinking about things. Only try not to think too long because I'm very worried about poor Jasper. He can be very trying to people who don't understand him."

"And with that," Kate said, relating the scene to Reed over her second martini, her first having been required simply to calm her down and stop her babbling, "she left with a lot more dignity than I was exhibiting. What the hell am I to do? Could you call some old pal from the DA's office to undertake a dog search on the side?"

Kate's husband answered her real question. "The doorman saw someone leave with the dog under his arm, as I understand it. The dog wasn't struggling, indicating that it wasn't being nabbed by a stranger but by someone it knew. You better find out more about the family."

"It doesn't sound like a family I want to know much more about. Perhaps we should offer to adopt Arrie and get her another Jasper."

"You have got to begin drinking less," Reed said with asperity. "We are a happy, adult couple, let me remind you—you have no trouble remembering it when you're sober. You aren't going to turn maternal on me after all these years?"

"Fear not. Just wait till *you* meet Arrie. Not to mention her father, the esteemed Professor Witherspoon."

"What is he a professor of, exactly?"

"Exactly is the word. He deals in manuscripts, the older the better, and in a foreign tongue. There is nothing about them he doesn't know, to do him justice. The trouble is, he doesn't know anything else. Confront him with an idea and he turns into a dangerous, oversized porcupine with a very loud voice. He detests every new discipline or theory or concept of teaching, and if he had his way the first woman faculty member would never have been hired. He's done his best to keep our numbers down. Women students, needless to say, are a different matter. He carries on with them in a manner designed to give sexual harassment a new name. Women students should be grateful to sit at his feet and submit themselves in other suitable poses; he doesn't want them as colleagues. He is also pompous and leering, but we might as well keep this discussion on an impersonal basis, as is my wont."

"That fills out the picture without getting us anywhere, wouldn't you say?"

"I've *been* saying, ever since I got home. What, dear man, is my next move?"

"Something will occur to you," Reed said with confidence.

The next day, Arrie's sister Roxanna Albright phoned Kate's office for an appointment. With enormous relief, Kate agreed to see her. Roxanna, being beautiful and older, could be counted on not to get to Kate in the same way Arrie had. No doubt they could arrive at a practical conclusion to the whole problem, insofar as it allowed of one. Perhaps it would be best to begin by advertising for Jasper, hanging plaintive signs on lampposts, that kind of thing.

Roxanna, whom Kate had unsuccessfully attempted to call to mind from some years back, exceeded all expectations. She was gorgeous—there was no other word. She must, Kate thought, have undergone some sort of transformation in the intervening years; not to have noticed her would have been like overlooking Garbo.

"I don't know whether to apologize or implore," Roxanna said when they had both sat down. "Arrie didn't consult me before coming. We'd talked about you once at dinner and I'd expressed my admiration. The fact that you had successfully undertaken some detective commissions was mentioned."

"As well as the opinion that I couldn't find a herd of buffalo in a white field; I know. But does the fact that your father despises me really qualify me to help Arrie? If so, I hope you'll tell me how."

"Oh, dear. Tact is something Arrie doesn't so much scorn as ignore."

"I quite agree with her," Kate said. "Tact should never interfere with one's getting at the facts. Your father, for example, lacks not tact but any concept of what the facts are."

"How well you put it." Roxanna paused as though considering how to go on. "I think the world of Arrie," she said. "Arrie's convinced she's an ugly duckling; I talk of a swan, which in time she will become. Arrie's going to do just fine. But, except for me, she doesn't get much undemanding affection, or really any affection at all. Except from Jasper, of course, which is what made this so awful. Jasper's a very responsive dog—he and Arrie have a relationship I can only call passionate.

"That's why I wanted to come in person to tell you that he's back, and apparently no worse for his strange adventure. We got a note, printed capitals on plain paper, saying he could be found at five P.M. tied to the gate of the playground at Seventy-second Street and Fifth Avenue. Of course Arrie was there on the dot, and so was Jasper. I've really only come to thank you for your kindness, not throwing her out, listening to her. It was a horrible three days. Even my father's glad the dog's back, and that's saying a good deal. You've been very kind."

"There was no ransom asked? No demand at all?"

"None. My father pointed out to Arrie that if she went ahead of time, as she wanted to do, the kidnaper might see her and not return Jasper. It's the only helpful thing he's said in living memory, so I suppose this whole affair is remarkable for that alone." Roxanna rose.

"I know," she said, "that Arrie will write to you and thank you for your sympathy and kindness. I think you, too . . ."

The next day, however, brought not a letter from Arrie, but Arrie herself. She had waited patiently during Kate's office hour until the last of the students had gone. She had Jasper with her, hidden in a very large sack. She let him out in Kate's office, explaining that she had brought him because she hardly dared leave him alone if she didn't absolutely have to, and because she thought Kate might like to meet him, having been so kind about his disappearance.

Jasper was a bundle of energy, perhaps ten inches high and eighteen inches long. He looked as though he could take on with ease anything five times his size. Having dashed about with relief at being out of the sack, necessitated by the university's No Dogs signs, Jasper sat down at Arrie's feet and looked up at her adoringly. Kate began to feel she was being forced to watch a Disney movie that threatened never to end. Arrie, perhaps sensing this, became very businesslike.

"Jasper and I are not here only to thank you," she said. "We wish to engage your services to find out who took him. Unless I know, you see," she added, "I'll never be able to feel safe in leaving him again. I'm sure you can understand that."

Kate was silent, which wasn't—as she was the first to admit—her usual part in a conversation. She had to recognize a clear reluctance to abandon this child to an additional unknown. Her father was clearly as reliable as a lottery and her sister affectionate but hardly able, and certainly not obliged, to provide parental attentions. The dog seemed to be the only steady factor, and Kate understood that Arrie's desire for assurance was certainly justified. How, on the other hand, to provide it?

"I've come with a suggestion," Arrie said, reaching over to stroke Jasper, who sat expectantly—Kate doubted if the dog ever sat any other way—at her side. "My father is relieved that I have Jasper back. So is my sister. I think they'd be willing to agree if I invited you to dinner."

"To case the joint?" Kate asked. Dinner with Professor Witherspoon, Roxanna, and Arrie, to name only the minimum cast of characters, struck Kate as likely to be bizarre. Apart from everything else, Witherspoon was the sort of man who, alone with three females, becomes either autocratic or flirtatious, neither of them modes dear to Kate's heart. On the other hand—

Arrie had smiled at Kate's question. "Tomorrow night?" she suggested. "Seven o'clock? I've written down the address and phone number. Jasper and I will be grateful."

Kate nodded. What else was there to do? Not for the first time, she thanked the gods—Kate, when not agnostic, was firmly polytheistic—that she had very little to do with children in this life.

At least one of Kate's trepidations about the dinner chez Witherspoon was allayed immediately upon her entrance: there were two men in addition to the professor. At least that cause of Witherspoon's pontification or sprightliness had been removed. Roxanna introduced a young man almost as gorgeous in his way as she was in hers—Desmond Elliott, an actor. What possibly else, Kate thought, shaking hands. Arrie she greeted with warmth and a wink. Jasper had been, it appeared, exiled for the duration. The other guest was an older man, who, it became immediately clear, was allied with Witherspoon and against the others. Why, Kate wondered, was that so clear? Equally clear, somewhat less inexplicably, was the fact that Mr. Johnson was a lawyer, who had joined them for dinner when Arrie's invitation to Kate superseded his planned dinner a deux with Witherspoon.

The professor had decided upon graciousness. He was the host, and while in his house Kate would be treated like a woman guest, neither more nor less. With relief, Kate sank into a chair, accepted a drink, and embarked upon a sea of meaningless chitchat. This torture was somewhat ameliorated by Desmond Elliott's amusing account of the actor's life—made up, it appeared, in equal parts of being a waiter and performing in small, unprofitable companies of great artistic integrity so far off Broadway as to be in another state.

Roxanna was a pleasant hostess, keeping an eye on everyone's comfort but not buzzing about or insisting upon anything. When they moved in to dinner, she brought things gracefully to the table. She and Desmond were the mainstays of the conversation, although Witherspoon made some acidic comments to Kate about their department which Kate did her best to ignore. It is difficult, while eating your host's meat, to convey to him that you disagree with everything he is saying and everything he is likely to say. They finally reached the blessed subject of the university's administration, in disdain for which even sworn enemies could agree.

As the company returned to the living room for coffee, Arrie asked Kate if she would like to say hello to Jasper. Kate eagerly agreed, and followed Arrie down the hall to a closed door, behind which sharp barks of anticipation could be heard. "Quiet, Jasper," Arrie said, revealing a history of complaints, from whom it was not hard to guess. "Up." The dog danced on his short hind legs and Arrie took from her pocket a chunk of chicken breast. She tossed it into the air and Jasper caught and swallowed it in one grateful gulp, then sat, hoping for more.

"You have a nice room," Kate said.

"Yes. I used to have a tiny room off the kitchen, but Roxanna took that since she doesn't really live here most of the time. There's really just me and my father now."

"And Jasper," Kate said, it being the only cheerful fact that occurred to her. "Did your father buy him for you?" she added hopefully.

"No. Roxanna did. Dad said I couldn't keep him. But then he changed his mind. Roxanna made him."

"Desmond's nice," Kate observed. It *was* odd how conversation deserted her in the presence of the very young.

"Very nice. I'm glad he was here. I don't care for Mr. Johnson."

"Does he come often?"

"No, he's never really been here before. I've just talked to him on the phone when he calls my father. Roxanna says he's simultaneously illiterate and imperious." Kate tried not to grin, and failed. They laughed together, and Jasper rose to his hind legs, joining in.

"I still need to know who took him," Arrie said before they rejoined the others.

Reed had promised that something would occur to Kate, but all that occurred to her was gossip. And for departmental gossip, the ultimate source was Richard Frankel. Dean Rosovsky, when he retired from his high post at Harvard, reported in *Harvard Magazine* that the first duty of a dean was to listen to gossip. Kate, not to be outdone by any dean, took the advice to heart. Richard, reached by telephone, was graciously pleased to make an appointment the following day for lunch.

Kate contemplated his face across the luncheon table with pleasure. Richard combined the best features of an imp and a youthfully aging and gay (in all senses of the word) uncle. He was, in fact, quite heterosexual and a convinced bachelor, having convinced everyone of this except himself. He still hoped to meet the right woman in the next day or so and launch himself on a satisfactory career of marriage and fatherhood. Like a number of people Kate had observed over the years, Richard, marvelously suited to his life and vigorously happy, was unaware that his deep satisfaction arose in part from the delusion that he was abjectly in need of passionate love, babies, and a deep and lasting relationship. Kate liked him enormously.

She did not immediately ask about Witherspoon. To have evinced that much interest would have started Richard's investigative motors and Kate did not wish to reveal her relationship with Arrie. But it was easy to work the conversation around to Witherspoon, whom Richard, together with the greater part of the department, despised with a vigor only mitigated by the pleasure they got in talking about how awful he was. Witherspoon, Kate was forced to realize, had provided a good deal of pleasure in his curmudgeonly life, none of it intended.

Richard knew all about the wife tucked away in a nearer version of Betty Ford's detoxification facility. "Before my time, of course, but the usual story. He pursued her with tales of his unsympathetic wife—now she's the unsympathetic wife. They never learn, poor dears. One hopes the graduate students these days are too smart to marry him, if not quite smart enough to dodge entirely. I met the wife once. He had me to dinner in the early days, before I turned out to be modern altogether. Obviously a lady, and punishing him and herself for her stupid mistake. They have two daughters, an absolutely mouthwatering creature called Roxanna and an afterthought called Arabella. The names are enough to give you an idea of the marriage. It's widely assumed that Arabella isn't his child."

Kate stared at him. "On what grounds?" she finally asked.

"I think it was the poor thing's final attempt to bolt, before she drowned herself in alcohol reinforced by prescription drugs. Considering his record of fornication and adultery, you'd think he'd have turned a blind eye, but not our Witherspoon."

"Why not?"

"Kate, my sweet, you don't seem your usual quick-witted self, if you'll forgive my observing it. Must you go on grunting monosyllabic questions?"

"I'm sorry, Richard. I'm always astonished at how much life is like prime-time soap operas."

"Which I'm certain you never watch. They are unreal only in the way outrageous situations follow hard upon each other and in the luxury of the surroundings. Actually, they are otherwise just like life, if your a shit like Witherspoon—which of course most of them are. Have you some special interest in him? A renewed fascination with manuscripts?"

Kate laughed. "If I could take the smallest interest in manuscripts, it wouldn't be renewed. It would be a new and sudden aberration. Actually, I had dinner there the other evening and was overwhelmed with curiosity. Roxanna used to be a student of mine, and she asked me." Richard would wonder why she hadn't mentioned this in the first place. The reason was clear to Kate: it had entailed lying.

"Ah—I wondered why your interest was so suddenly awakened. The rumor is that he now wants a divorce and most of what there is of her worldly goods. In exchange, he'll pretend to relinquish with infinite sorrow custody of Arabella."

"Do you mean he'll get her to pay him alimony?"

"Don't ask me the details, but that's often how it works out these days. The woman gets the children and the man gets the property."

"Surely the woman gets to keep what she brought into the marriage."

"No doubt," Richard drily said, "but since all this wife brought in was her misguided affection for Witherspoon that's unlikely to serve her very well. Of course, she may have some family bonds stashed away, in which case he'll do his best to get them. The man can always afford the better lawyers, alas."

"No doubt the men look at it differently," Kate said, her mind elsewhere.

"We certainly can guess how Witherspoon looks at it. And he's got two daughters from the former marriage, both unlikely to have great sympathy with the poor alcoholic. Maybe Roxanna and Arabella will come to her defense. I had the most awful row with him, you know, not too long ago. That's why it's an additional pleasure to contemplate his absolute awfulness. He worked every angle to get tenure for one of his acolytes, a twerp with his nose in manuscripts and his brain in a sling. Witherspoon got his way, of course, and I was marked down as an enemy—a mark not of distinction, since there are so many of us, but of honor. The only good part of the story is that the twerp left to devote himself wholly to some manuscript collection. Did Witherspoon behave himself at dinner?"

"Oh, yes. The older daughter is very gracious and I like the younger one. I'm surprised the wife had the gumption to have a love affair."

"Its end was no doubt the inevitable last straw. Witherspoon made no bones about the fact that if the child had been a boy he would have forgiven everything. He's that kind of monster."

"Do you think he's really the father?"

"God knows. Roxanna is pretty definitely his, and she's gorgeous, so who has an opinion about genes? Of course, the wife was pretty luscious in those days—he'd never have bothered otherwise, that being all women are good for."

"Do you know anything about the lover? He sounds mysterious, like the tutor who might have been Edith Wharton's father."

"I know the scuttlebutt. He was thin with glasses and buck teeth, and very sweet. He was an adjunct teacher in art history, which she dabbled in. I don't know what became of him. Gossip has it they used to walk around the campus holding hands. I feel sorry for her."

Kate was amazed, not for the first time, at the extent of her colleagues' interest in one another's lives. Richard was, of course, unofficial keeper of the gossip and since his heart was in the right place she was willing to decide that his was a valuable function. What Witherspoon would have thought of it was another question. Did she care what Witherspoon thought about anything, or only what he did?

What had he done, apart from being a failure as a human being and a father? Kate decided to walk for a while after bidding Richard a grateful farewell.

She wandered around the city streets, noticing dogs (no Jack Russell terriers) and the general air of menace which by now everyone in New York, and probably elsewhere, took for granted: it seemed the mark of an age. Compared to which, Kate told herself, the momentary absence of a dog was hardly to be counted. And yet that had been, somewhere along the family chain, a failure of trust which was how menace began. Was it Kant who said that trust was the basis of civilization?

Letting her attention wander unbidden over the cast of characters at that dinner, and in Richard's account of the Witherspoons, Kate found herself eventually at Central Park and East Seventy-second Street. She sat on a bench to observe the spot where Jasper had been tied when Arrie retrieved him. It was a well chosen location, easily approached and abandoned from four directions, sufficiently crowded with people and dogs entering and leaving the park to make one more man and dog unnoticed.

Man? A man had removed Jasper from the building, according to the doorman's report. Dogs were not allowed in the playground, so a number of them were tied to the entrance, waiting with accustomed patience or anxiety for their people on the other side of the fence. By the time Kate had to leave to meet her class, she had made up her mind.

"It is, of course, none of my business," Kate said to Roxanna as they had a drink before ordering their dinner. "That phrase is always a sign that someone thinks it is her business, or has determined to make it so. Do you mind?"

"Hardly," Roxanna said. "I used to wonder what it would be like to have dinner with Professor Fansler. Thank you for the privilege: my business is your business."

"Very graciously put. Perhaps you'd better order another drink."

"Oh, dear," Roxanna said.

"I intend nothing more sinister than blackmail," Kate said reassuringly.

"I know—on behalf of Arrie. Blackmail won't be necessary. From you, that is—I've already employed it on her behalf. Is that what you guessed?"

"It would hardly be fair to get you to tell me what happened and then claim to have guessed it all."

"Okay," Roxanna said. "You tell me. And I'll take that second drink. May I correct you as you go along?"

"Please do," Kate said. "My hope is that you'll end up assuring me about poor Jasper's safety."

Roxanna nodded.

"Your father, the revered Professor Witherspoon, has been after what money he can get out of your mother. Doubtless he has another young lady in tow. I say 'lady,' because I don't really think a *woman* would have anything to do with him. Did he try to retrieve from your mother something he had given her and now wanted to give to another? A ring? A brooch? It can't have been too big or Jasper wouldn't have swallowed it, however imbedded in a piece of meat. Although the way he gulps while dancing around on his hind legs, anything is possible."

"Not a ring," Roxanna said. "An emerald. He'd had it taken out of the ring and said he was going to get it reset. It's the most valuable thing my mother had—it was in her family for years. They may have pawned it, but they never sold it."

"He pretended to her it needed to be reset?"

"Nothing so civilized. She would have been suspicious at any kindly offer, I'm afraid. He talked her out of taking it to the detoxification place, said it might be stolen. She didn't believe him, but when he set his mind on something she didn't have a chance. I heard them arguing about it one night. So did Desmond, the guy you met—he was there with me. He held me back from interfering and he was right."

"He's very handsome, even for an actor," Kate said.

"He's especially handsome for a lawyer, which is what he is," Roxanna responded. "We were trying to allay my father's suspicions. He knew we'd overheard him. So when he emerged that evening, we pretended innocence, on Desmond's advice, and I introduced him to Dad as an actor. His looks, as you observed, made that easy."

"I've lost count," Kate said, "but I don't think I'm doing too well. Shall we order dinner?"

"The details need cleaning up, but you certainly seem to be onto the main story line. Go on."

"There isn't much more. Somehow, later, needing to hide the stolen emerald, the professor fed it to Jasper. Anyone who observed Jasper's routine with Arrie would have thought of it, whether the motive was greed or detection. Was he going to kill the dog?"

"Of course. Or pay someone else to. Fortunately, I guessed what he was up to. I had caught him examining the stone. I demanded it and he wouldn't give it to me. Sometime later, he came in to promise me he wouldn't take it out of the house. There was something about the exact way he said it that made me suspicious. I pretended to calm down and then went to look for the stone. It wasn't where it was supposed to be. My father went into calm assurances that he didn't have it and hadn't hidden it, urging me to search him. He was so smug about it! That, and the sight of Jasper dancing around, gave me the idea. He had fed it to the dog in a hunk of meat, intending to have the dog 'get lost.' When I figured this out, we really had a knockdown fight. I couldn't believe he'd really do that to Arrie."

"Where was Arrie?"

"Locked in the bathroom, crying. She hated the fights. She used to stuff her ears with toilet paper. He and I fought about a lot of things, though never as violently as this. In the end, I threatened him. You see, my mother had mentioned her ring when Arrie and I went to see her—she wanted Arrie to have it but Arrie said I should have it because I was beautiful. Mother hugged Arrie and said, 'You take care of Roxanna—it's far, far better not to be beautiful, believe me, my darling.' "

"And you got Desmond to leave with the dog under his arm. I gather Jasper had got to know him by now."

"Jasper takes a long time to get to know people well enough to let them pick him up. He may be small, but he's tough. That was me."

"In drag?"

She nodded. "Great fun. I got the idea from Sherlock Holmes. 'My walking clothes,' Irene Adler called them. Desmond borrowed the suit for me from someone my size. The doorman didn't raise an eyebrow."

"So you took Jasper—where?"

"To Desmond's, where I stay most of the time. I

walked him, and never have I used a pooper-scooper more diligently. At first we thought we'd keep him in, but poor Jasper is well trained. I tell you, retrieving that emerald from Jasper made me feel like someone in Dickens' *Our Mutual Friend*. I well remember you talking about that novel."

"You said you'd get the emerald back if he behaved?"

"More than behaved. I had Desmond as a witness and advisor. I said Arrie and Jasper were to live with me, that he was to give my mother a divorce under fair terms: he could keep the apartment, he had to continue to support Arrie till she finished her education, my mother was to get half his pension, and if he didn't agree I was going to drag him into court accused of theft and abusive conduct."

"And he bought it?"

"Not entirely. I had to give him the emerald and a few other things besides. But I figured I didn't need it and Arrie didn't need it. It hadn't done my mother much good—and it was worth her freedom and ours. I also told him I had a student lined up ready to bring charges of sexual harassment. I scared him. He even cooperated about Arrie's retrieving Jasper. I was going to make him leave the dog at the playground, but I didn't want him to take out his frustrations on the poor beast so I did that, too. Desmond came with me between two closings. Desmond's been great."

"He sounds rather unusual for a lawyer."

"He is. He's quitting. He says there's no point spending your life suing about water damage and helping one firm take over another. I don't know what he's going to do."

"You might suggest acting,' Kate said. "And being a waiter on the side."

"He's thinking of becoming a detective," Roxanna said. "A private eye. Perhaps he could get in touch with you for pointers."

Kate decided not to look for irony in this. "What next?" she asked.

"It's Arrie's vacation next week. We're going down with Desmond to visit my mom. I think with some real encouragement, and the knowledge that the professor is out of her life, she may actually make it. She never took up drinking or prescription drugs until she met him. But she's going to need a lot of help."

"Speaking of 'none of my business,' " Kate said, "may I ask an outrageous question? Just tell me to go to hell if you don't want to answer it. Is the professor Arrie's father or was there someone else?"

"I'll answer that question on one condition," Roxanna said. "That you agree to do me an enormous favor, no questions asked. Is it a bargain?"

"I'll have to think about it," Kate said. "I don't believe in blind promises."

"And I don't believe in gossip—not all of it. My mother did moon around with another guy. His main attraction was that he wasn't lustful. My father is very lustful. He insisted on his rights. That's how he thought of them—as rights. And he still wanted a son."

"You've been angry at him a long time, haven't you?" Kate said.

"I'm getting over it, with help. I don't want Arrie to go through the same thing. Of course, I couldn't have done it without Desmond—especially since the professor had that sleazy lawyer on his side. Mr. Johnson. You met him, too."

Kate looked into her coffee cup. "All right," she said. "It's a bargain."

Roxanna looked up questioningly.

"I'll keep Jasper for Arrie while she's gone. Reed will be overjoyed.—That is, I'll pretend we have him forever, and when he finds out it's only a week or so he'll be overjoyed."

"I think women are reprehensible," Roxanna said, "don't you?" And they laughed together. Kate even found herself wishing Arrie and Jasper had been there.

A CASE OF HEADLONG DYING

by Michael Innes

Sir John Appleby had been worried about Charles Vandervell for some time. But this was probably true of a good many of the philosopher's friends. Vandervell's speculations, one friend had wittily remarked, could be conceived as going well or ill according to the sense one was prepared to attribute to "speculations." His last book, titled (mysteriously to the uninstructed) *Social Life As a Sign System*, had been respectfully received by those who went in for that kind of thing; but it was clear that something had gone badly wrong with Vandervell's investments. He was what is called a private scholar, for long unattached to any university or other salary-yielding institution, and had for years lived very comfortably on inherited wealth of an unspecified but doubtless wholly respectable sort.

He was not a landed man. His country house, pleasantly situated a few miles from the Cornish coast, had extensive gardens but was unsupported by any surrounding agricultural activities. The dividends came in, and that was that. Nobody could have thought of it as a particularly vulnerable asset. Some adverse change in the state of the national economy might be expected from time to time to produce a correspondingly adverse effect on an income such as Vandervell's. But it would surely require a recession, a depression, or a slump of major order to result in anything like a catastrophe.

Vandervell himself was vague about the whole thing. This might have been put down to simple incompetence, since it would certainly have been difficult to imagine a man with less of a head for practical affairs. But there were those who maintained that some feeling of guilt was operative as well.

He was uneasy about living a life of leisure on the labors of others, and was unwilling to face up to considering his mundane affairs at all. He occasionally spoke in an old-fashioned way about his "man of business." Nobody had ever met this personage, or could so much as name him; but it was obvious that he must occupy a key position in the conduct of his client's monetary affairs. Vandervell himself acknowledged this. "Bound to say," he had once declared to Appleby, "that my financial wizard earns his fees. No hope of keeping my chin above water at all if I didn't have him on the job. And even as it is, I can't be said to be doing too well."

For some months this last persuasion had been gaining on Vandervell rapidly and throwing him into ever deepening gloom. One reading of this was clearly that the gloom was irrational—a depressive state generated entirely inside the unfortunate man's own head—and that a mere fantasy of being hard up, quite unrelated to the objective facts of the case, was one distressing symptom of his condition. One does hear every now and then, after all, of quite wealthy people who have stopped the delivery of milk and newspapers out of a firm conviction they can no longer afford to pay for them.

There was a point at which Appleby took this view of Vandervell's state of mind. Vandervell was a fairly prolific writer, and his essays and papers began to suggest that the adverse state of his bank balance (whether real or imagined) was bringing him to a vision that the universe at large was weighted against him and all mankind in an equally disagreeable way. Hitherto his philosophical work had been of a severely intellectual and dispassionate nature. Now he produced in rapid succession a paper on Schopenhauer, a paper on von Hartmann, and a long essay called *Existentialism and the Metaphysic of Despair*. All this didn't precisely suggest cheerfulness.

This was the state of the case when Appleby encountered Vandervell's nephew, Fabian Vandervell, in a picture gallery off Bond Street and took him to his club for lunch.

"How is your uncle getting along?" Appleby asked. "He doesn't seem to come much to town nowadays, and it's a long time since I've been down your way."

Fabian, who was a painter, also lived in Cornwall—more or less in a colony of artists in a small fishing village called Targan Bay. As his uncle was a bachelor, and he himself was his uncle's only near relation, it was generally assumed that Fabian would prove to be his uncle's sole heir. The prospect was probably important to him, since nobody had ever heard of Fabian's selling a picture. So Fabian too might well be concerned at the manner in which the family fortunes were thought to be in a decline.

"He muddles along," Fabian said. "And his interests continue to change for the worse, if you ask me. Did you ever hear of a book called *Biathanatos*?"

"It rings a faint bell."

"It's by John Donne, and is all about what Donne liked to call 'the scandalous disease of headlong dying.' It caused a bit of a scandal, I imagine. Donne was Dean of St. Paul's, you remember, as well as a poet; so he had no business to be fudging up any apology for suicide. Uncle Charles is talking about editing *Biathanatos*, complete with his own learned commentary on the theme. Morbid notion." Fabian paused. "Uncommonly nice claret you have here."

"I'm delighted you approve of it." Appleby noticed that the modest decanter of the wine with which Fabian had been provided was already empty. "Do you mean that you are alarmed about your uncle?"

"Well, he does talk about suicide in a general way. But perhaps there's no real cause for alarm."

"We'll hope not." Appleby decided not to pursue this topic, which didn't strike him as his business to discuss. "I have in mind calling on your uncle, incidentally, in a few weeks' time, when I go down to visit my sister at Bude. And now I want you to explain to me those pictures we both found ourselves looking at this morning. Puzzling things to one of my generation."

Fabian Vandervell proved perfectly willing to accept this invitation. He held forth contentedly for the rest of the meal.

Appleby fulfilled his intention a month later,and his first impression was that Charles Vandervell had become rather a lonely man. Pentallon Hall was a substantial dwelling, yet apart from its owner only an elderly manservant called Litter was in evidence. But at least one gardener must be lurking around, since the extensive grounds which shielded the place from the general surrounding bleakness of the Cornish scene were all in apple-pie order.

Vandervell led Appleby over all this with the air of a country gentleman who has nothing in his head except the small concerns which the managing of such a property must generate. But the role wasn't quite native to the man, and in an indefinable way none of the interests or projects which he paraded appeared quite to be coming off.

Vandervell had a theory about bees, but the Pentallon bees were refusing to back it up. In a series of somewhat suburban-looking ponds he bred tropical fish, but even the mild Cornish climate didn't suit these creatures at all. Nor at the moment did it suit the roses that Vandervell was proposing to exhibit at some local flower show later in the season: they were plainly (like so much human hope and aspiration, their owner commented morosely) nipped in the bud.

All in all, Charles Vandervell was revealing himself more than ever as a man not booked for much success except, conceivably, within certain rather specialized kingdoms of the mind.

Or so Appleby thought until Mrs. Mountmorris arrived. Mrs. Mountmorris was apparently a near neighbor and almost certainly a widow; and Mrs. Mountmorris came to tea. Litter took her arrival distinguishably in ill part; he was a privileged retainer of long standing, and seemingly licensed to express himself in such matters through the instrumentality of heavy sighs and sour looks.

On the other hand, Vandervell brightened so markedly when the lady was announced that Appleby at once concluded that Litter had rational ground for viewing her as a threat to the established order of things at Pentallon. Moreover, Vandervell took considerable pleasure in presenting Appleby to the new arrival, and Mrs. Mountmorris obligingly treated her host's friend as a celebrity.

It was, of course, a quiet part of the world. But Appleby, being well aware of Vandervell as owning a distinction of quite another flight to that attainable by a policeman, found in this piece of nonsense something a little touching as well as absurd.

Not that, beneath an instant social competence, Mrs. Mountmorris was in the least pleased at finding another visitor around. She showed herself at once as a woman of strong character, and perhaps as one who was making it her business to take her philosophic neighbor in hand. If that was it—if she had decided to organize Charles Vandervell—then organized Charles Vandervell would be. On the man's chances of escape, Appleby told himself, he wouldn't wager so much as a bottle of that respectable claret to which he had entertained Vandervell's nephew Fabian at his club. And Fabian, if he knew about the lady, would certainly take as dark a view of her as Litter obviously did.

"Charles's roses," Mrs. Mountmorris said, "refuse to bloom. His bees produce honey no different from yours, Sir John, or mine." Mrs. Mountmorris paused to dispense tea—a duty which, to Litter's visible displeasure, she had made no bones about taking upon herself. "As for his ships, they just won't come home. *Mais nous changerons tout cela.*"

This, whatever one thought of the French, was nothing if not forthright, and Appleby glanced at the lady with some respect.

"But a philosopher's argosies," Appleby said a shade pedantically, "must voyage in distant waters, don't you think? They may return all the more richly freighted in the end."

"Of *that* I have no doubt." Mrs. Mountmorris spoke briskly and dismissively, although the dismissiveness may have been directed primarily at Appleby's flight of fancy. "But practical issues have to be considered as well. And Charles, I think, has come to agree with me. Charles?"

"Yes, of course." Thus abruptly challenged, Vandervell would have had to be described as mumbling his reply. At the same time, however, he was gazing at his female friend in an admiration there was no mistaking.

"Has that man turned up yet?" Mrs. Mountmorris handed Vandervell his teacup and at the same time indicated that he might consume a cucumber sandwich. "The showdown is overdue."

"Yes, of course." Vandervell repeated with a nervous nod that appeared to be his leitmotif in Mrs. Mountmorris' presence. "And I've sent for him. An absolute summons, I assure you. And you and I must have a talk about it, tête-à-tête, soon."

"Indeed we must." Mrs. Mountmorris was too well-bred not to accept this as closing the mysterious topic she had introduced. "And as for *these*"—she gestured at an unpromising rosebed near the tea table—"derris dust is the answer, and nothing else."

After this, Appleby didn't linger at Pentallon for very long. His own call had been casual and unheralded. It would be tactful to let that tête-à-tête take place sooner rather than later. Driving on to his sister's house at Bude, he reflected that Mrs. Mountmorris must be categorized as a good thing. Signs were not wanting that she was putting some stuffing into Charles Vandervell, of late so inclined to unwholesome meditation on headlong dying.

It was almost as if a worm were going to turn. Yet one ought not, perhaps, jump to conclusions. On an off day, and to a diffident and resigned man, the lady might well assume the character of a last straw. Litter, certainly, was seeing her in that light. His gloom as he politely performed the onerous duty of opening the door of Appleby's car, suggested his being in no doubt, at least, that the roses would be deluged in derris dust before the day was out.

Appleby hadn't, however, left Pentallon without a promise to visit again on his return journey, which took place a week later. This time he phoned to announce his arrival. He didn't want to find himself again that sort of awkward extra whom the Italians style a *terzo incomodo*.

Litter answered the telephone, and in a manner which instantly communicated considerable agitation. Mr. Vandervell, he said abruptly, was not in residence. Then, as if recalling his training, he desired Appleby to repeat his name so that he might apprise his employer of the inquiry on his return.

"Sir John Appleby."

"Oh, yes, sir—yes, indeed." It was as if a penny had dropped in the butler's somber mind. "Pray let me detain you for a moment, Sir John. We are in some distress at Pentallon—really very perturbed, sir. The fact is that Mr. Vandervell has disappeared. Without a trace, Sir John, as the newspapers sometimes express it. Except that I have received a letter from him—a letter susceptible of the most shocking interpretation."

Litter paused on this—as if it were a phrase in which, even in his perturbation, he took a certain just satisfaction. "To tell you the truth, sir, I have felt it my duty to inform the police. I wonder whether you could possibly break your journey here, as you had proposed? I know your reputation, Sir John, begging your pardon."

"My dear Litter, my reputation scarcely entitles me to impose myself on the Cornish constabulary. Are they with you now?"

"Not just at the moment, sir. They come and go, you might say. And very civil they are. But it's not at all the kind of thing we are accustomed to."

"I suppose not. Is there anybody else at Pentallon?"

"Mr. Fabian has arrived from Targan Bay. And Mr. Truebody, sir, who is understood to look after Mr. Vandervell's affairs."

"It's Mr. Truebody whom Mr. Vandervell refers to as his 'man of business'?"

"Just so, sir. I wonder whether you would care to speak to Mr. Fabian? He is in the library now, sorting through his uncle's papers."

"The devil he is." Appleby's professional instinct was alerted by this scrap of information. "It mightn't be a bad idea to call him. Please tell him I'm on the telephone."

Within a minute of this, Fabian Vandervell's urgent voice was on the line.

"Appleby, is it really you? For God's sake come over to this accursed place quick. You must have gathered even from that moronic Litter that something pretty grim has happened to my uncle. Unless he's merely up to some ghastly foolery, the brute fact is that *Biathanatos* has nobbled him. You're a family friend—"

"I'm on the way," Appleby said, and put down the receiver.

But Appleby's first call was at a police station, since there was a certain measure of protocol to observe. An hour later, and accompanied by a Detective-Inspector called Gamley, he was in Charles Vandervell's library, and reading Charles Vandervell's letter.

> My dear Litter,
>
> There are parties one does not quit without making a round of the room, and just such a party I am now preparing to take my leave of. In this instance it must be a round of letters that is in question, and of these the first must assuredly be addressed to you, who have been so faithful a servant and friend. I need not particularize the manner of what I propose to do. This will reveal itself at a convenient time and prove, I hope, not to have been too untidy. And now, all my thanks! I am only sorry that the small token of my esteem which is to come to you must, in point of its amount, reflect the sadly embarrassed state of my affairs.
>
> Yours sincerely,
> Charles Vandervell

"Most affecting," Mr. Truebody said. "Litter, I am sure you were very much moved." Truebody was a large and powerful-looking man, disadvantageously possessed of the sort of wildly staring eyes popularly associated with atrocious criminals. Perhaps it was to compensate for this that he exhibited a notably mild manner.

"It was upsetting, of course." Litter said this in a wooden way. Since he had so evident a difficulty in liking anybody, it wasn't surprising that he didn't greatly care for the man of business. "But we must all remember," he added with mournful piety, "that while there is life there is hope. A very sound proverb that is—if an opinion may be permitted me."

"Exactly!" Fabian Vandervell, who had been standing in a window and staring out over the gardens, turned round and broke in unexpectedly. "At first, I was quite bowled over by this thing. But I've been thinking. And it seems to me—"

"One thing at a time, Fabian." Appleby handed the letter back to Gamley, who was in charge of it. "Was this simply left on Mrs. Vandervell's desk?"

"It came by mail."

"Then where's the envelope?"

"Mr. Litter"—Gamley favored the butler with rather a grim look—"has unfortunately failed to preserve it."

"A matter of habit, sir." Litter was suddenly extremely nervous. "When I open a postal communication I commonly drop the outer cover straight into the wastepaper basket in my pantry. It was what I did on this occasion, and unfortunately the basket was emptied into an incinerator almost at once."

"Did you notice the postmark?"

"I'm afraid not, sir."

"The envelope, like the letter itself, was undoubtedly in Mr. Vandervell's handwriting?"

"No, sir. The address was typewritten."

"That's another point—and an uncommonly odd one." Fabian had advanced to the center of the room. "It makes me feel the whole thing is merely funny business, after all. And there's the further fact that the letter isn't dated. I'm inclined to think my uncle may simply have grabbed it from the pile, gone off Lord knows where, then typed out an envelope and mailed it in pursuance of some mere whim or fantasy."

"Isn't that pretty well to declare him insane?" Appleby looked hard at Fabian. "And just what do you mean by 'the pile'?"

"I believe he was always writing these things. Elegant valedictions. Making sure that nothing so became him in his life as—"

"We've had Donne; we needn't have Shakespeare, too." Appleby was impatient. "I must say I don't find the notion of your uncle occasionally concocting such things in the least implausible, psychologically regarded. But is there any hard evidence?"

"I've been hunting around, as a matter of fact. In his papers, I mean. I can't say I've found anything. Uncle Charles may have destroyed any efforts of the kind when he cleared out, taking this prize specimen to Litter with him."

"Isn't all this rather on the elaborate side?" Truebody asked, with much gentleness of manner. "I am really afraid that we are failing to face the sad simplicity of the thing. Everybody acquainted with him knows that Vandervell has been turning increasingly melancholic. We just have to admit that this had reached a point at which he decided to make away with himself. So he wrote this perfectly genuine letter to Litter, and perhaps others we haven't yet heard of."

"Why did he take it away and mail it?" Inspector Gamley demanded.

"That's obvious enough, I should think. He wanted to avoid an immediate hue and cry, such as might have been started at once had he simply left the letter to Litter behind him."

"It's certainly a possibility," Appleby said. "Would you consider, Mr. Truebody, that such a delaying tactic on Vandervell's part may afford some clue to the precise way in which he intended to commit suicide? He tells Litter it isn't going to be too untidy."

"I fear I am without an answer, Sir John. The common thing, where a country gentleman is involved, is to take out a shotgun and fake a more or less plausible accident at a stile. But Vandervell clearly didn't propose any faking. The letter shows that his suicide was to be declared and open. I feel that this goes with his deepening morbidity."

"But that's not, if you ask me, how Mr. Vandervell was feeling at all." Litter had spoken suddenly and with surprising energy. "For he'd taken the turn, as they say. Or that's my opinion."

"And just what might you mean by that, Mr. Litter?" Gamley had produced a notebook, as if he felt there was too much unrecorded chat.

"I mean that what Mr. Truebody says isn't what you might call up to date. More than once, just lately, I've told myself that Mr. Vandervell was cheering up a trifle—and high time, too. More confident, in a manner of speaking. Told me off once or twice about this or that. I can't say I was pleased at the time. But it's what makes me a little hopeful now."

"This more aggressive stance on your employer's part," Appleby asked, "disposes you against the view that he committed suicide?"

"Yes, Sir. John. Precisely that."

There was a short silence, which was broken by a constable's entering the library. He walked up to Gamley, then hesitated—as if doubtful whether what he had to say ought to be communicated to the company at large. Then he took the plunge.

"Definite news at last, sir. And just what we've been afraid of. They've discovered Mr. Vandervell's body—washed up on a beach near Targan Bay."

"Drowned, you mean?"

"Yes, sir. Beyond doubt, the report says. And they're looking for his clothes now."

"His clothes?"

"Just that, sir. The body was stark naked."

Although the North Cornish coast was only a few miles away, Charles Vandervell had no regular habit of bathing there—this although he was known to be an accomplished swimmer. Even if the letter to Litter had never been written, it would have had to be judged extremely improbable that his death could be accounted for as an accident following on a sudden whim to go bathing.

For one thing, Targan Bay and its environs were not so unfrequented that a man of conventional instincts (and Vandervell was that) would have been likely to dispense with some decent scrap of swimming apparel. On the other hand—or this, at least, was the opinion expressed by his nephew—a resolution to drown himself might well have been accompanied by just that. To strip naked and swim straight out to sea could well have seemed to Vandervell as the tidy thing.

Yet there were other possibilities, and Appleby saw one of them at once. The sea—and particularly a Cornish sea—can perform astonishing tricks with a drowned man. It can transform into a nude corpse a sailor who has gone overboard in oilskins, sea boots, and a great deal else. It can thus cast up a body itself unblemished. Or it can go on to whip and lacerate such a body to a grim effect of sadistic frenzy. Or it can set its own living creatures, tiny perhaps but multitudinous, nibbling till the bones appear. What particular fate awaits a body is all a matter of rocks and shoals—shoals in either sense—and of currents and tides.

Appleby had a feeling that the sea might still yield up some further secret about Charles Vandervell. Meantime, it was to be hoped there was more to be learned on land. The circumstances of the missing man's disappearance plainly needed investigation.

Appleby's first visit to Pentallon had been on a Monday, and it was now a Monday again. According to Litter, the remainder of that first Monday had been uneventful, except in two minor regards. The formidable Mrs. Mountmorris had stayed on almost till dinnertime, which wasn't Litter's notion of an afternoon call. There had been a business discussion of some sort and it had been conducted with sufficient circumspection to prevent Litter, who had been curious, from hearing so many as half a dozen illuminating words. But Litter rather supposed (since one must speak frankly in the face of a crisis like the present) that the lady had more than a thought of abandoning her widowed state, and that she was in process of thoroughly sorting out Vandervell's affairs before committing herself.

When she had at length gone away Vandervell had made a number of telephone calls. At dinner he had been quite cheerful—or perhaps it would be better to say that he had appeared to be in a state of rather grim satisfaction. Litter confessed to having been a little uncertain of his employer's wavelength.

The next day, Tuesday morning, Mr. Truebody had turned up at Pentallon, but he hadn't stayed long. Litter had received the impression—just in passing this library door, as he had several times been obliged to do—that Mr. Truebody was receiving instructions which were being pretty forcefully expressed. No doubt Mr. Truebody himself would speak as to that. There had been no question, Litter said, of the two gentlemen having words. Or it might be better to say there had been no question of their having a row—not as there had been with Mr. Fabian when he turned up on the same afternoon. And about *that*, Litter supposed, Mr. Fabian would speak.

This sensational disclosure on Litter's part could have been aimed only at Appleby, since Inspector Gamley turned out to have been informed of it already. And Fabian seemed to have made no secret of what he now termed lightly a bit of a tiff. He had formed the same conjecture about Mrs. Mountmorris' intentions as Litter had done, and he was ready to acknowledge that the matter wasn't his business. But between him and his uncle there was some obscure matter of a small family trust.

In the changed situation now showing every sign of

blowing up he had come to Pentallon resolved to get this clarified. His uncle had been, in his view, quite unjustifiably short with him, saying that he had much more important things on his mind. So a bit of a rumpus there had undoubtedly been. But as he had neither carried Uncle Charles out to sea and drowned him, nor so effectively bullied him as to make him go and drown himself, he really failed to see that Litter's coming up with the matter had much point.

Listening to all this, Appleby was not wholly disinclined to agree. He had a long experience of major catastrophes bringing unedifying episodes of a minor order to light. So he went on to inquire about the following day, Wednesday, which looked as if it might have been the point of crisis.

And Wednesday displayed what Inspector Gamley called a pattern. It was the day of the week on which Pentallon's two maidservants, who were sisters, enjoyed their free half day together. Immediately after lunch Vandervell had started fussing about the nondelivery of a consignment of wine from a merchant in Bristol. He had shown no particular interest about this negligence before, but now he had ordered Litter to get into a car and fetch the stuff from Bristol forthwith.

And as soon as Litter had departed in some indignation on this errand (Bristol being, as he pointed out, a hundred miles away, if it was a step), Vandervell had accorded both his gardener and his gardener's boy the same treatment—the quest, this time, being directed to Exeter and a variety of horticultural needs (derris dust among them, no doubt). Apart from its proprietor, Pentallon was thus dispopulated until the late evening.

When Litter returned he was in a very bad temper, so that he retired to his own quarters for the night without any attempt to report to his employer. And since his first daily duty in the way of personal attendance was to serve lunch, and since the maids (as he explained) were both uncommonly stupid girls, it was not until afternoon the next day, Thursday, that there was a general recognition of something being amiss. And at this point Litter had taken it into his head that he must behave with discretion, and not precipitately spread abroad the fact of what might be no more than eccentric (and perhaps obscurely improper) behavior on the part of the master of Pentallon.

The consequence of all this was that it took Charles Vandervell's letter, delivered on Friday, to stir Litter into alerting the police. And by then Vandervell had been dead for some time. Even on superficial examination, it appeared, the police surgeon was definitely convinced of that.

Establishing this rough chronology satisfied Appleby for the moment, and he reminded himself that he was at Pentallon not as a remorseless official investigator but merely as a friend of the dead man and his nephew. That Charles Vandervell *was* now definitely known to be dead no doubt meant for Inspector Gamley a switching to some new procedure which he had better be left for a time to pursue undisturbed. So Appleby excused himself, left the house, and wandered thoughtfully through the gardens.

The roses were still not doing too well, but what was on view had its interest all the same. From a raised terrace walk remote from the house there was a glimpse of the sea. Appleby had surveyed this for some moments when he became aware that he was no longer alone. Truebody, that somewhat mysterious man of business, had come up behind him.

"Are you quite satisfied with this picture, Sir John?" Truebody asked.

"This picture?" For a second Appleby supposed that this was an odd manner of referring to the view. Then he understood. "I'd have to be clearer as to just what the picture is supposed to be before I could answer that one."

"Why should Vandervell clear the decks—take care to get rid of Litter and the rest of them—if he was simply proposing to walk over *there*"—Truebody gestured toward the horizon—"for the purpose of drowning himself? It was so unnecessary, and that worries me. He could simply have said he was going for a walk, or even that he was going out to dinner. He could have said half a dozen things. Don't you agree?"

"Yes, I think I do—in a way. But one has to allow for the fact that the mind of a man contemplating suicide is quite likely to work a shade oddly. Vandervell may simply have felt the need of a period of solitude, here at Pentallon, in which to arrive at a final decision. Anyway, he *has* been drowned."

"Indeed, yes. And his mailing that letter immediately beforehand does seem to rule out accident. Unless, of course, he was putting on a turn."

"A turn, Mr. Truebody?"

"One of those just-short-of-suicide efforts which psychologists nowadays interpret as a cry for help."

"That's often a valid explanation of unsuccessful suicide, no doubt. But what would the cry for help be designed to save him from? Would it be the embrace of that predatory Mrs. Mountmorris?"

"It hadn't occurred to me that way." Truebody looked startled. "But something else has. Say that Vandervell was expecting a visitor here at Pentallon, and that for some reason he didn't want the circumstance to be known. That would account for his clearing everybody out. Then the visit took place, and was somehow disastrous. Or perhaps it just *didn't* take place, and there was for some reason disaster in the mere fact of that. And it was only *then* that he decided to write that letter to Litter as a preliminary to walking down to the sea and drowning himself." Truebody glanced sharply at Appleby. "What do you think of that?"

"I think I'd call it the change-of-plan theory of Charles Vandervell's death. I don't know that I'd go all the way with it. But I have a sense of its being in the target area, of there having been some element of improvisation in the affair . . . Ah, here is our friend the constable again."

"Inspector Gamley's compliments, sir." The constable appeared to feel that Appleby rated considerable formality of address. "A further message has just come through. They've found the dead man's clothes."

"Abandoned somewhere on the shore?"

"Not exactly, sir. Washed up like the body itself, it seems—but in a small cove more than a mile farther west. That's our currents, sir. The Inspector has gone over to Targan Bay at once. He wonders if you'd care to follow him."

"Thank you. I'll drive over now."

Vandervell's body had been removed for immediate post-mortem examination, so it was only his clothes that were on view. And of these most were missing. It was merely a jacket and trousers, entangled in each other and grotesquely entwined in seaweed, that had come ashore. Everything else was probably lost.

"Would he have gone out in a boat?" Appleby asked.

"I'd hardly think so." Gamley shook his head. "One way or the other, such a craft would have been found by now. I'd say he left his clothes near the water, and they were taken out by the tide. Now they're back again. Not much doubt they've been in the sea for about as long as Vandervell himself was."

"Anything in the pockets—wallet, watch, that kind of thing?"

"Both these, and nothing else." Gamley smiled grimly. "Except for what you might call one or two visitors. All laid out next door. Would you care to see?"

"Decidedly, Inspector. But what do you mean by visitors?"

"Oh, just these." Gamley had ushered Appleby into the next room in the Targan Bay police station and was pointing at a table. "Inquisitive creatures that one gets in these waters. The crab was up a trouser leg, and the little fish snug in the breast pocket of the jacket."

"I see." Appleby peered at these odd exhibits. "I see," he repeated, but this time on a different note. "Will the postmortem have begun?"

"Almost sure to have."

"Then get on to them at once. Tell them—very, very tactfully—to be particularly careful about the bottom of the lungs. Then I'll put through a call to London myself, Inspector. We must have a top ichthyologist down by the night train."

"A *what*, sir?"

"An authority on fish, Inspector. And there's another thing. You can't risk an arrest quite yet. But you can make damned sure somebody doesn't get away."

Appleby offered explanations on the following afternoon.

"It has been my experience that the cleverest criminals are often prone to doing some single, isolated, stupid thing—particularly when under pressure and driven to improvise. In this case it lay in the decision to mail that letter to Litter, instead of just leaving it around the house. The idea was to achieve a delaying tactic, and there was a sense in which a typewritten address would be safer than one which forged Vandervell's hand. But it introduced at once what was at least a small implausibility.

"Vandervell, while obsessed with suicide, may well have prepared a dozen such letters, and without getting round either to addressing or to dating them. But if he later decided that one of them was really to be delivered—and delivered through the mail—the natural thing would simply be to pick up an envelope and address it by hand."

"Was that the chap's only slip-up?"

"Not exactly. The crime must be called one of calculation and premeditation, I suppose, since the idea was to get the perpetrator out of a tough spot. But its actual commission was rash and unthinking, so that it left him in a tougher spot still. Consider, for a start, the several steps that led to it. Charles Vandervell's supposed financial reverses were entirely a consequence of sustained and ingenious speculations on Truebody's part. They didn't, as a matter of fact, *need* to be all that ingenious, since our eminent philosopher's practical sense of such matters was zero.

"But then Mrs. Mountmorris enters the story. She is a very different proposition. Truebody is suddenly in extreme danger, and he knows it. His client's attitude stiffens; in fact, you may say the worm turns. Truebody is summoned to Pentallon, and appears on Tuesday morning. He is given only until the next day to show, if he can, that everything has been fair and aboveboard, after all.

"But Charles Vandervell has a certain instinct for privacy. If there is to be a row, he doesn't want it to be broadcast. When Truebody comes back on Wednesday afternoon there is nobody else around. And I suppose that puts ideas in his head."

"So he waits his chance?" Fabian Vandervell asked.

"Not exactly that. Imagine the two of them walking around the garden. Your uncle is a new man; he has this dishonest rascal cornered and is showing grim satisfaction in the fact. He says roundly that he'll have Truebody prosecuted and jailed. And, at that, Truebody simply hits out at him. He's a powerful fellow; and, for the moment at least, your uncle is knocked unconscious.

"It all happened beside one of those small ponds with the tropical fish. So it is *now* that Truebody sees—or thinks he sees—his chance. He will stage some sort of accident, he tells himself. In a moment he has pushed your uncle into the pond. And there he holds him under until he drowns. So far, so good—or bad. But the accident looks a damned unlikely one, all the same. And then he remembers something."

"*Biathanatos*, and all that."

"Precisely—and something more. Truebody has had plenty of opportunity, during business visits to Pentallon, to poke about among your uncle's papers. He remembers that batch of elegant farewells by a Charles Vandervell about to depart this life by his own hand—"

"But nobody would try to drown himself in a shallow fishpond. It simply couldn't be done."

"Exactly, Fabian. And as soon as Truebody had slipped into the empty house and secured that batch of letters he heaved your uncle's body into his car and drove hard for the sea. And there, let us say, he further did his stuff."

"And later mailed that letter to Litter. After which he had nothing to do but lie low—and get busy, no doubt, covering up on the financial side."

"He didn't quite lie low. Rashly again he took the initiative in holding rather an odd conversation with me. He thought it clever of himself to advance one or two considerations which were bound to be in my head anyway."

"And now he's under lock and key." Fabian Vandervell frowned. "Good Lord! I'm forgetting I still haven't the faintest notion how you tumbled to it all."

"That was the shubunkin."

"What the devil is that?"

"Small tropical fish—decidedly not found in the sea off Cornwall. A shubunkin deftly made its way into your uncle's breast pocket while Truebody was holding his head down in that pond."

"Well, I'm damned! But it doesn't sound much on which to secure a conviction for murder."

"It's not quite all, Fabian. In your uncle's lungs there was still quite a bit of the water he was drowned in. Full of minute freshwater-pond life."

CRUISE TO DEATH

by Alexandra Allan

Reg Symes glanced at his watch as he carefully pulled shut the door of his mother's cabin. Four fifteen. They would be sailing soon. In fact, he felt the change in the vibration of the ship's engines as he stood wondering where to go. Tea would be served outside on B deck, but he didn't feel like listening to more complaints about the breakdown of the air conditioning from the people who had gone on the bus trip. He grinned. Nor did he want to listen to his father gloat over the fact that those who had gone on the long, uncomfortable ride to the Tongass National Forest of Alaska to see blacktailed deer had seen nary an animal, while he, who had stayed in his comfortable deck chair all afternoon, had watched a beautiful specimen pose as if for its portrait on a bluff high above the town. He had kept binoculars on it for at least ten minutes.

On a ship as small as the *Lady Mary* there weren't many places to choose among if you wanted to be outside. A glance aft down the corridor showed him Helen Thorvald standing irresolutely before the door to her employer's stateroom. From her posture he inferred that she was feeling more put-upon than usual. He turned his back and fled up the nearby stairs to the upper deck where there was a small place at the stern that was seldom used. He lowered himself into the most sheltered of the chairs. Hardly had he opened his book, *The Russian Fur Trade in America*, when Helen perched on the chair two places over. He became absorbed in the book.

"Mr. Symes, I'm so sorry to bother you."

After five days of sitting at the same table with her for every meal, he was sick to death of that meek voice. Why couldn't she call him Reg like every one else did? Instantly, he realized how unfair that was. As a paid companion, she took her cue from her employer. Mrs. Ida May Bellamy would never approve of her dependent's being on equal terms with anyone else on the cruise. The old lady barely tolerated Helen's calling the other member of their table party Greta, even though the two women had discovered that they had known one another as children back in Norway.

With a repressed sigh, he closed the book. As a teacher at a boys' boarding school, he had learned to be tolerant of interruptions. "That's okay, Helen. What can I do for you?"

"I don't know what to do. Who to tell." With both hands, she smoothed back her already sleek blonde hair and tucked some wisps in the crossed braids at the nape of her neck. "There's no doctor on board, is there?"

It was obviously a rhetorical question. With only two hundred fifty passengers all told, everyone knew everyone else by this time. He supposed a nurse's instinct would be to find a doctor to whom to report.

"Is Mrs. Bellamy ill?"

The look of apprehension she habitually wore had deepened to one of fear.

"She's dead." The knuckles of her hands, now clasped in her lap, turned white.

"Good Lord!" Reg was surprised. Although they had all heard *ad nauseam* about Mrs. Bellamy's digestive troubles and recognized the lameness that confined her to the ship, Reg had considered her a hypochondriac, a match for his father. Some meals were made distinctly uncomfortable by their competitive anticipation of what one dish or another would do to them. Reg had not for a moment believed that the woman was really ill. "I'd better come with you," he said. "To the captain, I suppose. I don't really know the procedure."

He gestured to Helen to precede him, and she led the way down to Mrs. Bellamy's stateroom. There was no one in the adjoining lounge, but they could see through the windows that the deck outside was crowded with people drinking tea and showing off their purchases.

"I'm not a doctor," Reg was saying as Helen unlocked the door and he followed her in. Then, "Ah!" There was no need of a doctor to say how Mrs. Bellamy had died. She lay on the bed with a crumpled blanket over her legs. Her arms were flung wide, her mouth hung open, and half a pair of scissors jutted from her chest.

He bent over the body. "One wound. Straight to the heart. Would scissors penetrate deep enough?"

He was speaking almost to himself. Helen, however, answered in a calm voice. "They could. But she was old and not well; the shock might have killed her."

Reg looked rapidly round the room. "Have you touched anything?"

"No. I didn't need to touch her to know she's been dead for some time."

"When did you find her?"

"Just a few minutes ago. I came back to the ship before four o'clock."

"You didn't go on the bus trip." It was a statement, not a question, as he knew that the bus had been held five minutes for her.

"No. She kept me busy in here until it was too late. So I went into town with Greta."

Reg remembered his mother's reaction when the cruise director finally sent the bus off. "Really, Mrs. Bellamy is *too* selfish! To make the girl miss an outing at our last port-of-call! She doesn't need her; she'll only go to sleep as she does every afternoon. She's too selfish for words."

"Never mind," Reg had answered, looking back at the ship. "Her friend's waited for her." He nodded toward the railing where Greta Skaarl's distinctive hat—a large straw with a wreath of bright blue cornflowers and long scarlet streamers—contrasted with the white paint gleaming in the August sunshine.

All this time Reg had been looking for signs of an intruder. There were two portholes that opened onto the promenade deck, but they were not big enough to admit anyone. The door showed no signs of forced entry. "Did you come directly here when you got back?" he asked.

"No. We went to my cabin and sorted out our shopping. Mrs. Bellamy had said she would take her tea in the Wicker Room as usual, so I went forward to look for her there. Then I tried the deck in case she'd decided to go outside after all. Then I came in here and found her like that."

Although the stateroom was more spacious than a cabin, it was still small, and Reg had soon scanned the bed, sofa, chest of drawers, and tiny bathroom. Everything looked orderly. "Is anything missing, Miss Thorvald?" he asked, and then wished he'd called her Helen. Would she guess from his sudden formality that she was the best suspect?

Her worried expression lightened for a moment. "Robbery?" she asked.

She immediately opened a drawer in the bedside table, revealing her employer's handbag.

"Wait. Use this." He handed her a linen stole from the chair back. Helen quickly checked through the contents of the purse. Plenty of bills, both Canadian and American, in the wallet; her room key; traveler's checks apparently intact; three credit cards.

"It's all here," she said. The bleak look had returned to her eyes.

"Jewelry?" asked Reg.

Again using the stole, the nurse took a small velvet case from the top bureau drawer. "She didn't travel with anything valuable." She displayed a cameo brooch and earring set, a string of freshwater pearls, and an enameled brooch.

Reg suspected that there was another compartment in the box, but he didn't ask her to open it. He had suddenly remembered that the death was still unreported and that, anyway, he had no authority to investigate it. Hanging a "Do Not Disturb" sign on the door and ignoring the "Crew Only" sign on the stairwell to the top deck, they knocked on the door of the captain's private quarters and found him and the purser going over some papers. By this time Helen was trembling—delayed shock, Reg surmised—so he told the story. The two men were contrasts in appearance and personality, but their reaction to the news was exactly the same. "We can't afford any more delays or bad publicity!"

Captain Markle was short, plump, and nervous. With three extra people in the cabin, there was no room to pace, so he rocked back and forth on his heels.

"I'm sorry, Miss Thorvald, if that sounded insensitive. This is a shock for you." Then he burst out again. "It's as if the ship were jinxed!"

"I know," murmured Reg sympathetically. At the captain's inquiring stare, he explained, "Two of my friends are members of the syndicate that owns the *Lady Mary*."

"Yes, I remember, I was told so." Captain Markle shrugged. "Then you know . . ." Glancing at the woman passenger, he did not finish the sentence.

Reg merely nodded. He knew that this was the make-or-break season for the company, which had been plagued since its formation three years ago by a series of misfortunes to its ship. If they didn't make a profit this season, they were going to call it quits—

sell the *Lady Mary* and take their losses. One reason why Reg had urged his parents to take this ship instead of one of the big ones when his father came out of the hospital this time was to help out his friends.

"If there's nothing more I can do, Captain Markle, I'll leave you and Miss Thorvald to report the death." As Reg passed the purser, he signaled to him to follow.

Years ago, on another line, some passengers had told Bill Menzies that he resembled the young Jimmy Stewart. Since then, the purser had deliberately cultivated the likeness by imitating the actor's slow, sparse speech and loping walk. "What'd you think?" he asked Reg.

"Nothing yet," answered the other, moving farther away from the door. "While Miss Thorvald is busy with the captain, we should search her room."

"You think she did it?"

In the cabin, Reg warned, "We have no right to be here, so don't leave any traces."

The tall man nodded. "What're we looking for?"

"Anything belonging to Mrs. Bellamy. Jewelry. Money. Oh, and a pair of scissors."

After a few minutes, Reg asked, "Anything?"

"Nope. Say, you look pleased. Is that good?"

"No scissors. You'd expect a nurse to own a pair of scissors."

"Yeah! Where'd you suppose they are? In the old lady?"

Some passengers were waiting to see the purser in his office. He hurriedly arranged to meet Reg in half an hour in the captain's quarters and was only five minutes late. Captain Markle had been talking to the general manager of the steamship company and to the R.C.M.P. A policeman was due to come aboard from a launch out of Prince Rupert sometime in the night.

"Mr. Benson, our general manager, wants this kept quiet. Miss Thorvald has agreed to say that Mrs. Bellamy is ill. She's going to have dinner in her own cabin tonight. That's one good thing," he added, as if glad to find any consolation. "It won't be hard to watch her. We don't dock again until Saturday morning in Vancouver. She can't go anywhere."

"You think she did it," said the purser.

"I *hope* she did it!" answered Captain Markle. He had been fidgeting with a pencil and tapping his foot as he talked. Now he swiveled his chair around and looked almost apologetically at Reg. "I don't mean that exactly. But, if it wasn't her, the crew and passengers will all have to be questioned. It will get in all the papers, and we could be tied up for days. By the way, Mr. Symes, Mr. Benson instructed me to ask you if you'd work on the investigation on behalf of the company. Apparently you've had some experience?"

"Yes. I've helped the police on a few occasions."

"That's what he said. We'd be grateful if you could get this wrapped up before we dock on Saturday."

"A tall order, Captain Markle."

"I wish she was a man," declared the captain. "I'd soon get a confession!"

"*If* she did it."

"Who else?" demanded the little man. "Nothing was stolen, you say. We don't have any homicidal maniacs on board, I suppose."

The nearest thing to a madman, Reg thought, was probably his own father, who had just been discharged after his fourth stay in a psychiatric hospital. But Father was not violent. He *had* been alone on the deck, very close to Mrs. Bellamy's stateroom all afternoon. Reg suspected, however, that his father admired the woman for her imperious ways rather than disliked her. Dismissing any idea of his father's involvement as ridiculous, he turned again to what the others were saying.

"You sit at her table, Mr. Symes," Menzies said. "What kind of a woman is Miss Thorvald? What do you know about her?"

"Not much. I seldom speak to her except at meals.

The old lady didn't encourage her to talk about herself."

"How long had she been with Mrs. Bellamy?"

"Not quite a year, I believe. Before that she was working as a hospital nurse in Toronto. . . . What else? . . . She was born in Norway and trained there."

"She carries a Canadian passport," interrupted the purser.

"She came to Canada and wrote exams that allowed her to practice here, then became a Canadian citizen. Her parents are still in Norway, but she hasn't been back since she left. She plans on going home soon, I think."

Bill Menzies grinned. "You seem to be more interested in her than you admit."

Reg shrugged. "No, not really. I know all this because of the other woman at our table, Greta Skaarl. She's Norwegian. On a holiday. She and Helen got to talking and found out that they grew up in the same little coastal town in Norway. Larsund it's called. They went to school together, in fact, although they can't seem to have been friends. Helen's maybe two or three years older than Greta."

"Is that all? I would have guessed maybe ten years," Menzies said.

"It's the way they dress and the hair style. Helen's a nurse-companion; Greta's a business woman—real estate, I believe. They're both about thirty and they both left Larsund long ago. Helen said her parents still have property there even though they've lived in the city for years."

"Larsund," said Captain Markle. He had been idly tapping a pencil on his desk. Now he began to rap harder as if using the beat as an aid to memory. "Larsund. Where have I heard that name before?" As no inspiration came, he abandoned his efforts to remember. "What about Mrs. Bellamy?" he asked. "All I know about her is that she's a rich widow from an old Toronto family."

"She despised the current government," Reg replied promptly. "Believed very strongly in the privileges of the rich. Didn't like her daughter and son-in-law very much."

The phone rang. "That will be the dinner call," said the captain. "I will not be dining with the passengers this evening," he said into the mouthpiece. "All officers will eat in the mess tonight. Mr. Menzies is with me. Inform the others." He was frowning as he hung up. "I will have to tell them about the police coming on board and warn them to keep it quiet. What about the body, Mr. Symes?"

"The police will want to see it just as it is. You'll have to warn her steward, Mr. Menzies. Then perhaps, after the police finish, you and I could move it down to cold storage?" The purser nodded. "I'll tell Cindy, our waitress, that Mrs. Bellamy is sick and Helen's staying with her."

The three men rose and the junior officer opened the door for the others. As the captain passed him, he said, "Say! I've just remembered, sir, where we heard that name, Larsund."

"Where?" asked thc captain, walking toward the companionway.

"It was that oil fellow we had as a passenger on the first trip of the season. The engineer who got friendly with Scotty."

"I remember. Scotty brought him to the mess one night. He got drunk."

"Yup! And that's when he talked about this Larsund. Remember? He said his gang had found oil in the North Atlantic—off Scotland and Norway. Said we should all invest in property there because the oil companies would need lots of land for refineries or something."

"Telling secrets, was he?" laughed Reg.

"Yup, and mighty sorry the next morning. Didn't matter, though, none of us had any money to invest."

The buzz of conversation from passengers on their way to the dining room drifted down the corridor.

"I'll have you called when the police arrive, Mr. Symes," said the captain.

In the dining room, Cindy offered to send dinner to the absentees.

"Thanks, the steward's taking care of it," Reg replied. "What's wrong, Father? You're not feeling sick, too, are you?"

"No. Only sorry. I suppose I disturbed her this afternoon, but I didn't know she was ill."

"There, dear, don't fuss," said his wife. "Eat your soup before it gets cold. It really is good tonight."

"Delicious!" agreed Greta.

"What do you mean?" Reg asked his father.

"I couldn't help laughing when I saw the blacktail deer up on that rock. And the rest of you had gone for miles into the forest looking for one." He sprinkled salt and pepper into his bowl and stirred the soup as he spoke. "I thought Mrs. Bellamy would enjoy the joke, so I went and knocked on her door. It was two thirty; she's usually up by that time. But if she's sick, I'm sorry I disturbed her."

"She didn't answer you?"

"No. But if you don't believe I saw the deer, ask the watchman. He came along just then and I pointed it out to him. He told me they often see animals up there. Bah! I can't eat this soup! It's cold! You know I like my soup piping hot, Mildred. And it's salty, too."

The watchman would be able to tell the exact time he had spoken to Father, but it seemed safe to assume that Mrs. Bellamy was dead by two thirty. Reg chatted with Greta about her afternoon in town and discovered that the two women had been together constantly from the time they left the ship. Assuming Helen did it, she must have killed Mrs. Bellamy when they were all on the bus feeling sorry for her.

"Well, you didn't miss much when you missed the trip," he said.

Greta leaned back to allow the waitress to serve her red snapper. "I didn't care one way or the other," she said. "But Helen was upset."

"She didn't actually say anything against Mrs. Bellamy, did she?" asked Mrs. Symes.

Greta laughed. "No, she never does. Such patience! She wasn't herself, that's all. A bit nervous, preoccupied, not with it, as I told her in one store when she couldn't figure out the prices in Canadian dollars."

Later Reg was mulling over the meaning of Helen's preoccupation as he sat in a dim corner of the Wicker Room with his feet up on the coffee table and an open book face down on his lap. Bridge was being played rather boisterously at two tables in the middle of the room; the cruise director and her assistant were setting up for the concert which would start soon. Cheerful conversations were going on all over the room. So far, no one seemed to know that there had been a murder on board. Reg wondered how long it could be kept quiet. His mother sat down opposite him and took out her knitting. Another sweater for the grandchildren. When did they ever wear them all?

After a moment she asked quietly, "Is Mrs. Bellamy dead?"

"How did you know?"

"There was an empty tray outside Helen's door. None outside Mrs. Bellamy's."

Reg laughed. "You should be a detective."

"No. I leave that to you." She counted stitches for a moment, then asked casually, "Was it murder?"

"Mother!" He swung his legs off the table and sat upright.

"Oh, it's all right. No one else suspects. It's just because I'm your mother. I can always tell when you're detecting."

He grinned. "Well, you're right this time. It was murder. Stabbed with scissors."

Another passenger called a greeting from across the room and she nodded in reply before asking, "Who did it?"

"The captain strongly favors Helen Thorvald. You know, the rich woman and the ill-treated companion. Finally she rebels."

The knitting needles clicked loudly for a few minutes; a slight frown was the only other sign of agitation.

"But was she, dear? Ill-treated, I mean. Oh, I know Mrs. Bellamy was a wee bit demanding on occasion and a bit testy—but, Heaven knows, your father in one of his difficult times has said much worse things to me. And I haven't murdered him."

"That's true, but I sometimes think you have the patience of a saint."

"Well, I haven't, dear. Not at all. I often get very impatient with him. And I often get very depressed when one of his spells goes on and on and I know I'm tied to him for life. But, *not*, I assure you, to the point of thinking of murder. And that's another thing about Miss Thorvald. She hadn't to look forward to being companion to Mrs. Bellamy for very long. Don't you remember her telling us she was saving up to go back to Norway?"

"Are you saying Helen did not murder the old lady?"

"No, dear, I'm not saying that she didn't do it. You're the detective, not me. What I'm saying is that it wasn't because she was a downtrodden companion, because she wasn't."

"You mean, I must rethink the motive?"

"Yes, dear, that's all I mean." She jumped as the loudspeaker emitted a long, thin squeal. "Gracious, why can't they ever turn that thing low before they switch it on?" Rolling up her knitting, she added,

"Your father won't want to listen to the concert. I'll see if he'd like a game of cribbage."

"I'll play him, Mother. You stay for the music."

In the evenings, the small lounge off which the staterooms opened became a games room and library. Tonight there was a Scrabble game going on near the door, and two men were reading in opposite corners of the window wall. It was pitch black on the deck outside, but some sound wafted down from the bar on the deck above. Reg chose a table in the middle of the room and seated his father with his back to Stateroom A where Mrs. Bellamy's body still lay. The elder Mr. Symes wondered briefly whether it was something she ate for lunch that made the old lady ill, but he soon forgot her in anticipation of the game. Half of Reg's attention, however, was given to the murder. Supposing Helen hadn't killed her before she'd gone off the ship with Greta. Then the murderer must have gone into Stateroom A sometime between about one forty-five and two thirty when Mrs. Bellamy failed to answer his father's knock. Could Father have seen the person?

As he dealt the cards, Reg asked casually, "Did you spend the whole afternoon on the deck?"

"Yes, I did." The older man gathered the cards and held them in a fan close to his chest. "In blissful solitude."

"Nobody else stayed on board?" Reg frowned at his hand, muttering, "I hate these three and three splits."

His father chuckled. "These two cards won't sweeten the crib for you. No, after Miss Skaarl left, I didn't see another soul till the watchman came." He spoke with the satisfaction of one who had been watched over for too long.

"Oh, did Miss Skaarl keep you company? That was nice of her."

"I didn't need company! I meant I could see her sitting in here. In one of those chairs by the window.

No mistaking that hat of hers. She was waiting for her friend."

They played in silence until both had crossed the skunk line. The older man was slightly ahead and he watched sourly as his son counted up and pegged ten points in one hand.

"I can't stand that woman," he said suddenly.

"What woman?"

"That nurse. Mrs. Bellamy's companion." The jack turned up. "Ha! Two for his nibs! That's a good omen."

"You don't like nurses, period."

"They're all hypocrites. 'It's quite all right, Mrs. Bellamy. I don't mind a bit.' Talking about missing the bus. I saw her expression when we came up from lunch. She was ready to murder the old woman."

Reg threw his father a startled look, but it seemed to be just a figure of speech. "When did she say this?" he asked while counting up his hand.

"When she was leaving—before she closed the door."

So, thought Reg, Mrs. Bellamy was alive then. Or was Helen putting on an act for anyone who might overhear? Was she clever enough for that?

"She's stupid, too!" his father declared. Just six points short of winning, he was postponing having to look at his crib.

"Come on, Father, that's a little harsh."

"Wouldn't you call it brainless not to know her own handbag? She got them mixed up again today. I heard her when she came along the passage there. 'Oh, Greta,' " he mimicked, " 'look, I've got your bag.' Stupid woman."

"I thought you said Greta was inside."

"She came out and leaned on the rail there. Thought her friend was taking too long, I guess. Everybody's in a hurry these days—except me and Mrs. Bellamy."

Reg didn't agree that Helen was stupid, but taking the wrong bag reinforced Greta's impression that she had been upset. Unless she wanted something out of it? But what?

"Ha! I've won! Beat the schoolteacher again! Look here, four points in my hand and ten in the crib. Want another game?"

"Sure." As his father dealt, Reg stared at the door of Stateroom A. If Mrs. Bellamy had been killed *after* Helen left her, it must have been by someone who had a key or by a professional thief who knew how to open a door without leaving a trace. Could robbery have been the motive? Both the purser and the steward would have keys but they also had ample opportunity to enter when the cabin was empty. Why wait till Mrs. Bellamy was there? The same objection applied to a thief. Unless Helen was the thief. If she took a valuable piece of jewelry, Mrs. Bellamy would know. So, to get away with it, Mrs. Bellamy would have to die. The murder had certainly been premeditated; no one carries around a half pair of scissors. Who else on board knew the old lady well enough to want to murder her?

Throughout the game, Reg went on chatting and asking questions. His father was sure that he could see clearly from the deck into this room and that no one had entered from the time Greta left until he himself had knocked at Mrs. Bellamy's door. Of course, there must have been times when his attention was elsewhere; he had watched the deer, for instance. Shortly after the watchman had passed, two waiters had arrived on deck to set up for afternoon tea and passengers had begun to drift back aboard. No one would risk going into Stateroom A after that. It did look as if Mrs. Bellamy must have been dead when Father knocked on her door at two thirty. And, in spite of Mother's objections, it looked more and more as if only Helen could have reason to kill her. After all, they only had Helen's word that her employer carried nothing of value.

The next day, Reg tried this theory out on Inspector

Norm Follows when he, the inspector, and Constable Kennedy were alone in the captain's quarters after breakfast. The policemen had examined the body, photographed the scene, made maps after a tour of the ship, and heard reports from Captain Markle, Bill Menzies, and Reg. The captain and purser had now returned to their duties, leaving the other three men in the captain's cabin.

"She's going home to Norway soon. Maybe she wants to show off a bit—splash some money around?" suggested Reg.

"Does she strike you as that kind of person?"

"Frankly, no. Well, maybe she heard that property in her home town, what's its name?, Larsund, was going to be valuable and decided to buy some."

The inspector's black eyebrows joined into one thin line. "Not very likely, is it? The oil company would be keeping that pretty dark."

"The captain heard about it."

"Yes. Well, we'll keep it in mind. I'd better talk to the lady now. Since I agreed to cooperate with Captain Markle as far as possible in keeping this from the passengers, would you be good enough to bring her here? I imagine the presence of two strange men on board would start some talk, even though we're both in civvies."

"It would indeed! I'll get her."

Reg found Helen in her cabin with Greta, who was dressed for the sun in the briefest of yellow shorts topped by an oversized white and yellow cotton pullover. The nurse swayed and sat down abruptly on the bunk when he asked her to come with him.

"Now, there *is* something wrong, Helen!" said her friend. "Why should you be frightened of Reg?"

"Oh, Greta, Mrs. Bellamy's dead and they think I did it."

"What?" Greta looked in astonishment from the

trembling woman to the man leaning silently against the closed door.

"It's true. She was stabbed with scissors yesterday while we were in town." A sob choked her.

Greta held out a hand and Helen grabbed it convulsively.

"This is preposterous! They can't believe you killed anyone."

"Inspector Follows just wants a report from you, Helen," Reg said quietly.

"Who's Inspector Follows?" demanded Greta.

"A policeman who came on board last night. To investigate the murder."

"Murder! I can't believe this!"

Helen, more composed, stood up, and the other woman impulsively hugged her. "I'll come with you." She looked at Reg defiantly.

"At least you can come and speak to the inspector. He will say whether you can stay with her."

The policeman treated the request calmly. "We're not here to accuse you of anything, Miss Thorvald. At this time, I just want to get your account of how you found Mrs. Bellamy and a statement of your movements during the afternoon. Constable Kennedy will make notes of what you say. Mr. Symes is representing the steamship company, who naturally are anxious to get this cleared up as soon as possible. If you'd like your friend to stay, I've no objection at this stage."

"Thank you, sir, I would like it."

The inspector indicated chairs for everyone. Helen was directly opposite him on the other side of the desk. Reg noted with an inward smile that the best Greta could do was to cross her bare legs so that her shapely ankle and foot swung into the policeman's range of vision occasionally.

"Tell me about finding the body, Miss Thorvald."

Helen told him the same story she'd told Reg and went on to how she had gone first to Reg and then with him to the captain, who had asked her to stay in her cabin. "He thinks I did it. I know he does. But I didn't kill her. You know that when you saw her, Mr. Symes, she'd been dead more than a few minutes."

"Yes."

"Well, she was alive when I left her. I . . ." They all waited in silence. "Your father! Mr. Symes, your father was standing at the rail right opposite her door. I was talking to her after I opened it—looking back in, you know? He *must* have heard us. She was apologizing for keeping me late."

"He heard you speaking to her," Reg replied.

"Oh! Thank goodness!"

If Helen missed the implications of his reply, Greta didn't. "Mrs. Bellamy always spoke very quietly. One got the impression that a lady never raises her voice. She wouldn't be heard right across the lounge."

"That's so!" declared Helen.

Reg was not deceived by the inspector's mild and courteous manner into thinking that he accepted their version of events, but he wondered if the women were.

"Will you tell us, please, what happened from, say, the end of lunch. I understand you and Mrs. Bellamy were the last to leave the table."

"Yes. I felt sorry for Cindy—our waitress—because she wanted to go to town, too. I knew Mrs. Bellamy was deliberately dallying so I'd miss the bus. Anyway, there was nobody except the older Mr. Symes using the elevator, so we had a quick ride up and it was just one thirty when we got to her room and I thought I might still be on time. But she had me doing all sorts of little jobs."

"Like what, Miss Thorvald?"

"Oh, I don't remember—just time wasters. Like rubbing her good shoes, which didn't need it. Oh, finding her glasses; she'd slipped them under the pillow. Then we heard the bus go and she let me give her her tablets and she lay down. I covered her with a blanket and left her—alive!"

"How did you feel about missing the trip? Resentful, perhaps?"

"Not particularly. I know her, you see. She doesn't, didn't, like it when people paid attention to me. At lunch Mrs. Symes, and Greta, too, were both being kind, saying they'd save me a window seat, things like that. And I knew she was jealous."

"Because she couldn't go?" asked Reg, who doubted it.

"No, no. That sort of trip wouldn't interest her. No, just because they were treating her companion like a human being."

"And where did you go after you left her stateroom, Miss Thorvald?"

"To my own cabin."

"Meet anyone on the way?"

"Yes, our waitress. She came charging up the stairs just as I got to my door. She said something like, 'Oh, she kept you late, too!' Then she advised me to go into town and dashed off."

"And you decided to do that?"

"Yes, I thought I might as well. She said there were one or two good stores. So, I changed to a pants suit and then checked my purse to be sure I had enough American money. And discovered I had taken Greta's purse by mistake. They're so much alike." She indicated her straw bag as it lay on her lap and gestured towards her friend's. "It's happened before. We both put them under the table in the dining room."

Reg caught the inspector's eye and, receiving a small nod, asked, "How did you open your door if you had the wrong purse, Helen?"

"Oh, I carry my key in my pocket. Mine in my pocket and Mrs. Bellamy's in my purse so as not to get them mixed up."

"I see. So Mrs. Bellamy let you into her stateroom."

"Yes. Well, then I decided to see if Greta had waited,

seeing she had the wrong purse, so I went on deck and found her."

"I didn't even know," said the other woman, with a laugh. "Not until Helen told me."

"Yet you waited. That was kind of you, Miss Skaarl." The policeman rewarded her with a smile.

"Well, anyone could see the old lady was being deliberately mean. I didn't particularly care about going to the forest—we've got lots of trees in Norway. So, I thought I'd keep Helen company in town."

"Where did you wait?"

"On the deck till the bus left. Then I went in and sat in the lounge where I could see Mrs. Bellamy's door."

"And did Miss Thorvald come out of that door?"

"No. She must have gone before I sat down. So, I went back on deck and that's where we met."

"Do you know what time that was?"

"No, not exactly."

"There's a sailor who keeps watch on the gangplank when we're in port," Helen broke in. "He was there when we walked off; he might know the time."

"If we need to know, we'll ask him. Did you spend the rest of the afternoon together?"

"Yes, every minute," answered Greta emphatically, "until Helen went to look for Mrs. Bellamy, as she told you."

There was silence for almost a full minute. Only Helen fidgeted.

Then Follows asked, "Do you own a pair of scissors, Miss Thorvald?"

"Yes."

"Where do you keep them?"

"In my nurse's bag, in my cabin. They're not there. I looked to see."

Her voice cracked and Greta spoke up indignantly. "Lots of people own scissors, Inspector Follows. I daresay Mrs. Bellamy had a pair. I have some myself."

Helen had control of her voice again and she broke in. "They weren't my scissors that killed her. I looked to see. They didn't have my mark on them."

"Your mark?"

"At the hospital all the nurses' scissors looked the same. I scratched my initials on both sides of the join. If you look, you'll see there's no mark on the ones that killed Mrs. Bellamy."

The inspector made a note and then asked, "Where are your scissors, Miss Skaarl?"

"In my purse." She began to rummage energetically. "Funny! They're not here."

"May I see?"

She handed over the bag, but the inspector had no better luck.

"Are you sure they were in here?"

"Of course. That's where I keep them."

"Where do you think they are, then?"

"I'm beginning to wonder, inspector!" she said with a quick, grim look at Helen.

"Greta! You can't think I took them!"

"No. No, of course not. I must have used them and forgotten to put them back. I'll find them."

Not very likely, thought Reg. At least, not the missing half. They were likely at the bottom of Queen Charlotte Sound.

"For goodness sakes, Helen," Greta went on. "Pull yourself together. We'll get you a lawyer. That must be a right in this country, isn't it, Inspector Follows?"

"Miss Thorvald will be given all the help she needs, Miss Skaarl."

"If it's a question of money," she began belligerently.

"No! Greta! I forbid you to tell my parents!"

"You are both going much too fast," Follows said soothingly. "All we're asking of Miss Thorvald is that she be available to answer a few questions. Why don't you both go out in the sun while we check up on some of the times you've given us?"

"I'd rather be alone," said Helen somewhat stiffly as she walked to the door.

Her friend replied, "Whatever you say, Helen. But if you want me, I'll be on the sun deck."

"Do you want me to check those times, sir?" asked the constable as he closed the door.

"Yes, please, Rory, with both the waitress and the watchman. See if you can get the exact time that the waitress saw Miss Thorvald at her door. They must have to sign out. Also, ask if she actually saw her enter the cabin."

After he had gone, Reg said, "She *did* change her clothes. I don't know how long that would take."

"With my wife, usually half an hour. But she has done it in five minutes."

"Still, pretty tight timing. She'd have to be back in Mrs. Bellamy's stateroom before Greta sat down in the lounge and wait there till Greta got bored and went out again."

"Miss Skaarl was vague about times."

"Yes. So was Father. Even so . . . no, I think if Helen did it, she killed her before she met Cindy in the corridor." He paused for a moment. "Have you wondered why she made it look so much like murder?"

"It *was* murder," replied Follows.

"But surely, as a nurse and her constant companion, there were less obvious ways of killing her. Give her the wrong pills, or too many of them. Knock her downstairs—she was lame. It could have been made to look like an accident."

"I can think of one reason for making murder obvious," replied Follows, "but I don't see motive."

"I have a glimmer about motive," Reg replied. "Tell you in a moment. First let's see how it works out otherwise."

They discussed timing, the missing scissors, keys, and the psychology of the murderer, and by the time Constable Kennedy returned, they had decided that the R.C.M.P. would ask for the cooperation of the

Norwegian police in making certain inquiries in that country.

"Will you hold up the ship while you wait for an answer?" Reg asked.

"That depends . . . Oh, here's Rory now."

"Cindy Naumann booked out at one forty-five," the constable reported. "She looked back from the dock and saw Miss Thorvald at her porthole. The watchman says the two women came down the gangplank just a minute or two before he was relieved at two o'clock."

"That gives us enough to hold her for questioning. No, Mr. Symes, we won't have to detain the ship. I'll arrange for cars to meet us at the dock in Vancouver early tomorrow morning. The ship docks at seven thirty, I think?"

"Yes. And the passengers don't leave until after breakfast—say about eight thirty—so you should be able to get her and the body off without anyone's noticing anything unusual."

"We'll be as discreet as possible, but this *is* murder, Mr. Symes."

"Of course, of course. I'm not telling you how to do your job. I'll help in any way I can."

Mollified, the policeman said, "Keep an eye on her today and bring her to us in the morning."

Mindful of these instructions, Reg asked Helen and Greta to join himself and his parents in the bar for a pre-dinner cocktail. Everyone was dressed up for the captain's farewell party. Helen had loosened her hair, put on makeup, and wore a dress that Mrs. Bellamy would certainly not have approved. In the gaily-decorated dining room, Reg admired the professionalism of the officers and catering staff. It could not be usual to have a murderer among the guests, yet everyone from the captain on down acted as though they had nothing on their minds but the comfort and amusement of the passengers.

* * *

Next morning, Reg found his parents, Greta, and Helen all at their usual table for breakfast. Bending down, he said quietly to Helen, "Inspector Follows would like to see you."

The woman turned deathly pale and clutched the edge of the table. Mrs. Symes reached across and clasped one white hand. "Dear! Shall I come, too?"

"I will go, Mrs. Symes," said Greta firmly. She pushed back from the table, scooped up the two handbags, and stood up. "Come, Helen, be brave. You must get it over with."

Watching them leave, Mrs. Symes sighed and pushed away her porridge plate.

Her husband looked up from his bowl in time to see the gesture. "What's this?" he asked testily. "Is nobody eating breakfast but me?"

"You finish yours, dear. Here comes Cindy with your egg and toast. I need some fresh air."

From the deck she looked down on a police car and an ambulance. It should be a hearse, she thought, but I suppose that would frighten people. In a minute a procession started down the gangplank. It was led by two stretcher bearers carrying a blanket-swathed body. While they loaded their burden into the back, a young policeman helped Helen Thorvald mount to the passenger seat of the ambulance. An older officer escorted Greta Skaarl to the cruiser. Reg joined his mother.

"So, it was Miss Skaarl who killed her," she said.

"Yes."

"When?"

"Just after our bus left the dock. When Father was watching her flamboyant hat stuck up on something—maybe an ashtray—in the lounge window. She had taken Helen's bag with the key in it."

"Dear, dear! Why?"

"It's not proved yet, but I suspect she was cheating Helen's parents, among others, out of their property in Larsund. Somebody's going to make a fortune there in real estate."

"That's the business she's in," replied his mother. "I thought she'd be very good at making deals. Hard-nosed is what she is. Much more satisfactory as a murderer than poor Helen Thorvald."

"Mother! Anyway, the police have started inquiries in Norway. I wouldn't be surprised to find she's been buying up most of the property in that town."

Mrs. Symes looked puzzled. "But why murder Mrs. Bellamy?"

"To prevent Helen from going home before she got the deal finished. Helen might not have been so easy to cheat. I expect Greta came on this cruise deliberately. We know she had seen Helen's parents lately; they probably told her about the trip Helen was taking with her employer. And that she'd be coming home soon." He misinterpreted his mother's sudden frown. "Don't you see? If Helen was charged with murder, she wouldn't be allowed to leave the country. Why are you shaking your head? It makes sense. It might even hurry the deal up. Helen's parents might want money to help her with legal expenses."

"Oh, I understand all that perfectly. Her greed got the better of her morals. I was thinking of poor Mrs. Bellamy. The murder had really nothing to do with her. It was her companion who was important. She wouldn't have liked that! Not at all!"

THE DANGER POINT

by Margery Allingham

Mr. Albert Campion glanced round the dinner table with the very fashionable if somewhat disconcerting mirror top and wondered vaguely why he had been asked, and afterwards, a little wistfully, why he had come.

The Countess of Costigan and Dorn was the last of the great political hostesses, and she took the art seriously.

Sitting at the head of the preposterous table, she murmured witticisms in the ear of the bewildered American on her left in the fine old-fashioned manner born in the reign of the seventh Edward, although the decoration of the room, her gown, and her white coiffure belonged definitely to the day after tomorrow.

Mr. Campion had accepted the invitation to "a little informal dinner" because the great lady happened to be his godmother and he had never ceased to be grateful to her for a certain magnificent fiver which had descended upon him like manna upon the Israelites one hot and sticky half-term in the long-distant past.

At the moment he was a little exhausted. His neighbor, a florid woman in the late forties, talked with an unfailing energy which was paralyzing, but he was relieved to discover that so long as he glanced at her intelligently from time to time he could let his mind wander in peace. He observed his fellow-guests with interest.

There were sixteen people present, and Campion, who knew his godmother well enough to realize that she never entertained without a specific object in view, began to suspect that her beloved Cause was in need of extra funds.

Money sat round the table, any amount of money if Campion was any judge. The bewildered American he recognized as a banker, and the lady next to him with the thin neck and the over-bright eyes was the wife of a chain-store proprietor as yet without a title.

Campion's glance flitted round the decorous throng until it came to rest upon a face he knew.

Geoffrey Painter-Dell was still in his late twenties and looked absurdly youthful in spite of a certain strained expression which now sat upon his round, good-natured face. He caught sight of Campion suddenly, and immediately looked so alarmed that the other man was bewildered. His nod was more than merely cool and he turned away at once, leaving Campion startled and a little hurt, since he had known the boy well in the days before that promising youth had acquired the important if somewhat difficult position as Private and Confidential Secretary to one of the most picturesque and erratic personalities of the day, the aged and fabulously wealthy Lady (Cinderella) Lamartine.

That remarkable old woman, famed alike for her sensational gifts to charity, her indiscreet letters to the Press, and her two multi-millionaire husbands, was not present herself, but the fact that her secretary had put in an appearance indicated that the gathering had her blessing, and Campion suspected that his godmother's discreet cadging for the Cause was doing very well.

He returned to Painter-Dell, still puzzled by the young man's lack of friendliness, and caught him staring helplessly across the table. Campion followed his glance and thought he understood.

Miss Petronella Andrews, daughter of the famous Under-Secretary, sat smiling at her neighbor, the brilliant lights shining on her pale arms and on her honey-colored hair; and that neighbor was Leo Seazon.

Campion remembered that there had been rumors of a budding romance between Geoffrey and Petronella, and he quite understood any anxiety the young man might exhibit.

The girl was charming. She was vivacious, modern, and if gossip was to be relied upon, something of a handful. At the moment she merely looked beautiful and youthfully provocative, and Campion wondered, without being in the least old-maidish, if she knew the type of man with whom she was dealing so lightheartedly.

Leo Seazon was bending forward, his distinguished iron-gray head inclined flatteringly towards her.

He was a mature figure, handsome in the way that was so fashionable in the last generation and has never ceased to be fascinating to a great number of women. He seemed to be putting himself to considerable trouble to be entertaining, and Campion raised his eyebrows. In his own somewhat peculiar role of Universal Uncle and amateur of crime he had in the past had several opportunities to study the interesting career of Mr. Leo Seazon.

The man was a natural intriguer. He had a finger in every pie and a seat upon the most unlikely boards. His fortune was reputed to be either enormous or nonexistent, although his collection of *objets d'art* was known to be considerable. He was a man who turned lightly from jade and water colors to stocks and shares, from publicity to politics. He was also, at the moment, unmarried. It came back to Campion that he had last heard his name mentioned in connection with a certain foreign loan and it occurred to him then that Miss Andrews, and more especially Miss Andrews's family, might be very valuable allies to Mr. Seazon, could the matter be arranged.

He glanced back at Geoffrey with amused compassion. The young man still looked harassed, but now that Campion's interest was thoroughly aroused and he cast a more discerning eye upon him, he saw that his expression had an element of fear in it. Campion was startled. Irritation, alarm, bewilderment at the hideous taste of women in general, all these he could have understood; but why fright?

It was the florid woman on his right who answered his question, although he did not recognize it as an answer at the time.

"That's the Andrews girl, isn't it?" she murmured, bending a virulently red head towards him. "If she were my daughter I don't think I'd let her run about with that round her little neck."

Campion glanced at Petronella's pearls. As soon as they were pointed out to him he wondered why he had not noticed them before. It may have been that the face above them was sufficiently eye-taking. Now that he did see them, however, as they lay on her cream skin and fell among the draped folds of her pale satin dress, they impressed him.

The necklace consisted of a single string of carefully graduated pearls, with a second and much larger string arranged in scallops from the first so that a curious lace-like effect was produced. It was very distinctive. Campion had never seen anything quite like it before. It was such a sensational piece that even in that opulent gathering he took it to be an example of the decorative jewellery still in fashion. The Andrewses were a wealthy family, but not ridiculously so, and Petronella was very young.

"It looks very pretty to me," he said casually.

"Pretty!" said the woman contemptuously, and he was astonished to see that her small dark eyes were glistening.

It was not until afterwards that he remembered that she was Mrs. Adolph Ribbenstein, the wife of the jewel king.

At the moment, however, the conversation was cut short by his godmother, who swept the ladies upstairs to her new white and claret drawing-room on the first floor.

Campion saw Geoffrey watch Petronella follow the others, her white train rustling and the incredible necklace gleaming warmly on her small neck. His eyes were dark and questioning.

Their host, who only seemed to come to shaky life when his wife went out, developed an unexpected flair for interminable political stories, and Campion was unable to get a word with Geoffrey. Moreover, he received the impression that the young man was avoiding him intentionally and his curiosity was piqued.

Seazon, on the other hand, was in excellent form, and although a certain irritation with the elder man might have been excusable in Geoffrey Painter-Dell, now that the girl had gone any interest he might have had in the man seemed to have evaporated entirely, a circumstance which Campion found very odd.

Geoffrey sat with his head bent, his long fingers drumming absentmindedly on the mirror table, and when at last their host consented to move he was the first guest to rise.

Circumstances were against him, however. As the little party mounted the staircase a servant waylaid him, and when he did come into the drawing-room some minutes after the others he went over to his hostess, who was talking to Campion.

She listened to Geoffrey's worried excuses with gracious tolerance.

"My dear boy," she said, "Cinderella has always been difficult. Run along at once and see what she wants."

Geoffrey grinned helplessly.

"She either wants me to draw up a scheme for a Parrots' Home or ring up the Prime Minister," he said wearily.

The Countess of Costigan laughed.

"Then do it, my dear," she murmured. "She's a very powerful old lady. There aren't many of us left."

She gave him her hand and as he went off turned to Campion with a little grimace.

"Poor boy," she said. "His soul isn't his own. Cinderella's very difficult."

Campion smiled down at her. She was seventy, as keen-witted as a girl and quite as graceful.

"Cinderella?" he said. "It's a queer name."

His godmother raised her eyebrows.

"She adopted it when she was first married, out of compliment to her husband. He was a German prince," she said acidly. "That ought to give you the key to the woman. Still, she's absurdly wealthy, so we must forgive her, I suppose. Albert dear, do go over and talk to Mrs. Hugget. That's the thin one in the green dress. Dear me, money doesn't mix well, does it? I asked you and the Andrews girl to grease the wheels a little. I knew you wouldn't mind. Thank you so much, my dear. The one in the green dress."

Mr. Campion went dutifully across the room and passed Geoffrey Painter-Dell as he did so. The young man had paused to speak to Petronella on his way out and had evidently had some little difficulty in detaching her from a resumed conversation with Leo Seazon.

Campion passed by just as the young man was taking his leave and could not help overhearing the last half-whispered words. "Oh, don't play the fool, darling. For God's sake take the damned thing off."

A moment later Geoffrey had gone and Miss Andrews was looking after him, angry color in her cheeks and her eyes blazing. Seazon reclaimed her immediately and Mr. Campion bore down on the lady in green.

The party broke up early. Petronella fluttered away on Seazon's arm and Campion hurried off to see the final curtain of a first night whose leading lady was an old friend of his. But he could not get the odd scrap of conversation which he had overheard out of his mind, and Geoffrey's disinclination to talk to him rankled.

He saw Petronella again as he walked down Bond

Street the following afternoon. She was sitting beside Leo Seazon in the back of a gray limousine. They had passed in an instant, but Campion noticed that the girl was not smiling and that Leo was particularly elegant, a poem in spring suiting, in fact. He shook his head over them both, for he had liked the look of Petronella.

His thoughts returned to Geoffrey and his strange appeal to the girl which had annoyed her so unreasonably, but he could arrive at no satisfactory conclusion, and presently he shrugged his lean shoulders.

"Damn the young idiots," he said.

He repeated the observation on the evening of the following day when Superintendent Stanislaus Oates, of the Central Branch of the C.I.D., dropped in to see him in that peculiarly casual fashion which invariably indicated that he had come to glean a little information.

The two men were very old friends, and when Oates was shown into the Piccadilly flat Campion did not bother to rise from his desk, but indicated the cocktail cabinet with his left hand while he added his neat signature to the letter he had been composing with his right.

The superintendent helped himself to a modest whisky and lowered his spare form into an easychair.

"How I hate women," he said feelingly.

"Really?" inquired his host politely. "They haven't invaded the Yard yet, have they?"

"Good Lord, no!" Oates was scandalized. "Ever heard of Lady Lamartine?"

"Cinderella? I have."

"Seen her?"

"No."

Oates sighed. "Then you haven't the faintest idea," he said. "She has to be seen to be believed. I thought someone told me you knew that secretary of hers pretty well."

"Geoffrey Painter-Dell."

"That's the fellow. Know anything about him?"

"Not much, except that he's a nice lad. His elder brother, who died, was a great friend of mine."

"I see." The superintendent was cautious. "You can't imagine him being mixed up with any funny business? Not even if there were thousands involved?"

"I certainly can't." Campion laughed at the suggestion. "Sorry to disappoint you, old boy, but the Painter-Dells are absolutely beyond suspicion. They're the blood-and-steel brigade, *sans peur et sans reproche* and all that. You're barking up the wrong tree. Geoffrey is as innocent as driven snow and about as excitable."

Mr. Oates seemed relieved. "I practically told her ladyship that," he said, shaking his close-cropped head. "What a woman, Campion! What a woman! She's so darned important too; that's the devil of it. You can't say 'Run along, Grannie, you're wasting the policeman's time.' It's got to be 'Yes, milady, no, milady, I'll do what I can, milady' the whole time. It gives me the pip."

He drank deeply and set down his glass. "She's been at me all day," he said.

Mr. Campion made encouraging noises and presently his visitor continued.

"You were in the States in '31," he said, "and so you don't remember the Lamartine robbery. The house at Richmond was entered and nearly a hundred thousand quids' worth of jewellery was taken. It was her ladyship's own fault, largely. She had no business to have so much stuff, to my mind. No woman of eighty wants a load like that. Well, anyway, it was pinched, as she might have known it would be sooner or later. Fortunately we got most of it back and we put 'Stones' Roberts away for seven years. It was clearly one of his efforts, and we just happened to find him before he'd unloaded the bulk of the stuff."

He paused and Campion nodded comprehendingly. "Were you in charge?"

"Yes. I was Chief Inspector then, and Sergeant

Ralph and I cleaned the affair up as best we could. We didn't get all the stuff, though. There was a thing called La Chatelaine which we never did find. We put 'Stones' through it, but he swore he'd never seen the thing, and we had to let it go. Well, I'd practically forgotten all about it when the old lady sent for me this morning. She made it pretty clear that I'd better come myself if I was Police Commissioner, let alone a poor wretched Super, and the A.C. thought I'd better go. When I got there she was all set for me to arrest young Painter-Dell for knowing something about this Chatelaine thing, and I had an almighty job to convince her that she hadn't a thing on the poor chap. I had a talk with him finally, but he wasn't helpful."

Campion grinned.

"You didn't think he would be, did you?"

Oates looked up and his sharp, intelligent eyes were serious.

"There was something funny about the boy," he said.

Campion shook his head. "I don't believe it. The old lady was too much for you."

Still the superintendent did not smile.

"It was nothing *she* said," he insisted. "She simply convinced me that she wasn't quite all there. But when I talked to the lad I couldn't help wondering. He was so frightened, Campion."

At the sound of the word Campion's mind jolted and he remembered Geoffrey's face at the other end of the mirror-topped table. Fear; that had been the inexplicable thing about his expression then.

The superintendent went on talking.

"Lady Lamartine sent for me because her maid told her that Painter-Dell had been asking about the ornament. The robbery took place a couple of years before he took up his appointment. He'd never seen the thing and had never asked about it before, but yesterday he seems to have put the maid through it, making her describe the jewel in detail. The maid told her mistress and her mistress sent for me. I explained that no one could base a charge on anything so slight, and to pacify her I saw the boy. I kid-gloved him, of course, but he was very angry, naturally. He handed in his resignation and the old lady wouldn't accept it. I apologized and so did she. There was a regular old-fashioned to-do, I can tell you. But all the same I didn't understand the boy. He was sullen and quiet, and in my opinion terrified. What d'you know about that?"

Campion was silent for some moments. "La Chatelaine," he said thoughtfully. "It sounds familiar."

Oates shrugged his shoulders. "It's one of these fancy names some jewels get," he explained. "It's a necklace which is supposed to have belonged to one of the French queens, Catherine de Medici, I think. It's an unusual-looking thing, by the photographs. Like this."

He got up and crossing to the desk, scribbled a design on the blotting-paper.

"There's a single string and then another joining it here and there, like lace, see?" he said.

"Dear me," said Campion flatly. "What are the stones?"

"Oh, pearls. Didn't I tell you? Perfectly matched pearls. The finest in the world, I believe. Interested?"

Campion sat staring in front of him, bewilderment settling over him like a mist. In his mind's eye he saw again Miss Petronella Andrews at his godmother's dining-table, and round her neck, falling into the soft satin folds at her breast, was, only too evidently, Lady Lamartine's La Chatelaine.

It was then that he repeated under his breath the observation he had made in Bond Street on the morning before.

The superintendent was talking again.

"It's a funny thing that this should come up now," he was saying, "because 'Stones' Roberts came out a fortnight ago and we've lost sight of him. He didn't report last week and we haven't hauled him in yet. I always thought he knew something about those pearls, but we couldn't get a word out of him at the time. Well, I'll be getting along. If you say the Painter-Dell lad is above suspicion I'll believe you, but if you do happen to hear anything, pass it along, won't you?"

Campion came to himself with a start.

"I will, but don't rely on me," he said lightly, and rose to escort his visitor to the door.

He did not put the extraordinary story out of his mind, however, but actually set out that night on a pilgrimage round fashionable London in search of a young lady whom the superintendent would have liked very much to meet. Campion's conscience insisted that he take this step. It had clearly been his duty to tell Oates all he knew and, since he had not, he felt in honor bound to do a certain amount of investigating on his own account. Petronella was not easy to find. She was neither dancing at the Berkeley nor dining at Claridge's. He looked in at the Ballet and did not see her, and it was not until he remembered the Duchess of Monewden's Charity Ball at the Fitzrupert Hotel that he found her, looking like a truculent little ghost and dancing with Leo Seazon.

He caught sight of Geoffrey almost at the same moment and accosted him, demanding an introduction to Miss Andrews. Geoffrey Painter-Dell grew slowly crimson.

"I'm frightfully sorry, Campion," he said awkwardly. "I'm afraid I can't. We—er—we're not speaking. Terribly sorry. Got to rush now. Goodbye."

He retreated in considerable disorder before Campion could murmur his apologies, and disappeared among the throng.

Campion was aware of a growing sense of uneasiness. He had been fond of Geoffrey's elder brother and was genuinely alarmed at the prospect of seeing the young man involved in any sort of mess. He looked about him and espied old Mrs. De Goncourt, who was only too happy to introduce him to her niece. She took him by the arm and waddled happily across the floor with him, annihilated the frowning Mr. Seazon with her magnificent smile, and pounced upon the girl.

"The cleverest man in London, my dear," she said in a stage-whisper which would have carried across Drury Lane. "There you are, Albert. Take the child away and dance with her. Ah, Mr. Seazon, you look younger than I do. How on earth do you do it?"

Miss Andrews glanced up at Campion and, although her smile was charming, her gray-blue eyes were very much afraid. He suggested that they should dance, but she hung back.

"I'd like to, but—" she began and glanced nervously at her escort, who was doing his best to extricate himself from the clutches of his redoubtable contemporary.

Campion did not press the matter. He smiled down at the girl.

"I saw you at dinner the other night," he said. "We weren't introduced and I don't suppose you remember me. You're not wearing your beautiful pearls tonight."

She stared at him, and every vestige of color passed out of her face. For a dreadful moment he thought she was going to faint.

"Not very beautiful pearls, I'm afraid." It was Seazon who spoke. He had escaped from Petronella's aunt and now stood, sleek and very angry, a little behind the girl. "Miss Andrews was wearing a pretty little imitation trinket she did me the honor to accept from me. Now, unfortunately, it is broken. She will not wear it again. Shall we dance, my dear? It's a waltz."

He had not been actually rude, but his entire manner had been coldly offensive and there was an old-fashioned element of proprietorship in his attitude towards the girl which Campion saw was resented even while she was grateful to him for his interference.

Campion went home depressed. He liked Geoffrey, had been prepared to like Petronella, and he disliked Mr. Leo Seazon nearly as much as he disapproved of him, which was considerably. Moreover, the mystery of La Chatelaine was becoming acutely interesting.

He had business which took him to the other end of the town the following morning, so that he lunched at his club and returned to his flat a little after three o'clock. His man, who admitted him, mentioned that there were visitors in the study but did not remember their names, so that he went in entirely unprepared and unheralded.

Standing in the middle of his own Persian carpet, clasped in each other's arms with a reckless enthusiasm which could neither be disregarded nor misunderstood, were Petronella Andrews and Geoffrey Painter-Dell. They turned to him as he appeared, but neglected to relinquish hands. Petronella looked as though she had been crying and Geoffrey was still harassed in spite of a certain delirious satisfaction in the back of his eyes.

Campion surveyed them politely.

"How nice of you to call," he said fatuously. "Will you have cocktails?"

Petronella looked at him pathetically.

"Geoffrey says you can help," she began. "Somebody must do something. It's about those utterly filthy pearls."

"Of course the whole thing is fantastic," put in Geoffrey.

"Paralyzing," murmured Miss Andrews.

Campion restored order. "Let's hear the worst," he suggested.

Geoffrey looked at Petronella and she sniffed in an unladylike and wholly appealing way. She took a deep breath.

"I've got a flat of my own," she began unexpectedly. "It's in Memphis Mews, at the back of Belgrave square. You see, I've always wanted to have a place of my own, and Mother stood up for me, and after a tremendous lot of trouble we persuaded Father. He said something awful would happen to me and of course he's right, and I am so sick over that. Still, I needn't go into that, need I?"

She gave Campion a starry if somewhat watery smile and he mentally congratulated Geoffrey on the possession of his family's celebrated good taste.

"It begins with the flat, does it?" he inquired.

"It begins with the burglary," said Miss Andrews. "My burglary—the one I had, I mean."

Campion's lean and pleasant face invited further confidence and the girl perched herself on the edge of his desk and poured out her story, while Geoffrey hovered behind her with helpless but adoring anxiety.

"It was last Monday afternoon," she said. "The day of the dinner party. I was out and my maid let a man in who said he was an inspector from the electric light people. She left him in the big room I call my studio and went back to the kitchen. Then she heard a crash and hurried in to find that he'd pulled my bureau out from the wall, caught the legs on the edge of the carpet, and spilt everything off it onto the floor. She was still scolding him when I came in and then he just fled. Margaret—that's the maid—rang up the electric light company and they said they hadn't sent anyone. That's how we knew he must have been a burglar."

"I see. Did you tell the police?"

"No. He hadn't taken anything. How could I?"

Campion smiled. "It's sometimes just as well," he said. "And then what happened?"

"Then I found the loose board," said Miss Andrews calmly. "I said I'd put the room straight if only Margaret would get some tea, and as I was doing it I found that one of the floorboards, which is usually under the bureau, had been sawn off at some time and put back again. It was very wobbly and I pulled it up. There was an old cigarette tin in the hole underneath and I took it out and put the board back. I thought the tin had been stuffed there to make the board fit, you see.

"It took us some time to get the place straight and then I had to dress. I didn't think of the tin again until I was just setting out. Margaret had gone home. I took a last look round, because I do like the place to look tidy when I come in, or it's so depressing, and I saw this dirty old tin on the edge of the carpet. I picked it up to throw it into the wastepaper-basket when I thought it felt heavier than it ought to have done, so I opened it. The pearls were inside in some cotton-wool."

She paused and blushed.

"I suppose I ought not to have worn them," she said, "but I didn't dream they were valuable, and they looked so lovely against my frock. It was natural to try them on and then I hadn't the heart to take them off."

Geoffrey coughed and his eyes sought Campion's appealingly.

"Yes, well, there you are," he said. "I suddenly looked across the table and there they were. I recognized them at once. They're the famous La Chatelaine. The rooms I spend my life in are littered with paintings and photographs of Lady Lamartine wearing them. I knew they'd been stolen and never recovered, and I was pretty nearly bowled over. I realized there'd been some mistake, of course, but I knew how Lady Lamartine felt about her necklace. She's a very—well—impulsive woman, you know, Campion, and I'm afraid I said all the wrong things when I did get a moment with Petronella."

Miss Andrews turned to him with a wholly delightful gesture.

"You were sweet," she said magnanimously. "I was a pig. He just rushed up to me, Mr. Campion, and said, 'Where on earth did you get those things? Who gave them to you? Take them off at once.' I thought he was being a bit possessive, you know, and I was rude. And then of course he had to go. What made it so much worse was that when he 'phoned me early next morning I was still angry. I refused to give him any information, and I told him I didn't want to see him again, ever. When he rang up again after that, I was out. I didn't want to talk about the wretched things by that time, you see, naturally."

A puzzled expression passed over Campion's face.

"Why was that?" he inquired.

"Because I'd lost them," said Miss Andrews blissfully. "I lost them that night, the night of the dinner party. They just went. They got warm, you know, as pearls do, and must have slipped off without my noticing it.

"I've been everywhere to look for them. Leo Seazon took me everywhere the next afternoon. We went to the Carados first, and then on to the Spinning Wheel Club in Bellairs Street, and even to the coffee-stall where a crowd of us had some awful tea about four in the morning, but of course nobody remembered seeing them. I daren't advertise and I daren't go to the police because Lady Lamartine is so unreasonable and so difficult, and Geoffrey being her secretary makes it so much worse. You know what she's like. She'll make a frightful scandal and think nothing of it. Daddy will never forgive me and it will be ghastly for Geoffrey. What on earth shall I do?"

Campion considered the problem. It was not an easy one. Lady Lamartine was indeed, as even Superintendent Oates was prepared to admit, a very difficult old woman.

"It's all those people," Petronella continued. "All those people at the dinner party and at the Carados afterwards. You see, everybody seems to have recognized the wretched things. Apparently they're famous. The story is bound to go back to Lady Lamartine eventually and, of course," she added thoughtfully "there is Leo Seazon."

Campion avoided Geoffrey's eyes.

"Ah, yes, of course, Seazon," he said casually. "Why did you tell him about it in the first place?"

"I didn't," said Miss Andrews. "He told me. I had no idea what they were until he came out with it. I've met him two or three times lately and he was always very attentive and all that. When we discovered that he was going on to the Carados too, we decided to go together. He seemed quite amusing. He left us at the Spinning Wheel and I didn't think of him again until he 'phoned the next morning and asked if I could see him on 'a private matter of great urgency'—you know how he talks. I told him to come along and when he arrived he started off by asking me in a fatherly fashion if I'd be a good girl and take La Chatelaine to the police."

She took a deep breath.

"I was simply staggered, of course," she said, throwing out a pair of small gloved hands, "but he made me understand what he was talking about at last and I got rather frightened. He put it so badly and he would keep begging me to 'do the sensible thing' and 'own up.' "

"You told him you'd lost the pearls?"

She nodded and her little diamond-shaped face grew grave.

"I'm afraid he didn't believe me," she said. "He didn't believe the story of the cigarette tin either, even when I showed him the loose board."

Geoffrey made an inarticulate sound and she turned to him.

"Oh, he didn't actually say so, of course, darling," she protested. "He pretended to be very helpful. But he did let me see that he didn't really trust me. And now he's come out in the open. He spends hours exhorting me to 'be wise,' to 'trust him,' and not to 'force him to do anything he'd hate to have to do.' "

She looked directly at Campion and he saw that behind her flippancy there was genuine distress in her eyes.

"It's almost a sort of blackmail," she said. "I'm getting to loathe him. I can't move him off the doorstep and I daren't shoo him away in case he goes roaring round to Lady Lamartine. The trouble is I'm afraid he's stewing up to the point where he's going to make an offer to marry me and keep quiet. I can feel that in the wind. I think he rather fancies an alliance between the two families."

Geoffrey snorted and Campion intervened.

"Don't you think that's a little old-fashioned and melodramatic?" he ventured gently.

Miss Andrews met his eyes with an unexpectedly forthright glance.

"Leo Seazon is old-fashioned and melodramatic," she said. "He must be nearly seventy."

Campion, who knew that debonair and conceited man to be but fifty-six, felt a sneaking sympathy for Leo Seazon. However, it was not of long duration. Geoffrey took the girl's hand.

"When Petronella rang me up today and poured out the whole story I was beside myself," he said. "Lady Lamartine is on the war-path already. She's heard something. There was a Yard man down there yesterday asking nervous questions. He practically apologized to me for bringing up the subject, but I felt pretty guilty. What can we do, Campion? What on earth can we do?"

Campion made no rash promises. The two young people standing so forlornly in front of him touched his heart, however. He gave them a cocktail and sent them away with the assurance that he would do what he could.

Just before they left, Geoffrey turned to him wistfully.

"About this fellow Seazon," he began diffidently. "I can't pitch him out yet on the street, can I "

"My dear boy, no!" Campion was mildly scandalized. "I'm afraid Mr. Seazon must be placated at all costs. He's the danger point, you see."

Geoffrey nodded gloomily. "The man's practically ordered Petronella to go to the ballet with him tonight."

"Then she must go," said Mr. Campion firmly. "I'm sorry, but it's imperative. The one thing we must avoid at all costs is publicity, I take it? Mr. Seazon has a devastating tongue."

"Here, but I say . . . !" Geoffrey protested in sudden revolt. "If we're going to accept that premise, Petronella may have to marry the fellow if La Chatellaine doesn't turn up."

Campion's pale eyes were hidden behind his spectacles.

"Let us hope it doesn't come to that," he said solemnly. "Bless you, my children. Let me have your card, Miss Andrews. I'll ring you in the morning."

As soon as his visitors were safely off the premises, Campion sat down at his desk and drew the telephone towards him.

Superintendent Oates was even more helpful than usual. His curiosity was piqued and he listened to the Memphis Mews address with considerable interest.

"Yes," he said, his voice sounding lazier than ever over the wire, "it does strike a note in my memory. That's the place where 'Stones' Roberts's girl lived. Her father was a chauffeur, I remember. They've turned all that Mews into society flats now. What's the excitement?"

Campion did not answer him directly. Instead he put another question and once again the Superintendent was helpful.

"It's funny you should ask," he said. "I was just thinking about Roberts when you rang. One of our men reports that there's a fellow very like him acting as a waiter at the Spinning Wheel Club. He couldn't be quite sure and didn't want to frighten him. He wants Ralph or me to go down and identify him."

"Fine." Campion sounded relieved. "That's a real bit of luck. Look here, Oates, do me a favor. Don't pull the man in, but have him tailed. I've got a very good reason for asking."

Oates began to grumble.

"When is your lordship thinking of taking the humble police force into his confidence?" he demanded.

"Right away," said Campion cheerfully. "I'll come round. Oh, Stanislaus, heard from Lady Lamartine today?"

Mr. Oates made a remark which the telephone department would have considered vulgar, and rang off.

Petronella Andrews was entertaining Mr. Leo Seazon to tea when Mr. Campion telephoned to her the following afternoon. She was paler than usual and there were definite signs of strain in her young face. It seemed to her that she had been entertaining Mr. Seazon for several hundreds of years without respite.

He sat, grave and handsome, in the quilted armchair by the fireplace and regarded her with the half-reproachful, half-sympathetic expression which she had grown to hate.

They had been talking, as usual, of La Chatelaine, of Mr. Seazon's considerable fortune, and of the advisability of a young girl having a husband who could protect her in times of trouble.

Petronella had skillfully led the conversation away from the sentimental whenever it had appeared, but it had been growing steadily more and more apparent that his evasion could not last forever, and the telephone call came as a heaven-sent interruption.

Campion was very discreet on the wire.

"Miss Andrews," he said, "do you remember some earrings you lost? No, don't speak; I said earrings. You lost them when your flat was robbed and you told the police. You may not remember all this, but I want you to know it now. Will you come down to

Scotland Yard at once and get them? Mr. Seazon is with you, isn't he? Perhaps he'd bring you in his car, which our man reports is outside your door. Don't be alarmed. Just come along. Explain who you are when you arrive and you'll be taken straight up to Superintendent Oates. I shall be there. Goodbye."

An excellent training by a mother of the old school had taught Petronella both self-possession and adroitness, and within half an hour the courtly Mr. Seazon, who was not unadroit himself, was handing her gracefully out of his gray limousine in the courtyard of the ugliest building on the Embankment.

The square high-ceilinged room in which Superintendent Oates received them with the avuncular charm he kept for pretty ladies was already half-full of people. Petronella's heart leaped as she caught sight of Geoffrey sitting next to Mr. Campion in a corner, and when he smiled as he rose to greet her she blushed very charmingly.

Mr. Seazon, who observed the incident, did not seem so pleased.

Besides the superintendent there were two other officials present, a thin man in uniform with a box and a fat man in a brown suit with a portfolio. It was very impressive.

Mr. Oates beckoned the thin man, took the box, and smiled encouragingly at the pretty girl.

"Now, Miss," he said.

"My—my earrings?" stammered Petronella.

Oates regarded her blandly.

"A clerical error," he said magnificently. "The necklace, I think. Now would you identify this, please?"

He opened the box with a flourish and took out the shimmering string of loveliness within. La Chatelaine hung over his stubby fingers and glistened like frozen tears in the gray and ugly room. Petronella took them and her face lit up.

"Oh, this is marvelous!" she said. "Oh, bless you! Where did you find them?"

"One moment, Miss." Oates turned to a plump and shining little man who had been sitting unnoticed on the other side of Mr. Campion and who now came forward.

"Yes," he said, taking the string delicately from the girl. "Yes, definitely. I can identify them. This is La Chatelaine. It has been through our hands several times for restringing and so on. We attend to all Lady Lamartine's magnificent collection of jewellery. Dear me, I never thought we should see this in its present lovely state again. You are to be congratulated, superintendent. If these pearls had been separated it would have been a sin, a major sin."

He dropped them back into the cotton-wool with a little gesture which was almost a caress.

Leo Seazon coughed. His face was expressionless but quite composed. He conveyed the impression of a man gallantly concealing a deep disappointment.

"Well, now are you satisfied, my dear?" he murmured. "The necklace goes back to its—ah—rightful owner, I suppose?"

"I am taking the pearls to her ladyship tonight personally, sir," said Oates. "She'll be very glad to see them."

"I have no doubt of that," said Seazon drily and a little unpleasantly, but Petronella silenced him.

"How did you get them?" she demanded.

The superintendent smiled.

"Police methods," he said airily, avoiding Campion's eyes. "The crook who performed the robbery in the first place was arrested and sent to jail. That was nearly seven years ago. We recovered practically everything he had had his hands on except the pearls. He'd hidden those in a place we didn't think of searching, under a floorboard in his young lady's father's flat. He didn't even trust her and the family left while he was in jail, so that when he came out and went back for his swag, he found the place had been done up and turned into fashionable little residences. As soon as he was certain he was not being watched, he made an attempt to get into the flat by telling the maid there that he was from the electric light company, but he was disturbed and went off without finding out if his cache was still undiscovered. At this time he was working as a waiter at the Spinning Wheel Club in the West End and the same evening he saw a guest come in wearing the very necklace he was after."

Oates paused and a laugh of pure relief escaped Petronella.

"And so he stole them again?" she said. "Oh, how wonderful! Oh, Geoffrey!"

Leo Seazon watched the young man go over to her and his round dark eyes were not pleasant.

"Very interesting," he said briefly. "It'll make a delightful story. I must add it to my repertoire."

There was a moment of silence. The young people stared at him in consternation and Petronella put out her hand.

"You wouldn't," she said huskily. "Oh, you wouldn't?"

He regarded her coldly.

"My dear child, I don't see why not," he said drily and turned towards the door.

Campion rose.

"I say, don't go," he murmured affably. "Hear the rest of the story, since it interests you. Our Mr. Roberts, the original crook, didn't steal La Chatelaine *in* the Spinning Wheel."

Leo Seazon swung round slowly and Campion went on, still in the light and pleasant tone that his enemies disliked so much.

"Oh, no," he said. "Our Mr. Roberts, Mr. 'Stones' Roberts, merely saw the jewels at the club. He followed them and found it impractical to attempt to recover them that night. He hung about long enough to see where they were hidden, however, and made his plans to steal them. Unfortunately for him he took so long reconnoitering that by the time he made his successful attempt last night he had a couple of policemen on his tail. They caught him just as he was coming out of the house with La Chatelaine in his pocket. It was a 'fair cop,' as he said himself. Does that improve the story, Mr. Seazon?"

The handsome man with the distinguished iron-gray curls attempted to bluster, but his face was haggard.

"I don't understand your inference," he began.

"Don't you?" said Campion. "Oh, well, then, you're going to get a jolly surprise as well, because the house from which Mr. Roberts took La Chatelaine last night was your house, Mr. Seazon, and Mr. Roberts, in the statement which he has made to the police, distinctly says that he followed you home after seeing you slip the necklace off Miss Andrew's shoulders as you were helping her off with her evening cloak in the Spinning Wheel. It may be a lie, as I see you are about to suggest, but he was coming out of your house when he was taken with the pearls on him and he has described the drawer in the desk in your study from which he says he took them."

"Ridiculous! Why should I steal? I'm a rich man." Mr. Seazon's voice was not too steady.

Campion looked at Miss Andrews.

"There's a frightfully trite old saying about wealth not being able to buy one everything one wants," he said. "Well, there you are. I've said my piece. It's up to Miss Andrews to prosecute."

Petronella turned a pale, horrified face from her erstwhile admirer.

"I won't. I won't, of course, if only he doesn't *talk*," she said.

Campion held open the door to the retreating Leo Seazon.

"He won't, I'm sure," he said clearly. "But if he

should, well, you can always change your mind, can't you? It remains at your discretion, my children."

In the background Oates chuckled.

"Lay you six to four he don't send you two a wedding present," he said.

HOLOCAUST AT MAYHEM PARVA

by Julian Symons

A fine summer morning in Mayhem Parva. Through the leaded light windows of her cottage in the High Street, Mrs. White, who thought of herself as the merry widow, watched Professor Plum walking along erratically as always, taking care to dodge the cracks in the pavement. He looked deplorably untidy in that old pullover, but still she thought he was a fine figure of a man, and one said to be susceptible to feminine charm. If she was at his table at the Vicarage tea party that afternoon, and sparkled—and she knew how to sparkle, who better?—anything might follow. A supper tête-a-tête, a little gentle dalliance, and then—well, she had really exhausted the pleasures of being a merry widow, and although the Professor had the reputation of being a permanent bachelor, interested only in the odd concoctions he brewed up in his laboratory, he had never seen the merry widow really sparkling. But of course it was necessary to arrange that she *should* sit at the same table. She picked up the telephone.

Outside Mr. Bunn the baker, the Professor had to sidestep dexterously to miss a couple of tricky hairline cracks in the pavement. An ancient Morris pulled up behind him with a shriek of brakes. The window was wound down and the Reverend Green's round shining countenance looked out at him.

"Is it not a beautiful day, Professor? All the live murmur of a summer's day, as the poet puts it. And where can the summer day murmur more seductively than here in Mayhem Parva?"

"Ha," said the Professor.

"We look forward so much to seeing you this afternoon." At that, Professor Plum merely nodded. The Reverend Green put his head on one side and said coyly, "A certain temptress has asked my dear Emerald if she may share your table."

"Ha," the Professor repeated.

"That makes you curious, I'm sure." In fact, the Professor had shown no sign of curiosity. "I fear you must wait for curiosity to be satisfied. What I can promise is that Emerald has prepared a sumptuous spread. But I have duties, I must fly." The ancient Morris moved off in a series of jerks.

The infernal Mrs. White, I suppose, the Professor thought. Stupid, simpering woman—not a patch on that fine little filly Mrs. Peacock, what's her name, Paula. Now if it had been Paula Peacock who'd asked to sit at his table— But that wasn't likely, and it wasn't the problem—which was what to do about the Vicar. Should he go to the boy's parents or confront the Vicar face to face and tell him he was a disgrace to the cloth? But suppose the man just laughed at him and the boy's people sent him off with a flea in his ear? Difficult, difficult. Better have a word with the Wise Woman, he thought, which was his name for Miss Harple.

Back in his ugly little house near the station, the Professor retired to his lab. He was working at the moment on a mixture made from spotted hemlock, which he believed to be good for asthma. Multiplex Chemicals had shown interest in taking it up on a commercial basis. But the problem of the Vicar was on his mind and he found it hard to concentrate and after half an hour gave up. He telephoned Miss Harple and asked if she could come over, as there was a confidential matter he couldn't discuss on the telephone . . .

"A garden is a lovesome thing, God wot," the Reverend Green said as he leaned over the fence that separated the untidy Vicarage garden from Miss Harple's neat rosebeds, primrose and polyanthus borders, and rock garden cleverly devised in stripes of red, white, and blue. Miss Harple, who was weeding the rock garden, straightened up but did not reply. Even in gardening clothes, she looked elegant, her beautiful white hair perfectly dressed, her china-blue eyes innocent—or, as some said, icy.

"What does the philosopher tell us? That God Almighty first planted a garden, and that it is the purest of human pleasures."

"But it was entered by the serpent," Miss Harple said.

"Ah, you are too clever for me." She did not deny it. "Dear lady, may I venture to remind you that Emerald and I look forward to seeing you this afternoon in our rambling wilderness?"

"I have a guest coming down from London." She elaborated. "A gentleman."

"Of course he will be welcome—the more so because he comes as the escort of our dear Miss Harple, solver of all our mysteries, elucidator of every puzzle."

The Reverend Green passed a handkerchief over his face, smiled, bowed, opened his green gate. Miss Harple looked after him for a moment, finished her weeding, and went into the kitchen. She had much to do before her guest arrived.

The letter plopped onto the mat.

Mrs. Peacock, eating her single slice of dry toast, drinking her sugarless tea—she knew the importance of preserving her figure—heard it and shivered a little. When she saw the square envelope with its carefully printed capitals, she had to force herself to open it. She read:

I KNOW WHAT YOU WERE DOING WITH PROFESSOR PLUM IN THE CONSERVATORY—GET OUT OF MAYHEM PARVA YOU FILTHY WHORE

She put the letter beside the two others, deliberated during a long hot bath, and then went round to see Miss Harple.

Mrs. Peacock had come only recently to the village and almost the first person she met was Miss Harple. They had met before, when Miss Harple solved the mystery of the missing Egyptian diplomat, at a time when Mrs. Peacock was the Egyptian's mistress and was known as TouTou, the Peacock Fan dancer. Her maiden name, which she had never changed, was Betty Sludge, but, not unnaturally, she preferred Paula Peacock and—as she told Miss Harple—she wanted only to live quietly in Mayhem Parva, her days as TouTou forgotten.

Miss Harple read the letters, and then looked at Mrs. Peacock with those blue eyes that, as TouTou had said when being questioned by her during the Egyptian-diplomat affair, could see through a brick wall.

"Is there any truth in these stories?"

"None at all." She giggled, then stopped as she saw Miss Harple's frown. "Though Professor Plum is an attractive man."

"But you were not with him in the conservatory—or the library, as another letter says—or his study?" A shaken head. "And you have met nobody else in the village who knew you in the past?" Head shaken again. The china-blue eyes looked hard at her. "Of course, if you left Mayhem Parva and returned to London—"

A third headshake, and the most decisive. "I've bought my house. And I love it here. It's so peaceful—so *English*."

"Very well. Leave the letters with me. I will think

about them. And don't worry. Every problem has a solution."

With TouTou gone, Miss Harple returned to her kitchen preparations, but not for long. This time when the doorbell rang, it was Miss Scarlett, who lived only a few yards away, in a lane leading off the High Street. Miss Harple didn't care for Miss Scarlett, whom she regarded as a malicious gossip, but she could be kind and gentle in the presence of distress and she saw that Miss Scarlett was upset. She sat her down now in the little sitting room crowded with knick-knacks and asked what was the trouble.

"I have had such a shock. This morning earlier, I was in Payne's the chemist. I went in to get some indigestion tablets, but also because—I wonder if you have heard the story about Elfrieda Payne and the grocer's boy. It seemed to me that he—I mean, Mr. Payne—was looking very *tense*, and when Elfrieda came down the stairs—"

"Miss Scarlett, I don't want to know about Mrs. Payne and the grocer's boy. Something has upset you. You were going to tell me about it."

"Yes, my tongue runs away with me. I got my tablets, turned round to go out, and came face to face with Colonel Mustard."

"The man who has taken a short lease on old Mrs. Cunningham's house now she's gone to live in Malta. I have met him once or twice—he seems pleasant enough."

"Oh, yes, he *seems* pleasant. But his name is not Colonel Mustard, and he is a swindler. He called himself Commander Salt when I knew him and persuaded me to invest in his company. It was called Electric Car Electrics. They were going to make very cheap electricity out of old newspapers soaked in sea water, which would run a new electric car. He said I should make a fortune, but he disappeared and I never saw a penny of my money back. Oh, it was such a shock."

If Miss Harple thought that a fool and her money are soon parted, she didn't say so. She gave Miss Scarlett a cup of tea and one of her homemade scones, found out by a few adroit questions that it was unlikely Miss Scarlett would have a case for legal action against Colonel Mustard, spoke soothing words, and said she would speak to the Colonel. She reflected that there were several fools with money in Mayhem Parva, but she did not say that to Miss Scarlett.

Colonel Mustard, alias Commander Salt, alias Group Captain Fairweather, did his usual hundred morning press-ups, ran round the garden half a dozen times, ate a hearty breakfast which he cooked himself, said "Top of the morning to you" to Mrs. Middleton the cleaner, and retired to his study to look through the draft prospectus for Uniworld Military Disposals, a company which according to the prospectus was being formed to buy out-of-date military equipment in European countries cheap, and sell it to the Third World. As the Colonel read through the draft, he talked to himself.

"Agents all over Europe—old uniforms, cooking equipment, armoured cars, all sorts of electrical gear, out-of-date planes—going for a song, my dear sir, going for a song—no question of military use, m'dear madam, planes converted for commercial use, armored cars turned into jeeps, uniforms retailored as dungarees—endless possibilities—you'll see thirty percent a year on your money—and helping people who need it, shouldn't consider taking it on otherwise."

The Colonel made a few amendments, stood up, looked at himself in the glass, admired the soldierly look, the erect stance, the clipped moustache. "Ready to go, m'boy," he said. "If I'm not much mistaken, there's rich pickings in Mayhem Parva."

But Colonel Mustard was mistaken.

Miss Harple met her visitor, whom we will call simply the Author, at Mayhem Parva station, which had no waiting room and was hardly more than a halt. He was an awkward, shambling figure, who was writing a book about Agatha Christie. Miss Harple had known her well, and had an encyclopaedic knowledge of the works. As they walked back through the village, she told the Author of her busy morning, the Vicar's call, Mrs. Peacock's visit followed by that of Miss Scarlett, her own call on Professor Plum, whom she had found messing about in his laboratory. The Author listened, enthused about the well preserved village street, and was suitably impressed by Miss Harple's little Georgian home; Mayhem House, the Waterford glass on the shelves, and the bits of Minton china in cabinets.

"It will be rather a scrap lunch, I'm afraid," Miss Harple said when they were sipping dry sherry. "My maid of all work, Marilyn, is in bed with a gastric upset, and I must apologize for the place looking so untidy." In reality it could hardly have been neater. "And that means, I'm afraid, I shall have to give the Vicar's wife, Emerald Green, a hand this afternoon. There's a tea party at the Vicarage, and Marilyn was going to help with cutting bread, making sandwiches, all that sort of thing. If you'd like to come, Emerald would be very pleased, but perhaps you'd be bored by a Vicarage tea party."

On the contrary, the Author said, it would be a new and no doubt exciting experience. He wandered round the garden while Miss Harple laid lunch, noting the abundance of roses without a trace of blackspot or mildew, the pretty yellow jasmine climbing up the wall, the weedless grass, the yew tree that separated this tidy garden from the overgrown one next door.

After lunch, his hostess talked about Agatha Christie, her shyness, her love of true English villages like Mayhem Parva, her endless curiosity about tiny details most people overlooked or didn't notice, her relaxed charm with friends. The Author listened and made notes.

When lunch was over, and they had drunk coffee

in a shady part of the garden, Miss Harple went round to lend a hand at the Vicarage, leaving the Author to look round the village before putting in an appearance at the tea party. He admired the old-fashioned colored bottles in the chemist's window and the sign outside the butcher that said BUTCHER AND GRAZIER, HOME-KILLED PORK; went into the well kept church, was amused by the name of the pub, which was called the Falling Down Man, went into one of the flourishing antique shops and considered buying a Victorian mother-of-pearl card-case, but decided it was too expensive. Then he made his way back to the Vicarage, where the tea party was in full swing.

There were little tables with four or six people sitting at them, plates of sandwiches, scones, and little cakes, dishes of trifle, ice cream. His hand was pressed by one that seemed damp with oil rather than water.

"You must be the friend of our dear Miss Harple. *So* good of you to come. Now let me see, where can we find room for—ah, but here is the lady herself. Thank you, my dear, I must confess to being a trifle parched." The Reverend Green accepted gratefully the cup of tea handed him, and wandered away.

"Here you are, then," Miss Harple said a little sharply. "Do you like trifle?"

"Well—I think perhaps—not after such an excellent lunch."

"You'll find chairs in the corner, and there's a place over here." She led the way to a table where three people sat, and introduced him. "This is Mrs. Peacock—Mrs. White—Professor Plum. And here is Emerald with a cup of tea."

Little Mrs. Green said it was nice to see any friend of Miss Harple, and recommended the tuna-paste sandwiches which she had made herself. The Author considered his companions. Mrs. Peacock sipped her tea delicately, Professor Plum drank his noisily while eating a piece of fruitcake, Mrs. White was occupied with a plate of creamy trifle decorated with hundreds and thousands. Mrs. White spoke to the Professor.

"This is really delicious, Professor, do try some."

"Don't fancy it." The Professor made a harrumphing noise, and said to Mrs. Peacock, "Settling down all right, are you? All very neighborly here in the village. That garden fence of yours could do with a bit of attention. Quite a handyman myself, it you need one."

Mrs. Peacock murmured that he was very kind, in a voice that sounded extremely refined. Mrs. White tittered slightly, leaned forward, and said, "I hear your laboratory is quite fascinating, Professor, that you make all sorts of wonderful old medicines there. I believe myself that the old remedies are much the best—"

She was interrupted by a prolonged, high-pitched scream. There was a crash, a sound of breaking crockery. Mrs. White stopped speaking to the Professor and said, in quite a different voice, "Whatever's the matter with Colonel Mustard?"

The Author turned and saw that a tall, red-faced man wearing a blue brass-buttoned blazer was on the ground, writhing and crying out unintelligible words. He had pulled over the table as he fell and lay in a welter of spilled tea cakes and sandwiches. The Reverend Green, Emerald, Miss Harple, and a man wearing spectacles were beside him. The woman who had screamed put a hand to her thin chest and cried: "I had nothing to do with it, it was nothing I said to him!" Miss Harple took her arm and said, "He's been taken ill, Miss Scarlett, nobody's blaming you. Doctor Playden will be able to help."

The man with spectacles looked up from beside the body and shook his head. "I'm afraid not. This man is dead."

Sometime later the Author sat on a sofa in Mayhem House, listening while Doctor Playden and Chief Inspector Haddock discussed the case with Miss Harple. He was amused by the way in which both men deferred to her.

"You're sure you feel up to the mark?" the doctor said. "I know you've been sleeping badly."

"I am perfectly well now," Miss Harple said, with her agreeable touch of acidity.

The Chief Inspector coughed. "Up to a point, it's straightforward enough. There was cyanide in his tea. The question is who put it there. The only other person permanently at his table was Miss Scarlett, though the Reverend Green sat there in between getting up to say hallo to people as they arrived, and chatting with them."

"And I believe three cups of tea were taken to the table by Emerald—Mrs. Green," Miss Harple ventured. The policeman nodded. "And she just put them down on the table? So it was by pure chance that the cup with cyanide in it came to Colonel Mustard." Miss Harple paused. "Unless Mrs. Green was the poisoner."

Doctor Playden protested. "You surely can't believe that."

Miss Harple spoke gently, her blue eyes innocent. "I am simply pointing out the possibility."

The policeman and the doctor were drinking whisky, the Author and Miss Harple her home-brewed mead. She spoke again, slowly. "Miss Scarlett had reason to dislike Colonel Mustard, but I don't think any cause to wish him dead. I think in the circumstances I should tell you about it." She did, and then went on: "But I have a feeling—"

"Yes?" the Chief Inspector said eagerly.

"That perhaps this is only the beginning. There was an old farmer we used to visit when I was a child, and he could always tell the weather after there'd been a storm. The sky might be blue again, not a cloud in sight, but he'd say: 'This was only the beginning, the real storm's still to come.' I feel like that old farmer. The real storm's still to come."

* * *

Miss Harple, as so often, was right. The Author, curious to follow the case and anxious to talk with her again about Agatha Christie, spent the night in the Falling Down Man, and at breakfast heard the news from the distraught landlord.

"Reverend Green's dead, sir, and that's not all. Ambulances been in and out the village all night, taking 'em to hospital. Doctor's not had a wink of sleep. There be so many taken ill, sir, it's an epidemic like except it's not. They say the Reverend died in his sleep, and I hear tell he was poisoned—they say it was all that tea party at the Vicarage."

The Author spent the next two days talking to people in the village. He paid a couple of calls on Miss Harple, but there seemed to be always a policeman in discussion with her—a Sergeant with the autopsy reports, a harassed-looking Chief Inspector, or the Chief Constable himself. She was obviously too busy to talk about Agatha Christie, and seemed disinclined to discuss the case, or cases, with him. The Author paid a visit to Professor Plum's house, in the company of Doctor Playden, and saw the laboratory. The Doctor, indeed, was friendly enough to tell him the detailed results of the autopsies on the six victims. It was after he had learned these that the Author paid Miss Harple another, and, as it proved, his last visit.

It was late evening, and his welcome was friendly, although not overwhelmingly so. Miss Harple was wearing a blue-brocade dress with a little lace round the neck and a matching piece of lace on her white hair. She looked elegant, but also frail and tired. She apologized for her failure to look out papers she had mentioned about Mrs. Christie, but said she would send them on to him.

"I didn't come to talk about Agatha Christie. I came to talk about the case."

"The case is solved. Mr. Haddock agreed with me

that there was only one possible culprit—Professor Plum."

"But Professor Plum is dead."

"Precisely. He had always been eccentric, and it is plain that the eccentricity turned to madness. He had the means of making poisons in his laboratory, and had actually produced some of those used. What he did was the work of a madman, and when it was done he felt remorse. Why are you shaking your head?"

"I think there is a different explanation. Would you like to hear it?"

"It has been a long day. Will the explanation take long?"

"A few minutes."

"Talking is thirsty work. I know you enjoy a glass of mead. And perhaps you would like a biscuit."

The Author watched as she filled two glasses from a decanter and placed one beside each of their chairs. When she left the room to fetch the biscuits, he changed the glasses. On her return he began to talk, aware of his similarity to a detective in an Agatha Christie story gathering the suspects together to explain the case. Here, however, he had an audience of one.

"There were six victims. Colonel Mustard, who died at the tea party, Mrs. Peacock, the Reverend Green, and Professor Plum, who died during the evening or early night, Miss Scarlett, who died in her sleep, and Mrs. White, who died early on the following morning. Each died of a different poison. Colonel Mustard drank tea laced with cyanide, Mrs. Peacock an infusion of hemlock. The Reverend Green was poisoned by taxine and Professor Plum by gelsemium. Miss Scarlett took an overdose of chloral hydrate and Mrs. White was poisoned by arsenic."

"She was an exceptionally tiresome woman."

"It's interesting that you should say that. She was the only one to suffer a prolonged period of pain before death." Miss Harple looked at him sharply, then sipped her mead. The Author drank a mouthful of his.

"It would seem at first glance that the killer was somebody with a passion to try out the effects of different poisons, chosen at random. Nothing at all appeared to link them. But that was not the case."

The Author waited as if for questions, but Miss Harple did not speak.

"The link was Agatha Christie. All of these poisons were used in her stories. Cyanide, of course, quite often, most notably in *Sparkling Cyanide*. Coniine, which is derived from spotted hemlock, was used in *Five Little Pigs,* taxine in *A Pocket Full of Rye*, gelsemium in *The Big Four*. One of the victims in another novel took an overdose of chloral hydrate, and arsenic was used in a story called 'The Tuesday Night Club.' The murderer, then, was somebody with an expert knowledge of the Christie canon, something that ruled out Professor Plum, who hardly had a work of fiction in his house."

"But he made coniine in his laboratory."

"Quite true. Doctor Playden told me he was in hopes of it being adopted as a remedy for asthma. You were friendly with him, often visited the laboratory. I think you took a phial with you on one visit and filled it from his jar of coniine."

"And where do you suggest I found those other exotic poisons?"

"Two of them from your garden. Gelsemium is derived from yellow jasmine, which grows plentifully up your house wall, and taxine comes from the berry of the yew tree. I noticed a fine specimen at the bottom of the garden. Cyanide is still an old-fashioned way of getting rid of wasps and arsenic of rats, although of course they have to be extracted with some care."

"Chloral hydrate is not easily obtainable."

"Doctor Playden prescribed it for you because you told him you were sleeping badly. You saved it up and then, with your usual thoughtfulness, gave it to

Miss Scarlett as a sleeping draught. I remember that after our discussion when Colonel Mustard died, you said you were worried about Miss Scarlett, and went round to see her."

Miss Harple straightened the lace round her neck. "And I suppose you think I gave little Marilyn something to upset her stomach so that I could replace her as Emerald's assistant at the tea party?" The Author nodded. "You are really very ingenious. Ingenious but ridiculous. Nobody will believe this nonsense. Have a biscuit."

He shook his head. "When I tell the Chief Inspector about the yellow jasmine and the yew tree, I think he'll take notice."

"You really suggest I put those various poisons into the teacups?"

"Yes. You carried round most of the cups and some of the cakes. It wouldn't have been difficult to give them to the right people."

"Arsenic in tea would taste distinctly bitter."

"Of course. I should have mentioned that. You knew Mrs. White liked trifle and copied the Christie story in which the arsenic was in the hundreds and thousands on top of the trifle."

"There is one thing you have forgotten."

"I don't think so."

"The three teacups were taken to Colonel Mustard's table by Emerald Green, not by me. I couldn't possibly have known he would take the cup containing the cyanide."

"Oh, that was clever. But then of course you took that from Agatha Christie, too, and adapted it for your own purposes. There is a story in which the poisoner wants a victim and doesn't care who it is, anyone in a group will do. You didn't mind which of the three at their table took the cup with cyanide, because all of them were going to die. The other cups contained the hemlock and the taxine." He yawned. He felt very tired.

"I congratulate you. You are perfectly right."

"Thank you."

"You may have been puzzled by my motives. I simply wanted to preserve the reputation of this unspoiled English village."

Miss Harple leaned forward and looked at him intently. The Author found it hard to meet the gaze of those icy blue eyes. "Colonel Mustard had plans for inducing some of our credulous residents to invest in his companies, and they would have been ruined. Mrs. Peacock had a past which—I won't dwell on it, but she was really not the kind of person we want here. I did my best to get her to leave by sending some letters suggesting she was carrying on an entirely fictitious affair with Professor Plum and telling her she would be happier back in London, but she insisted on staying here. A pity—I rather liked her. Miss Scarlett I did *not* like. She was a busybody, mischief-maker, tale-teller, really no loss. Neither was Mrs. White, who always thought of herself as the merry widow—which meant that she set her cap at any eligible man she met, in a way I found most distasteful. The Reverend Green's conduct was scandalous—I shall say no more than that. And Percy Plum—" her voice, which had been jarring as a clatter of steel needles, softened to little more than a whisper "—was part crazy, but part a wonderfully clever scientist. I was very fond of Percy."

"Then why—?"

"Because of his discovery." Miss Harple looked down at the carpet, her manner almost coy. "In his experiments, Percy had stumbled by chance on what crime writers have feared might exist for years, the undetectable poison. He told me the secret, and of course it is safe with me, but the silly fellow insisted it should be made public. Can you imagine the result for books like Mrs. Christie's? It would no longer be possible to write them. Why didn't I use the poison, you may ask? That wouldn't have been fair play, would it? And when we try to imitate crime writers, we must always observe fair play." She broke off. "You worked things out very well, but you made one mistake. Shall I tell you what it was?"

The Author nodded. He found it hard to keep his eyes open.

"You failed to notice that when I left this room to get the biscuits I could see what you were doing in the looking glass placed just over there beside the bust of Agatha Christie. I had expected you to take the precaution of changing the glasses, and had prepared my own glass of mead accordingly. Of course, if you had not changed the glasses, I should have knocked over my own by accident."

"You mean—" The Author tried to rise, but found that his legs refused to obey him. He saw Miss Harple now as through a mist.

" 'To cease upon the midnight with no pain'—a beautiful line, I always think. It is a minute to midnight now, and I think I can trust you with the secret of the undetectable poison. The three elements are—"

Those were the last words the Author heard.